David Burnell comes from York. He studied maths at Cambridge and taught it in West Africa. His remaining career was spent on management problems in Health, coal mining and the water industry. On "retiring" he completed a PhD at Lancaster University on the deeper meaning of data from London's water meters.

He and his wife split their time between Berkshire and North Cornwall. They have four grown-up children.

David is now turning his mind to the next "Cornish Conundrum".

Earlier Cornish Conundrums

Doom Watch: "Cornwall and its richly storied coast has a new writer to celebrate in David Burnell. His crafty plotting and engaging characters are sure to please crime fiction fans." Peter Lovesey

Slate Expectations: "combines an interesting view of an overlooked side of Cornish history with an engaging pair of sleuths, on the trail from past misdeeds to present murder." Carola Dunn

Looe's Connections: "A super holiday read set in a super holiday location!" Judith Cutler

Tunnel Vision: "Enjoyable reading for all who love Cornwall and its dramatic history." Ann Granger

Twisted limelight: "The plot twists will keep you guessing up to the last page. This is a thrilling Cornish mystery." Kim Fleet

Forever Mine: "An intriguing mystery set to the backdrop of a wedding in sleepy Cornwall, where all is not as it appears." Sarah Flint

Crown Dual: "A page-turning contemporary thriller with a deeply compelling narrative." Richard Drysdale

Peter Lovesey holds a Crime Writers' Cartier Diamond Dagger.
Carola Dunn writes Daisy Dalrymple and Cornish Mysteries.
Rebecca Tope pens the Cotswold and West Country Mysteries.
Judith Cutler created the DS Fran Harman crime series.
Ann Granger authors the Campbell and Carter Mysteries.
Kim Fleet writes the Eden Grey Mysteries.
Sarah Flint authors the DC Charlotte Stafford series.
Richard Drysdale pens political thrillers on Scottish Independence

UNSETTLED SCORE

A Cornish Conundrum

David Burnell

Skein Books

A Cornish Conundrum

UNSETTLED SCORE

Published by Skein Books, 88, Woodcote Rd, Caversham, Reading, UK

First edition: May 2020.

This book, although set in real locations, is entirely a work of fiction. Truro's magnificent Cathedral with its crypt and upper passage, the Royal Cornwall Museum, Charlotte's Tearoom and the Old Grammar School Cocktail Bar and Restaurant all exist, as does the nearby village of Shortlanesend. No modern character is based on any real person, living or dead and any resemblance is purely coincidental.

ISBN: 9798628289471

The front cover shows the Upper Passage, high in the southeast corner of Truro's Cathedral. Other photographs appear inside. I am grateful to Dr Chris Scruby for taking and fine-tuning the main photographs; and to my wife, Marion, for the photo of me in the Cathedral Nave on the back cover.

TRURO, CORNWALL

NOVEMBER 2019

PROLOGUE

Both sides had known it would be a battle to the bitter end. The episode was to last the best part of two days and its consequences would continue for much longer.

The French schooner, The Scipion, was the larger of the two warring vessels, lying deep in the heaving waves and sunk even lower by its excessive loads of sugar and coffee. These had come from the nearby slave plantations and were tightly packed, intended for delivery and consumption in Europe. The weight of cargo made it less manoeuvrable than the English warship. On the other hand the French boat was larger and more heavily armed, with an extra tier of weapons.

The English naval vessel, HMS London, was captained by James Kempthorne of the Lizard, newly promoted and keen as mustard though relatively untested in battle. Mere chance had given his lookout, perched on top of the forward mast, a distant glimpse of The Scipion through the thrashing waves. This was a bonus at the end of a long shift. Kempthorne's boat had almost completed its first patrol of Hispaniola – one of the largest islands in the West Indies.

At that particular moment, autumn 1782, the English and the French were not technically at war. But even in times of "peace", conflict between the two was never far away. The countries had been rivals for centuries and the slave trade, with its impact on the fertile plantations across the islands of the West Indies, was at its height.

Both countries had long term ambitions to expand their Empires around the world. For the French, the Revolution that would tear up the old order and lead, after much bloodshed, to the Republic was but a few years distant.

But once The Scipion had been spotted, and especially when its flag was recognised, it could not be ignored. This was the challenge of Kempthorne's patrol to every ship he came across: what was it carrying and where was it being taken? And if the questions led to a search, were there any crucial messages from the French colonials to their masters in Paris hidden amongst the cargo?

It did not take long for a suitably arresting signal to be hoisted high between the masts of The London, but much to his frustration Kempthorne's message was completely ignored.

Not far away the sky was darkening as a major tropical storm was brewing. Kempthorne's First Mate, who had many years' experience in the West Indies, counselled caution but the Captain believed that a storm was no good reason to delay. The subsequent chase by HMS London led the two vessels for mile after mile around the eastern end of Hispaniola, then on to the more peaceful, palm-tree lined tropical beach of Samana Bay.

The trouble for The Scipion was that this was an inlet with only one exit. In those days maps of the western hemisphere were limited but to his dismay the French captain could see with his own eyes that there was nowhere else to flee. A fight was inevitable and slowly, reluctantly, the two vessels trimmed their sails and squared up to one another.

3

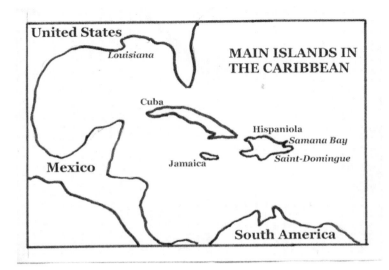

The range of both sets of cast-iron cannons was limited and the era of mobile artillery was still many years away. At this time the weapons on both ships were mounted in fixed positions, one deck of guns above another, along each side. But The Scipion had the advantage of one extra row of guns.

A battle was inevitable. Broadside on, less than fifty yards apart, the vessels sought to pound each other to smithereens. At first there was some order to the firing of the weapons on both sides. Soon, though, panic had taken over and the guns were loaded and fired more or less at random. It was a struggle which was to last for many hours.

By now the eye of the storm had arrived overhead. The regular sparks of ignition and the roar of cannon-fire were interleaved with rolls of thunder and the intermittent but fierce flashes of lightning. As the vessels fought and the hours went

4

by, both captains could sense the wind speed ramping up to near-typhoon strength. The storm was almost beyond human endurance.

In the end darkness came suddenly, as it always does in the tropics. But it was not the persistent English cannon fire that finished the French schooner. It was that, in the gloom, the vessel was driven onto a massive, viciously sharp rock, half submerged in the waters of Samana Bay. Even that might not have been terminal except that it coincided with a mountainous wave.

The crew cried out in alarm as the sounds from below deck signified The Scipion taking in huge volumes of water. These shouts turned to deep cries of distress as they sensed their vessel was starting to go down.

It was no consolation to the French captain, but he could see that the fate of HMS London was not going to end much better.

In its desire to bring the battle to a close, the British warship had ventured too close to the schooner and taken massive punishment in the final stages of the day-long battle. Two dozen of the London's crew members had been mown down by cannon-fire and most of the rest were badly wounded. The few that were not badly injured were torn between struggling to care for their stricken colleagues and trying, heroically but in vain, to continue the onslaught.

As night approached, the task of steering their terribly damaged vessel away from the steadily sinking Scipion in the ferocious storm was beyond the strength of the remaining able-bodied crew. The two ships drew ever closer together, like Torville and Dean collapsing together after an epic ice-skating performance of the Bolero.

Even worse was to follow. The tropical storm did not abate; it grew ever more intense as the tropical darkness fell. By now The Scipion was lower than ever in the water. HMS London tried to implement a full-scale retreat but in truth was in no better shape than its French opponent.

It was the final stage of mutual disaster in a battle that would end with both vessels shredded, torn to pieces in the once-peaceful bay.

Only one of the two hundred men taking part in that deadly skirmish would reach the shore alive. But it was not land in a guise that he had ever known. Captain James Kempthorne was battered and broken, crushed to a point beyond despair. What he had been left with seemed to him almost like life beyond the grave.

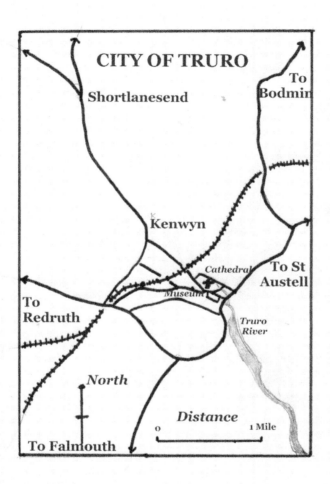

CITY OF TRURO

Shortlanesend

To Bodmin

Kenwyn

Cathedral

To St Austell

Museum

To Redruth

Truro River

North

Distance

0   1 Mile

To Falmouth

CHAPTER 1

A cheerful, convivial atmosphere enveloped the common room of Truro Cathedral's Diocese House. Joy Tregorran, a slim, cheerfully attractive vicar in her early forties, usually based on the Lizard, glanced around and started to feel reassured. Despite her earlier anxieties it might after all be working out for the best.

'Have another drink, Joy,' urged one of the delegates. Everyone was casually dressed by this stage – it was Wednesday evening and the conference was now well under way – but Joy turned and recognised the speaker, even without his clerical collar: it was Neil, a hearty, middle-aged vicar from Newquay. She had little doubt that he might have expected to be leading the conference in earlier times. No doubt he had dealt with issues around "Assisted Dying" in many contexts over the years.

But there was a reason the Bishop had chosen her to lead this "Encounter Conference", she told herself. Her earlier career had included teaching sixth form science and later battling to hold together the conflicting expectations of science and faith. She had accepted the Bishop's challenge; now she just had to live up to the expectations.

'Just half a cider please, Neil,' she replied. 'Then I'd better circulate, put some names to faces. I may have processed all these folk's applications but I don't know most of them at all.' She mustn't appear to be part of a holy huddle, she thought; she could chat with Neil anytime. She took the proffered glass and slid adroitly away.

A timid looking woman, also aged around forty but with her hair a lot less tidy, was standing alone at the far of the room. Joy decided that she was a priority and headed in her direction. All the delegates had been given identity badges on arrival. Most had put them away by this stage of the evening but "Miss Timid" was still wearing hers. They must use a larger font next time, Joy told herself, as she struggled to read the name.

'Hello, I'm Joy,' she began. 'I'm the overall convenor for this event.'

The woman seemed uncertain whether to disclose her name, then relented. 'Hello, I'm Fiona. This is a pleasant room for the conference social, I must say.'

Joy mentally went through her delegate list seeking a Fiona. There were twenty-five delegates and the only occurrence of Fiona was right on the end, which meant the woman must have been a late addition to the gathering.

'It's important that we relax with one another, Fiona. We use this building for all sorts of church-based conferences and we always take this Common Room for socials. It's been designed for it – the bar stocks a wide range of drinks, hot and cold. Where d'you come from and what kind of things have brought you here?'

Fiona gave a hesitant smile, paused and plunged in. 'I live in a small cottage just up the road from St Mawes. On my own.'

'Roseland's a beautiful part of Cornwall, Fiona. I'm based

just down the coast on the Lizard, been working there for a few years. I was brought up further down, near Penzance. Am I right, you were a last-minute applicant?'

Her companion nodded. 'My Mum only passed away two months ago. She'd had a dreadful time over the past year, mostly in terrible pain. She pleaded with her doctor for an escape from it all, said she'd had enough of this earthly life, but he'd had a very strict upbringing. Kept quoting the Hippocratic Oath and saying death was in God's time, not man's.'

'But that made you wonder why your mum had to suffer so much?'

'It made me really angry, to be honest. So when it was all over and Mum had finally left us I decided I'd do more research on the subject. This conference was fairly close and looked to be exactly what I was after.'

Joy felt relieved. 'That's encouraging. It's one of a series just started by our new Bishop. A result of Brexit, you see. He reckons a key thing for our country is that we learn to talk to one another again – and more importantly, to listen to one another. We're only a small country. We can't afford to be separate tribes in our own little villages, writing one another off. Even where we've got different opinions or have assumed different identities, we're still fellow human beings.'

Fiona looked reassured. 'That's certainly true, Joy, it's a good thought. I'll do my best to make it work.'

'That's great, Fiona. Please take courage and talk to some of the others. They may not look it but they're probably as nervous as you are – many of them will have issues of their own. But don't assume they'll all think the same way that you do.'

Joy glanced around for someone else to talk to. She spotted a confident-looking woman, standing for the moment on her own and moved towards her.

'Hello, I'm Joy. I don't think we've met before?'

'My name's Roberta. I'm a senior social worker, over in St Austell.'

'Great. So what brings you to this particular conference?'

'Several of my charges live in Care Homes around the town. While on my visits I've seen dozens and dozens of residents, many with different degrees of dementia.'

'Which makes you wonder . . .?'

'It's the extreme cases that worry me most. They're the saddest: folk with no memories at all. I see their relatives come to visit them and making no impact at all. Often they can't remember who their visitors are. I mean, these poor old dears aren't really living – they barely exist from one day to the next.'

Joy frowned. 'But why does that worry you, Roberta?'

'Well, care in these homes isn't cheap: it all costs money – and most of that money has to come, in the end, from some other part of the care system.'

A horrible thought occurred to Joy. The application forms had been carefully designed, but she and the Bishop had seen no way to exclude extreme views from conference attendees if they were determined to attend. 'You're not suggesting there should be an upper age limit on life?'

Roberta looked shocked. 'No, no, no. But there must be some way to ask questions about it all in a civilised manner. I mean, shouldn't we at least ask if there's some way of managing this better? Would you like to linger on, Joy, taking up space like an out-of-date vegetable that's long past its sell-by date? I'm sure I wouldn't.'

'It's really important to ask searching questions like that, Roberta. The trouble is, it's not that easy to do so in the right way. That's one of the things the Bishop is hoping we can explore, on this and on other conferences that he's planning.'

'What else will be on offer in the future?'

'The next one is issues around the Environment: what should be our response to global warming? Are holidays which require us to fly abroad a luxury or an evil? Should we all be following Greta Thunberg and sailing across the Atlantic? Ought we all to give up eating meat? How seriously, really, do we need to take it?'

One of the other delegates, a florid-faced man in his fifties, caught the flavour of their conversation as he wandered past. 'Hello, can I join you? I'm Tom Smyth – Dr Tom Smyth. I'm a GP over in Bodmin.'

Joy and Roberta introduced themselves and the conversation returned to dementia.

'What do you do about dementia patients, Tom?' asked Roberta.

'We don't have many of them coming to our surgery, thank goodness. But I do have a couple of Care Homes on my visiting list. If there's no hope of recovery and a patient's in a lot of pain, I do my best to give them regular doses of morphine. In generous quantities, shall we say. Not that I'd admit that on the public record – not with the law as it stands, anyway.'

Tom's final point caused them all to pause.

'There are so many aspects to all this,' said Joy. 'When we get down to unpacking some of these tomorrow, I hope we can all share our views and experiences in a constructive manner.'

'Will there be any more drama to help us?' asked Tom. 'I know it simplifies the issues but even so, it's less traumatic to start with a simplified problem rather than delving into anyone's own experience.'

'We've more sketches planned for the next few evenings,' replied Joy. 'Did you enjoy our visit to the Crypt today?'

Earlier in the evening they had eaten a meal together in the nearby Chapter House refectory, then made their way through the dimly-lit Cathedral and down to the Crypt, which was located under the Quire. There an amateur drama group had put on a short play to illustrate some of the topics raised by the questions of Assisted Dying.

'It was certainly chilling,' said Roberta, shivering as she remembered. 'Especially when you turned the lights out as the drama began.'

'But not too frightening, I hope? I'm afraid most of the Cathedral lights are turned off in the evening.'

'The drama was well acted anyway,' responded Tom. 'How on earth did you find the actors?'

'It was the other way round, actually,' laughed Joy. 'A couple of the folk who applied to come on the course happened to mention on their entry forms that they were involved in a drama group, so basically they found us. That's what gave me the idea, you see. I used to produce plays in my earlier life as a teacher, so I contacted them. Then we sat down to write a suitably provocative script between us.'

'Is the man who played the heartless doctor somewhere

13

here?' asked Tom.

The sketch had been based around an ill man at home in relentless pain pleading to end it all, a doctor who was reluctant to act to hasten the ending, a frustrated wife seeing her partner in terminal suffering and a visiting social worker. In the end the wife and a friend with some medical knowledge had given her husband the fatal dose.

'Barry, the man who was playing the doctor, is one of the delegates, certainly. As is Donald, the patient who ended up being hastened away by his wife.'

'I'd love to chat with Donald,' said Roberta. 'He seemed to be really into the part. Find out what he felt about it all.'

Joy glanced round the gathering. She could see Barry, the man playing the doctor, holding forth on the far side but couldn't see Donald. 'He must be around somewhere. Maybe he's slipped out for some fresh air – or gone for a consoling drink?'

'Maybe he's still lying in a back room in the Crypt?'

'I doubt it, Roberta. I asked for realism from the drama but I didn't want that much.'

The evening went on. Joy kept an eye out for Donald as she circulated but he didn't appear.

A little later she caught up with Barry. 'D'you know where Donald might have got to?'

'I'd been wondering that myself. He's normally sociable enough. Maybe the shepherd's pie disagreed with him. He lives on his own but somewhere or other I've got his phone number. Shall I try giving him a ring?'

He slid away to make the call in the corridor and came back a few minutes later, looking puzzled. 'It's slightly odd, Joy.

Donald's not answering his phone. I can't get hold of him.'

Joy was mildly concerned but she had a whole conference to run and it was already ten o'clock. Several of the delegates had already headed off for an early night and more were inching towards the door. All those attending, including members of the drama group, had guest rooms on the upper floors.

'I don't see what more we can do at this time of night, Barry. Let's hope he reappears in the morning.'

CHAPTER 2

Dr Harry Jennings, Senior Lecturer in History at Exeter University, stared out of the window as his train trundled over the viaduct that Thursday morning. The city of Truro lay below him, its magnificent Cathedral in the centre of a huddle of slate and whitewashed buildings. As the track crossed over Truro towards the station, he felt an odd combination of excitement and uncertainty.

It had all started months ago, with a restructuring at the University coinciding with his ongoing tussle with the

Departmental authorities. At one point he'd feared he would be dismissed. Harry was far too unconventional for Exeter students, who to his mind were simply interested in passing their exams and moving onto lucrative employment.

He'd tried to tone down his lectures and stay within the official syllabus but history, to his mind, wasn't that sort of subject. Curiosity was its most vital feature, not something to be squeezed out and eliminated.

Then, when the writing had not just appeared on the University wall but seemed to be scorched deep into the plaster, the offer had arrived.

A rich donor, anonymous but presumably based in Cornwall, had made a donation to start a History Outpost in Cornwall. It was to be linked to Exeter but with a remit to take in mature Cornish students to conduct PhD calibre studies of Cornish life and history.

A senior historian from Exeter was required to head up the unit. Harry had made his application and thus removed the mismatch headache from the Exeter HR officials.

It was not a move without risk. Harry would become a big fish in a very small pond indeed. Research was always something of a gamble; the Outpost might fail to produce a single item of lasting academic value. If so, it would be an obvious candidate for closure on the next round of University restructuring. Harry knew he wouldn't be invited back to Exeter if that were to happen.

The historian, though, was not much driven by the notion of keeping risks at bay. In his mind life was too short to be played safe. He hadn't always been an academic and the remit of the Outpost – he had already named it the Exeter Cornish History

17

Outpost, or ECHO for short – stirred up hopes of conducting more research himself, alongside his role as leader and mentor of the students he had selected.

And Harry had another reason for wanting the move. Earlier that year he had met, and fallen headlong for, a woman based on the Lizard: the Associate Vicar of Gunwalloe Church, Joy Tregorran. Harry hadn't yet found a flat in Truro – which was why he was still commuting from Exeter – but anything which brought him nearer to the Lizard was worth having.

Harry had first come to Truro in the context of ECHO in July. He'd hoped to rent a large house, probably Victorian, not far from the Cornwall Records Office. That would be conveniently located just up the hill from the station. If he could find something at a rent he could afford, on a three-year tenancy, that would be long enough for the students based there to complete their PhDs – as long as they were focussed enough.

But it wasn't as straightforward as he had hoped. For the time being he'd had to make do with a Portakabin, built not long after the war, round the corner from the Records Office.

After that he'd set himself to find an array of historical questions, each connected with Truro, that might be a tasty bait to attract bright students. He was after ones that would appreciate more subtle problems, not just check that the items were on the syllabus.

He had spent a long time in the city's Royal Cornwall Museum, which he discovered had a serious academic library facility upstairs, holding a vast array of Cornish documents and diaries, as well as some interesting galleries at street level.

He'd struck a chord with the Head Librarian, Angela, and made an impact on one of her younger assistants. He'd also spent time in the local Records Office.

Harry had of course taken an interest in Truro Cathedral. He'd been amazed to discover that the Cathedral had only been started in 1880 and finished in 1910. So despite its traditional, Early English appearance, it was in fact fairly modern. How, where and why it had been built had also suggested a number of possible research projects.

As the train drew in, more or less on time, Harry recalled the first Outpost meeting in late September. It hadn't started well: his train from Exeter that morning had been running an hour late. There were four graduates in the meeting room when he arrived, all aged around thirty. They had looked pretty fed up and impatient by the time he got there.

'I'm so sorry,' he'd begun, holding up his hands in mock surrender. 'Our wonderful railway, First Great Western, send their apologies as well. There was a potential suicide sitting on the viaduct at St Austell. I'm trying to move down to Truro from Exeter but there's been a hiccup on the flat I'm buying. It should be sorted within the next month.'

He'd glanced around. 'I assume you've all introduced yourselves while you've been waiting? Now if we're with a client you'd better call me Dr Jennings but at the working level please call me Harry. We don't need much of a hierarchy. So have you all got places to stay in Truro?'

His unreserved apology seemed to clear the air. No-one wanted to start the first session on the wrong foot.

The only woman present, Ellie Masters, tall, slim and a

honey blond, responded first. 'I'm already living in Truro with my sister and mum, Harry. On the other side of the Cathedral, up in Kenwyn. It's not that hard to cycle in. There are hills at both ends but that helps me keep my weight down.'

'I've found a flat near the centre,' said Simon Quentin. 'Just past the Museum, in fact. I'm sharing it with three others, but it's walking distance from here. It'll do for the time being.'

The other two students, Bill Towers and Ben Williams, both had relatives living near enough to Truro that they could stay with them for as long as was necessary. 'But you'll be alright getting in?' checked Harry. 'It's important we support one another: I want you all here most of the time.'

Both assured him that they had cars, which they'd managed to park without charge in a nearby side road.

Of the men, Simon was the smartest: small and dark haired with a trim beard. Ben was built like a rugby three quarter while Bill, rather like a younger version of himself, was lanky and tousle haired. Harry had interviewed them with two colleagues from Exeter a few weeks ago. They had all gained good first degrees in history for different eras. Ellie had studied the ancient Greeks, Simon medieval England and the other two modern Europe. Harry had high hopes of what they might achieve if he could coax the best out of them.

'Great,' said Harry. 'Right, let me begin by outlining the basis of ECHO. It's been funded by an anonymous donor who wants to promote interlinked historical research on Cornwall. That's what's funding your bursaries; and also my salary and the costs of this building. It's been set up as a Trust, with half a dozen local worthies to keep an eye on what's going on.'

'How will that work?' asked Ben. He sounded dubious.

'It'll doubtless evolve. To start with, I'll meet with the Trust every two months. That means I'll need something to say by the end of October. This is really important, guys. We must keep them on our side.'

'As you can see,' he went on, 'there are only five of us. But you've all been carefully chosen: quality not quantity. I want to take advantage of that and find ways that we can work together – for example, with topics of research that overlap. If we can manage that, I'll find some broader topics to investigate that will set each of your projects in a broader context. Hopefully that will give our individual projects a wider resonance.'

The focus turned to possible research topics. All the students had been outside Cornwall for their first degrees and were happy to consider suggestions from Harry.

'One possible topic is Truro Cathedral, which as you know dominates the town. In fact, compared with most cathedrals in Britain it's not that old. But that means most of the information about how and where it was built will still be available. For example, how was it funded? what was the mix of gifts and the rate at which they came in? Who gave them? And what lessons are there on fund raising for such a project starting today?'

Harry glanced around. He could see he'd got their attention.

'Another, slightly related project is music in Cornwall – maybe starting here in Truro. One character that I learned about in the Royal Cornwall Museum is an amazing person called Joseph Emidy.'

'What was amazing about him?' asked Bill.

'Well, he was a black man who started off life in Guinea, in West Africa. He was captured by the Portuguese and sold as a

21

slave to Brazil. For some reason or other his slave master there started teaching him to play the violin. But Emidy was a musical genius. He became so good at it that he was taken back to Portugal as a performer.'

'Interesting, Harry – but what's that got to do with Truro?'

'A British seaman took Emidy on board as an entertainer. But the captain was so impressed that he wouldn't give him back. Eventually he put him ashore at Falmouth.'

'That's still not Truro.'

'No. Somehow or other – I don't know how – Emidy found his way here. Then he joined and later became leader of the Truro Philharmonic Orchestra. He lived here for thirty years. You can see his grave up in Kenwyn.'

'So what is there left to research?'

'Oh, there's plenty we don't know. And we're fairly ignorant about the growth of music across Cornwall.'

There was a silence as his words were digested. Then Ellie asked, 'Harry, is that the end of your possibilities?'

'Oh, no. I've plenty of others. Mining, for example. That's well documented on individual mines but we might learn more from a county-wide view. I mean, we've centuries of developments down here: what's the balance between competition and cooperation?

There had been silence as these ideas were absorbed.

'What about ports?' asked Bill.

'Good suggestion. Truro has history there, too. It was once a significant port but gradually it silted up. All that's left now is the passenger boat service to Falmouth – and that's only for summer months.'

An animated discussion had ensued. Some had other ideas.

Ellie was keen to pursue feminism in Truro life. Harry suggested that she looked into some of the diaries that he'd located at the Museum. Simon had an Anglican background and was intrigued by the history of the Cathedral. Bill wanted to pursue the history of the port of Truro while Ben wanted to take a broader view of musical developments.

Harry had felt encouraged by their enthusiasm. In turn he had suggested that he began a series of weekly seminars on the history of Cornwall to help set their research in context. That was the purpose of his trip today. He would also have weekly sessions with them individually to keep track of their progress.

In the long run ECHO might succeed or it might fail; but to Harry's mind it had certainly made a promising start.

CHAPTER 3

One Chapter House refectory "special" was an extended breakfast, available from eight to eleven. Many workers in the city centre used it regularly. Joy Tregorran didn't approve of late rising, least of all when attending a conference, and had encouraged all the delegates who wanted feeding – 'whether it's full English or just a Danish pastry' – to be there by eight.

'Our first meeting will begin at nine sharp,' she added. Joy feared she would miss breakfast herself, she had to use the time to find out what had happened to Donald.

The first task was to check his room: had he returned late from a foray into Truro? Was he still slumbering away? As conference convenor Joy had been given a master key to all the guest rooms in Diocese House in case of emergencies. But when she knocked hard and then peered round the heavy oak door to his room, she could see the man wasn't there, his bed hadn't even been slept in.

The next place to try was the Crypt. Had the missing man been taken ill in his dressing room, shortly after the drama finished? It would be a sad indictment of the Cathedral's hospitality – and of her pastoral efficiency – if he hadn't been missed and had lain there all night.

Joy had also been lent a set of keys for the Crypt. One of the less spectacular parts of the Cathedral, it was used mainly as a place for the choir and clergy to robe for the services.

24

Their robes were kept there. It was also the storage place of last resort, with a clutter of items in obscure corners that still awaited a proper home. The Crypt was no part of any Cathedral tour.

Joy slipped from the Chapter House into the aisle alongside the Quire and along to the Crypt stairway, then down a dozen stone steps into the rooms below.

The Crypt itself was fairly large, matching the area taken by the Quire above. The place was laid out as she'd left it the evening before, with a few rows of chairs facing a temporary raised stage. She was hoping to have further dramatic events during the conference.

There were several side rooms adjoining the main area, none locked. Security depended on the Crypt itself being secured when not in use. Quickly Joy went through these one by one. It wasn't hard to identify the room used by Donald: there was the tartan dressing gown which the man had worn for the drama. After all, she reminded herself, he'd been playing the part of a dying man.

But of Donald himself there was no sign.

Carefully Joy went round the rest of the Crypt. It was just possible that if Donald had fallen ill, say if he'd fainted and then recovered consciousness after everyone else had gone, he might have ended up anywhere down here in a frantic quest for an unlocked exit.

Surely, though, if he was locked in, he would have shouted for help? But Joy wasn't sure he'd have been heard. She was only a short-term visitor to the Cathedral for the conference, so wasn't into security. Was there an overnight patrol that might have heard him? She had no idea. So to be sure she went round all the other rooms in turn: but still there was no sign of Donald.

More anxious now, Joy returned to Diocese House and found the folder of conference application forms. Donald's was one of the first she had received. It gave a landline number and address for his home in the village of Shortlanesend, three miles out of Truro. She rang the number but there was no sign of life there either.

Looking for someone to share this with, Joy returned to the refectory. Most of the delegates had left to get ready for the conference but Barry was still on his toast and marmalade, seated in the far corner. As far as she knew he was the only person who had known Donald in earlier times. Quickly she joined him and voiced her concerns.

'I don't know Donald that well,' said Barry, 'but I recall him mentioning some sort of heart condition – he had to go into hospital every so often for treatment. Maybe he's gone there again?'

'But if he knew he'd an appointment, surely he'd have told someone – not just wandered off? Don't you think we'd better report his disappearance to the police?'

Barry frowned. 'He's not been gone that long. We need more information. If you like, Joy, I could go to his home in Shortlanesend, look through the windows and make sure he's not collapsed there. A neighbour might have a key. Once I'm in, I could look for a diary or calendar, see if he had any appointment for today that had slipped his mind.'

He continued, 'If there is, of course, that'd give us somewhere else to check – might well solve the whole thing.'

Joy wasn't completely convinced. If she hadn't had a

conference to run she would have gone to Shortlanesend herself. But Barry was concerned too. He knew the missing man; and his proposal sounded sensible.

'OK then, Barry. I'll be here all morning. Please let me know as soon as you have any news. Then we can decide between us what to do next.'

Most conference sessions would take place in the main meeting room in Diocese House. When she got there, Joy could see that her delegates were eager to get going. Mercifully her concerns about Donald had not yet been widely noted.

'Good morning, ladies and gentlemen. I'd like to begin by inviting comments on last night's drama. I'll summarise on the whiteboards as we go along. But please remember,' she urged, 'we're expressing our own feelings. We can't impose them on anyone else. For some this will be a set of ideas on right and wrong. For others it will be a live issue on a personal level – it may affect someone we're living with. Whatever our views we must all be considerate with one another.'

Whatever its effect on Donald, the drama had been a good icebreaker. Every aspect had prompted reactions and Joy was kept busy jotting them all down. An hour later they'd assembled a potential agenda for the whole conference.

Joy glanced around at their handiwork. 'Great. Later, after coffee, we'll break into groups and unpack some of these ideas. Where we've seen problems, how might they be mitigated? What other resources do we need and where could they come from? Do we need any changes in the law?

'But before that I'd like us to list some wider aspects of

Assisted Dying that you'd like to talk about. Or other items that you'd hoped we'd be covering. I'll give you ten minutes to write down your thoughts, then we'll put our ideas together.'

Later that morning the delegates were divided into groups, carefully balanced by Joy, to work out their ideas on various questions. They were scattered in seminar rooms all over Diocese House. Joy retreated for a few moments of reflection to her office.

But she wasn't alone for long. There was a knock at the door; one of the delegates, faintly familiar, stood there. The new arrival was tall and willowy, her shoulder length hair a strawberry blonde. It was someone she'd had dealings with before, but it took a few seconds to remember her name.

'Hello, Frances. I didn't recognise you with your hair down.'

The two had met briefly a year ago. Then her visitor had been in uniform: Frances Cober was a local police sergeant in Helston. Joy recalled Frances saying she'd been sent on the conference as a representative of the law. She was here in place of her boss.

'Hi, Joy. Could I bother you for a few minutes?'

'Sure.' Frances was invited in and took the spare seat.

'Forgive me if I'm adding two twos and making twenty,' Frances began, 'but I overheard a comment at breakfast that worried me. Is there something going on that the authorities should know about? Have you . . . have you mislaid a delegate?'

So much for the notion that no-one had noticed anything. But on balance Joy felt relieved. She had lost the burden of being the one to decide what might need reporting to a higher authority.

'I might have. It's very odd. But I'm still making inquiries. I didn't want to report anything until I was more certain.' Quickly she told Frances all that she knew about the missing Donald.

'So now,' she concluded, 'I'm waiting for Barry to come back from Donald's house. He shouldn't be too long. Once he's back, things might be clearer. The whole problem might go away.'

'Mm,' responded Frances. 'That's an optimist's view of things. My perspective is always to fear the worst.'

But it wasn't her place to spread alarm. 'I can see the whole thing's a little tricky. And why you're so uncertain.'

Don't damn her, Frances, she told herself. 'What you've done so far sounds fine. Tell me, do any of the delegates here know I'm with the police?'

'I haven't given anyone's background on the material I've handed round. And we're not using titles; they probably don't even realise I'm a vicar. D'you want yours kept secret?'

'It's probably unnecessary, Joy. But in the worst case, if something needs investigating, it wouldn't do any harm. Right, I'll get back to my group. We're comparing Assisted Dying in the UK with what happens in other countries. But I am here if there's anything you need to share. You can take me as a listening ear.'

'Thank you, Frances. Let's hope Barry comes back with some good news.'

CHAPTER 4

A sombre-looking Barry came back just before lunch. Joy was surprised to see Roberta the social worker with him, then remembered the woman had also been part of their conversation the previous evening. She too must have been concerned about Donald.

The rest of the conference delegates had finished their work in teams and were all off for lunch. Joy was waiting on one of the smart blue seats in the foyer to intercept Barry as he came through the Diocese House entrance.

'Why don't we slip away to eat,' suggested Joy. Barry's face told her that the news wasn't going to be good. 'We'll never get a table to ourselves in the Chapter House. And whatever you've found or heard, I'd like to keep it to ourselves for as long as I can.'

The new arrivals were not minded to disagree and they headed into the city centre. Joy spotted a small restaurant down a side street. 'That'll do.'

The place wasn't busy. They found an isolated table towards the rear where they wouldn't be overheard. They each ordered a round of toasted sandwiches and a mug of tea.

As soon as the waiter had gone, Joy turned to her companions. 'Right. So how've you got on in Shortlanesend?'

'Bad news, I'm afraid, Joy,' began Barry. 'Donald is dead.'

Joy was silent for a moment, mentally voicing a prayer.

'As soon as we got to Shortlanesend we sensed something was wrong,' explained Roberta. 'Donald has a bungalow in Cranfield Close. There were lights on inside but even though we knocked several times no-one came to the door. So we started peering through the windows.'

'I got as far as a bedroom,' went on Barry. 'The curtains weren't drawn. But inside I could see a figure. It looked like Donald, face down on the floor. He was horribly still. I knocked as hard as I could on the window but it was no good, he didn't move.'

Barry paused, clearly distressed as he replayed the events in his mind. Then he shook himself and continued.

'We found a man who lived opposite who had Donald's spare key. His name's Jim . . . Jim Temple. He came over with us and we all went inside and into the bedroom. Roberta was in front. She felt for Donald's pulse and checked his breathing but there were no signs of life. His body was stiff and cold, he must have been dead for hours.'

Barry stopped, distraught with the memories.

Roberta sensed his distress and took over the tale. 'There were some boxes of pills by Donald's bedside – his regular medication, I assume. He had plenty. I looked at the box labels and that gave me the name of his pharmacy.

'So I rang them, explained what we'd found and they gave me the number for Donald's surgery. I got through to their reception – it took a while, but I'm pretty forceful – and between us we identified his regular GP, a Dr Shaw. I was put through to her, explained what we'd found and she came out at once. She was with us in half an hour. Trouble was, there was nothing to be done. It didn't take long before she declared

Donald to be dead.'

'We'd all been expecting it but it was still a shock. Jim asked her what came next,' said Barry. 'Ought we to call the police or the ambulance?

'Dr Shaw explained that Donald had been under her for regular treatment, due to an irregular heart condition. "In fact," she said, "I saw him only last week." So his death in his own home, although sad, was not a medical surprise. As his regular doctor she could forego the post-mortem. In consequence, she added, she could give us his death certificate right away.

'"Next you'll need to contact an undertaker," said Dr Shaw. She gave us the name of a firm in Truro. "Sam Coleridge: we usually refer people to them, they're very reliable."

'Donald's neighbour said that he would wait in the front room until the undertaker arrived,' concluded Barry. 'He was a sensible sort of chap, seemed content to stay there on his own. We thought we should get back here to tell you the news face to face, as soon as possible.'

'Thank you,' said Joy. She reflected for a moment. 'Poor old Donald. What a terrible occurrence – and what horrible timing. Do you think we'd better close the whole conference?'

'Barry and I are the only two that have been affected directly,' replied Roberta. 'Speaking for myself, I'm fairly used to old folk dying in the homes I visit. I would say life needs to go on. I wouldn't feel too upset if the conference was to continue.'

Barry concurred. 'I'd rather not have to share any of the details, though. Could you make a brief announcement at the start of this afternoon's session – but leave Roberta and me out of it?'

The conference attendees looked shocked when Joy told them of Donald's sudden death in his home the night before, as she began the afternoon session. But being an experienced vicar she was able to set his death into the wider context of the conference itself.

'Donald's death reminds us all that, whether we like it or not, dying is part of life,' she concluded. 'One day it's going to happen to us all. That's why I think it is right for our conference to continue. Of course, I'd be happy to talk privately to anyone who's feeling upset.'

Even so Joy felt relieved that the first event of the afternoon was going to be led by an outside speaker, a visiting chaplain to a local hospice. He spoke reassuringly and movingly about the journey to death of patients that he had known there, leaving several delegates in tears. The extended tea-time that followed saw much informal ministry between members of the conference.

Later, when the delegates had been packed off on their second group exercise of the day and Joy had retreated to her office, she was joined once again by Frances Cober. 'Can you tell me what you know about Donald's death in more detail, Joy?'

Joy was relieved to be able to share the news with a fellow professional. Carefully she retold Barry and Roberta's feedback, reassured that Frances took notes as she did so. This was a situation where two heads were better than one.

'So the doctor was comfortable signing off Donald's death, saw no reason to call in the police?' probed Frances, when Joy had finished.

'That's what I understand. Why, d'you think there's something suspicious about it?'

Frances was silent for a moment. 'If his regular doctor was comfortable then I guess that should be enough for all of us. It's just that the timing is bizarre. The man plays the part of someone being helped to an assisted death; then he goes home and dies himself. That's an odd coincidence. Is there really no connection? What was Donald's frame of mind when he got home? Might playing the part have pushed him towards suicide?'

Joy pondered for a moment and then frowned, shaking her head. 'I was at the same table as Donald, talked to him over supper. He was cheerful, said nothing that sounded suicidal. I gather he'd not long retired, had a number of plans and dreams.'

Joy went on, 'And I doubt he'd be stressed by the drama. After all, he'd helped to write the words. We'd rehearsed it in the Crypt a dozen times beforehand.' She shook her head. 'No, I'd say there was no evidence of distress at all.'

'Right. So it's probably OK. But I'd be grateful, Joy, if you don't mention my profession. I'll listen hard to conversations over the next few days and make sure there's nothing else going on. And please, please, do let me know if anything worries you.'

As she left the room, Frances had no reason at all to make the case official. But she was in charge of Helston police station. She could initiate a few unofficial enquiries of her own.

CHAPTER 5

Frances Cober's regular position was Police Sergeant in charge at Helston, though she had to maintain close links with Truro as her boss, Inspector Kevin Marsh, was based there.

Marsh had something of a reputation. His operating slogan was said to be "let sleeping dogs lie". He knew only too well that his teams were busy. In his view there was no point in widening the police workload unless it was unavoidable. So in this case Frances knew he wouldn't be interested in a death which even the man's doctor had declared was almost medically inevitable.

Frances had been asked to come on the Assisted Dying conference by Inspector Marsh in his place. He hadn't given her much choice. He in turn had been asked to come by the Assistant Chief Constable, a direct invitation that had come to him from the Bishop himself.

Frances had no-one of lower rank that she could pass the invitation on to. In any case, the topic might be of some long-term value to the Police Force. That made her comfortable to attend.

Now she didn't want to spend any time away from the conference. It wasn't often she'd have the chance to mingle incognito with others who'd been close to a dead man, hours before he died. She had no idea how that might help any future inquiry but she wasn't going to miss the chance to try.

But Frances had access to low-level resources in Helston. A few minutes later, away in her guestroom, she was on the phone back to her office.

Tim Barwell was Helston Police's newest recruit. He was gangly and mop-haired but tried to think for himself. Frances had seen his potential at the recruiting interview and assigned herself a role to mentor him. Tim was razor sharp; potentially he might one day be her replacement.

'Hi, boss,' he answered, when she called him. 'You got all the details on assisted dying yet? We're looking forward to the training when you get back.'

Frances reminded herself that there'd been animated discussion of the conference when she'd told her colleagues she was attending. It wasn't clear to most of them what she could possibly get out of it. "High-minded skiving" was probably the unspoken thought of the day.

'Tim, something's happened here that I need help with,' she retorted. 'Are you on anything right now that couldn't wait a day?'

'Everything here is classified as "urgent". But the tasks you give me are usually more interesting,' he replied. 'What d'you want me to do?'

'Get your notebook out,' said Frances crisply. 'It's like this.'

Quickly the sergeant summarised the events as so far known about the death of Donald McKay in Shortlanesend.

'It's almost certainly a natural death,' she said. 'But it

happened so quickly after he was performing in a drama, where he played the man who was mercy killed, that I'm left wondering. My copper's sixth sense is nagging me. I wouldn't mind one of us having a look round the bungalow for ourselves.'

Tim had been on a basic law course for new officers. 'But shouldn't we wait on a post-mortem?'

'Well, it's unclear. There doesn't need to be one if the man died in his own home and his regular doctor thought it was expected. But it would only need one unexplained object or one item that doesn't fit to shift the default position.'

Tim wasn't convinced. That wasn't what his notes had said. He had learned, though, that sometimes it was best not to argue. 'OK. How will I get into the bungalow?'

'The man who lives opposite – he's called Jim Temple – has a spare key. I expect he'll be around, he's retired. He's meant to have called the undertaker. I don't know how long it'll take for them to get there and take away the body. If the body's still there then you can slow things down – but you'll need to be diplomatic.

'Mind, you'll need a good story so Jim's happy to let you in. And remember, Tim, it's not a crime scene yet, but it might become one. So be careful what you touch or taste.'

'That's alright, boss. I'll plan as I go. Can I take a police car from the pool to boost my credibility? I'll ring you once I'm inside.'

Forty minutes later, Tim Barwell was in Cranfield Close, where Donald McKay had lived and died. He parked outside the dead man's bungalow, which was unlit and uninviting.

There was a house directly opposite. A casually-dressed man in his late fifties answered his knock.

'Good afternoon, sir. Are you Mr Temple?'

'Hello. Ah, you've come about Donald, over the road? It's good the police are taking an interest.'

That was better than he'd feared. 'I'm Constable Tim Barwell. My sergeant is looking into Donald's last known activity in Truro. Could you let me into his bungalow, please?'

The pair crossed the road and Jim Temple unlocked Donald's front door.

'Would you mind coming in with me, sir, and telling me exactly what you saw earlier today?'

'Certainly. A middle-aged couple came, about ten o'clock this morning. They were worried that for some reason Donald hadn't reappeared at the Cathedral. There was some event there that he was part of. They'd seen what looked like a fallen body through the side window and wanted to get in. I'm his nearest neighbour, they guessed I might have a spare key. Which as it happens, I did.'

'Right. So which room was he in?'

'This one here.' Jim opened a door off the hall which led to the main bedroom. 'Poor Donald was lying on the floor, face down, with one arm stretched out. He was fully clothed. One of the couple, the woman, checked his breathing and his heart rate but there were no detectable signs of life.'

'Mm. Which direction was he facing?'

Jim thought for a second. 'He was heading towards the bed.'

Tim turned and noticed a phone and a notebook on the bedside table. 'Maybe he was trying to reach that phone to call an ambulance?'

'Could be. Whatever had got him had obviously been very swift.'

There was nothing suspicious about the bedroom. It was tidy enough, didn't look like someone had searched it or given it an exhaustive clean.

'Can I see the rest of the bungalow, please?'

Jim led him down the hall and into the kitchen dining room. That was neat enough for a retired man living on his own. Tim noted a single empty wine glass on the table.

'Hm. Looks like he was here on his own.'

'He was usually. I don't think he had many visitors. He'd go down to the Old Plough for the pub quiz on a Thursday evening, but that and his drama group were about the limit of his regular socialising. '

Tim jotted down the name of the Inn. Maybe he could drop in on his way home?

Then a different question occurred to him. 'Have you any idea who was his nearest relative?'

'Annie and I've been wondering about that all day.'

'That's your wife?'

'Yes. She remembered that he has a nephew in Australia. But he hasn't been here for years. Donald was talking about flying over to visit him next year. It was one of his retirement projects.'

'We'll need to get in touch with him. You don't happen to know the nephew's name or which part of Australia he's in, do you?'

'No idea, I'm afraid. But his address book will be in his desk. There are probably not many entries for folk in

Australia.'

'That's a good idea. Well, you can leave me here to look for it. I'll lock up and bring the key over when I've finished.'

One further thought occurred to him as Jim reached the front door. 'By the way, sir, can I assume no-one else was here last night or this morning, besides you and the couple?'

Jim paused before he answered. 'It's quiet enough here. I didn't hear any other cars in the Close last night, apart from Donald's. No-one else came today between the couple and the undertaker and his crew. I was waiting here for them, but I went home as soon as they'd taken away the body. The poor man was as deserted in death as he seems to have been in life.'

CHAPTER 6

Tim Barwell recalled his boss's comments and slipped on some latex gloves. Then he sought McKay's address book. The desk was tidy and uncluttered. Jim was right: there was only one address in Australia, it was another McKay – Neville. So this was most probably the next of kin.

Tim reflected for a moment. He computed that a brother was needed to complete the familial link between Donald and his nephew. Had he also passed on? Further perusal showed no more McKays in Donald's address book so that seemed pretty likely.

Tim wanted to have a proper look round whilst he had the chance. First, though, he must contact his boss, report back on what he'd found so far. When he called she answered at once.

'Hi, Frances,' he began. 'I'm calling from Donald McKay's kitchen.'

'Well done, Tim. Have you found anything of interest?'

'The neighbour, Jim Temple, was very cooperative. He said he'd been hoping the police would take an interest. He showed me where Donald was found, lying on his bedroom floor. There was no sign of disturbance, everything seemed in order. I can send you the photographs if you like?'

'Yes, please. What about the rest of the bungalow?'

41

'As far as Jim knows, Donald was here on his own. He says no more cars came to the Close, anyway. And there's just a single wine glass on the kitchen table.'

Frances pondered for a minute before her next question. 'So what was his final drink?'

Tim glanced round. 'Can't say, boss. It's an empty glass and there's no bottle. Hey, should I put it in an evidence bag?'

'Best leave everything exactly as you find it, I think.'

But Frances was still in detection mode. 'Come to think of it, Tim, where did the contents come from? Is there a wine bottle in a kitchen cupboard? Or an empty bottle in the waste bin?'

'Good questions, boss. I'll have a look when we've finished talking. One other thing I have found is a likely next of kin. It's Neville McKay. According to Jim Temple's wife, he's a nephew. Trouble is, he's not local, he lives in New South Wales.'

'Does he have an email?'

'I'm afraid not. Just an address.' Tim read it out carefully and Frances noted it down. Joy Tregorran would be happy to have that, no doubt she'd see it as her responsibility to send a message of condolence round the world.

'So right now, boss, Jim's gone back and I've got the bungalow to myself. What d'you want me to look for?'

Frances mused for a moment. 'You know, I don't have a good feeling about this. The timing is so very odd. Let's just imagine for a moment that someone had intended Donald harm. In that case we'd be after evidence that he wasn't alone at home last night and possible reasons for him being harmed.'

Tim had been pondering as well. 'One thing we haven't

eliminated yet is that Donald could have brought someone else home with him. . .'

'Good thought. Right, I'll do my best to check on that from this end. The convenor here, Joy, mentioned that the drama group are also invited to this conference. Someone might have seen him leave the Crypt or the Cathedral. It'd be good to know if there are any witnesses to him having company.'

'Even if he was on his own, boss, there'd be questions. If I had some keys I could take a look outside, see if there's anything else that might point to a motive for murder.'

'Mm. A straightforward search would be enough for now, Tim.' She didn't want him to be too radical.

Even so, Tim had respect for his boss's intuitions. They didn't come very often but when they did they weren't often wrong. And if she was correct, for the first time in his life he would be alone at a suspected serious crime scene.

If there really was something amiss, he didn't want to muck up the chance to shine. It would be good to make a distinctive contribution.

Back in Diocese House, Frances had borrowed Joy's folder of conference application forms. They were all hand-written so, in case they got lost, she had photographed all twenty-five entries on to her mobile phone.

Frances had also made her own list of the delegates. She was ready to add new facts when these emerged.

After this she had studied Donald McKay's application at some length. It wasn't particularly expansive but it seemed to have been one of the first to arrive. He had explained that he was single and had recently retired from a small engineering business in Truro. But he'd left empty the section given to explain why he wanted to come to a conference on Assisted Dying.

Now she browsed the forms again. There was a section on "other interests". Between them the delegates had identified a wide range of activity. It didn't take her long to identify two more members of the drama group, both into middle age.

One was Barry – the man who had taken the lead in visiting Donald that morning. The other was a woman called Suzanne. Frances guessed that she'd been the woman playing the long-suffering wife in last night's drama.

Soon it was time for the conference supper in the Chapter House. Frances made sure she was there early. She was able to pick out Suzanne from the drama the evening before and then to grab the seat beside her.

Donald's death, which had only been announced just after lunch, was the main feature of discussion everywhere. That made it easier for Frances to ask probing questions without it seeming odd.

'You were in last night's drama, I believe?' she asked Suzanne.

The woman nodded, almost in tears. 'Our group had been together for ages. We didn't have many chances to perform so we tried to make each one count.'

'What was your last sight of Donald?'

Suzanne sighed. 'In that sketch, you'll remember, Donald was supposed to be the one dying. He was meant to be ill so he was wearing tons of makeup,' she explained. 'The trouble was that afterwards it took him ages to scrape it all off. He was fairly image-conscious – he didn't want to go outside with any

44

still on.'

Frances tried to guess what that might imply. 'So Donald had his own dressing room?'

'That's right. When we first got there, he made some comment about being the oldest, so that was his prerogative – or so he said. The rest of us weren't that fussed. Anyway, we'd got into the habit of leaving him on his own in his room to clear off the makeup after the rehearsals. I guess we carried that over to the live performance. I didn't have to change so I came out of the Crypt fairly quickly. Then I headed back to Diocese House for the reception.'

'Were there any signs that Donald wasn't well?'

'He seemed perfectly normal. To be honest, Donald was a bit of a hypochondriac, he'd moan quite a lot, but last night he didn't complain at all. He seemed in fine form. That's why his death is such a shock.'

'Were the members of the drama group close?' asked Frances. 'I mean, did you see much of one another socially, apart from during rehearsals?'

'Not much. I mean, we weren't from the same village or anything. We were scattered around Truro; we'd met through a workshop put on by a drama team from Exeter. In fact, I've never been to Donald's house at all. And now I guess I never will.'

Suzanne looked very upset. Frances decided she had learned as much as she could. Swiftly she moved the conversation onto the afternoon's poignant stories from the man based in the local hospice.

Meanwhile Tim was searching Donald's bungalow without

much success.

He had ransacked every cupboard in the kitchen, high and low, without coming across a bottle of wine or any other drink.

He'd found a second rubbish bag in the drawer and used it to empty out the kitchen waste bin over the floor. But no wine bottle came to light.

Lastly, he had gone outside and found the dustbin. That too was fairly full – encouraging, it meant the dustbin men hadn't just been round and emptied it – but it contained no bottle that might have filled the wine glass.

Frustrated, Tim stopped for a mug of tea from his flask. This wasn't just an oddity, he thought, it didn't make sense. There were plenty of tumblers but no-one would use a wine glass for anything but wine. Donald's wine must have come from somewhere. But if so, where was the bottle?

Then he had an idea. What if Donald had got a glass out of the cupboard but then discovered he'd nothing to put in it? But the policeman smelt the glass: yes, there was a faint alcoholic aroma. It had certainly been used.

Tim was going to ring Frances again, then he remembered he hadn't yet found Donald's keys. The trouble was, though he walked through every room, he couldn't spot them anywhere.

Once more the policeman went through the bungalow, searching everywhere he could think of, but without success. He even went through the pockets of Donald's clothes.

Bizarre. The man must have had car keys to drive home and a key to let himself in, so what on earth had he done with them?

All Tim could think of was that the key were still in the clothes Donald had been wearing when the undertakers had taken away the body. That seemed unlikely: it would be a gross unprofessional error.

He would get the funeral name from Jim and check tomorrow. Tonight, though, was far too late for anybody to be in the office.

CHAPTER 7

There had been only time for a brief phone conversation between Tim and Frances Cober on Thursday evening. So they had arranged to meet for an early breakfast, away from the Cathedral, in central Truro.

Tim went over his findings in Donald McKay's bungalow. He noted the absence of a wine bottle and the missing keys. He concluded with a further conversation with Jim Temple, as he'd taken back the spare bungalow key in mid evening.

'I told him there were one or two things that were odd,' he said. 'On no account was he to let anyone else into Donald's residence. I said I'd be back this morning for a further chat.'

Frances nodded in approval. 'Good. The missing items don't prove that something criminal happened but they make it more likely. The question is, Tim, what we should do next?'

'Warn the undertaker to expect further enquiries?'

'That's a good idea. Since they've not yet been given a next of kin, they haven't anyone to consult or charge. That'll mean his body will be kept in the background. Your aim is to make sure it stays there. Sound official, tell 'em they mustn't let anyone see it without talking to us first.'

Frances paused to consider. 'I'll talk to the doctor – Dr Shaw, I think Joy said her name was – and see if I can persuade her to backtrack on signing the death certificate.'

'A post-mortem would make it a lot easier for us to take it

further,' opined the young policeman. 'Hey boss, d'you think Donald might have been poisoned?'

Frances could see no evidence for the idea at this point, only a question mark over the wine glass. But no reason to dismiss it completely. There was silence as both tucked into their cooked breakfasts.

'So what did you find out from the other delegates?' asked Tim.

'I focussed on other members of the drama group who were also attending the conference. There were two: Barry and Suzanne. Suzanne said she was one of the first actors to leave the Crypt when the drama had finished. She also said Donald was always the last one out.'

'What about Barry?'

'He told me he hadn't hung about, either.'

'But how many were taking part in this drama?'

Frances thought for a moment. 'Five, I think. There must have been a couple of actors that didn't come back to the conference, went straight home. Right, I'll get their names from Joy.'

Tim was still undertaking regular police training. 'Ought you to alert Inspector Marsh? Put what we're doing on a firmer footing?'

Frances gave a sigh. 'At this stage, Tim, that might be a disaster. The only evidence we've got so far is the two items that are missing – his keys and a wine bottle. Marsh would dismiss the whole thing, order me to leave well alone. Probably dig out some time-consuming task to make sure I've no time for anything else. That would make further enquiries much harder.'

Frances paused, considering options. Then she added, 'I reckon we could give ourselves a couple more days to poke around unofficially. I'll ring Dr Shaw later. If she changes her mind and asks for a post-mortem, as she's entitled to do, we could see what that tells us.

'In the meantime, Tim, I'd like you to go back to Shortlanesend, get the names of Donald's local friends from Jim and his wife, and visit as many as you can. Find out all you can about him. I mean, if he was killed, what might he have done to provoke it? Had he any dubious contacts? And while we're about it, did he have a criminal record?'

Her comment had jogged Tim's memory. 'By the way, I asked Jim what time Donald came home on Wednesday evening. He told me that he heard his car arrive at about nine fifteen.'

Frances considered. 'Well, the Crypt drama ended by eight forty five. Donald would have to remove his makeup and get changed out of his dressing gown and pyjamas, then walk to his car and drive out to Shortlanesend. Even at that time of night that must be a fifteen minute journey. No time to go anywhere else on the way. So if he did have anyone with him, it was almost certainly someone from the conference.'

'That's a limited cast, boss. Could you interview them all – say in between sessions?'

'I'm better off staying under cover and listening hard. What I could do, perhaps, is to get Joy Tregorran – she's the conference convenor – to talk to everyone in private, one by one. She could check they hadn't been affected. But also ask, did any of them know Donald before the conference started?'

Frances suddenly noticed the clock on the café wall. It was

already showing quarter to nine. 'Hey, the first session starts in fifteen minutes. I'd better be going. I don't want to stand out from the crowd.'

Tim decided he'd time for another coffee. He didn't think the undertakers would be open any time before nine.

CHAPTER 8

Saturday evening. Truro Cathedral had not long closed its doors on its first, but certainly not its last, Encounter Conference. The written conclusions and delegate observations were modest but in other ways it had been a success. The final, sociable gathering in the common room had seen some impromptu but moving scenes of acceptance and friendship between hitherto non-empathising delegates.

And there had been no more deaths, assisted or otherwise.

Frances Cober was having supper in her own home in Gweek, a former fisherman's cottage twelve miles from Truro and four miles out of Helston. She had a guest, invited long before the conference date had forced its way into her diary. The timing, though, might be fortuitous.

George Gilbert was an acquaintance of similar age who Frances had encountered less than a year ago, on a previous policing escapade. George was as slim as Frances, but she was short with dark curly hair. The two women were both unattached. George had been left a widow a decade earlier when her husband was declared dead in a faraway plane crash, while Frances found it hard to meet anyone she felt secure with amidst her intensive police work, which she took very seriously.

The two had become firm friends over a series of incidents,

a friendship which meant they would stay over with one another from time to time as circumstances allowed. These visits often concluded next day with a walk along the Coast Path and a pub lunch.

George was an industrial mathematician who turned out to have a knack of detecting key links in complicated cases. Her day job was management consultancy, these days predominantly in the West Country. George owned a small cottage close to Tintagel, on Cornwall's north coast, but from there she would take on projects all over Devon and Cornwall.

Her current work was connected with maximising internet security. It was sponsored by Newquay airport and meant she needed regular contact with British Telecom's staff in Truro – and in particular with their data.

Tonight's meal was no banquet. The police officer could cook elaborate meals when required but this time she'd had no chance after arriving back from Truro. But the Sainsbury's beef bourguignon was still something of a treat, especially with Aunt Bessie's roast potatoes. She'd also brought back some red wine from Diocese House and made sure there was water on the table. She knew the beef might be quite salty.

'Right. I think that's all ready now, George. Would you like to eat?'

The two sat down at the small dining table. George reflected how well her friend had done to prepare the meal straight after her previous commitment. 'So, Frances, was the conference as bad as you'd feared?'

'No, it was illuminating. I'd never have thought there was so much you could say about assisted dying. Turns out there are good arguments on all sides and the delegates were forceful in expressing them. The person running it, Joy Tregorran – she's an associate vicar near here, down at Gunwalloe – has a real gift at getting people to drop their guard and relate to one another.'

George nodded, but sensed that her friend was holding something back. 'But perhaps that wasn't all?'

Frances smiled at her friend's perception. 'By no means. I'll share it with you, if you like – on a strictly private basis.'

George was surprised. Frances normally kept her police work well away from her social life. 'Only if you want to bounce a few ideas off me?'

'Well, it is highly confidential. But it's not yet a police case.'

'Stories are hardly worth sharing, Frances, if there's not some sort of secret. But go ahead if you want. I could do with a fresh challenge. My project is heavy going, I don't have as much time as I'd like for human interaction.'

So as they started to eat, Frances expounded the mystery of the death of Donald. 'It was straight after he'd played the part of a pain-ridden man who'd been assisted to take his own life by his stressed-out wife.'

By the time she'd finished the bare outline, with regular questions and diversions, their plates were empty. In the excitement of the story-telling, though, their wine glasses were still fairly full.

George knew Frances, could see this wasn't just a question of a recent crime story to entertain her guest. The case – if indeed it was a case – had an intriguing beginning but in truth hadn't got very far.

She frowned: was she being invited to contribute? Or

simply to act as devil's advocate? Perhaps what Frances was really after was candid advice to stop her stressing over an incident that had grown large only in her over-excited imagination?

The analyst took a deep breath. 'So maybe something did happen to Donald, Frances. But you must admit, the hard evidence so far is non-existent.'

Frances wasn't easily dissuaded. 'Well, by Tuesday we should know one way or the other. I finally got through to the relevant doctor on Friday afternoon. Told her about the missing wine bottle and the lost keys. That's negative evidence, I agree, but it is evidence of a sort.'

She glanced a pleading appeal at George, but her friend gave a sniff of derision.

Frances continued to defend her interpretation. 'Well, it turned out that the doctor had been worrying as well. Feared she'd been too quick to sign the form and wondered what she might have missed. Doctors are under such pressure, you know, these days.'

'So anyway,' suggested George, 'she's asked for a post-mortem?'

'That's right. That'll take place in Truro General on Monday, with my favourite pathologist, Emily Barton. That could be a vital piece of the jigsaw. And if she finds something striking I can go to my boss and open an official case.'

George saw that her friend needed to be humoured. 'Right, Frances. Let's assume, just for the sake of argument, that something is found.' She shrugged. 'I don't know, let's say Donald might have been poisoned. If that happens, how would you see the case moving forwards?'

'Let me think about that as I sort the dessert. Could you manage some blackcurrant cheesecake?'

Frances returned with the cheesecake and a jug of fresh cream. George had used the intervening silence to plan her line of questioning. But she began first with a gentle observation.

'Neither of us has made much headway on the wine, Frances.'

'We'll have some more once we've had the dessert, if you like. Right: you asked about moving the case forward. Well, I got Joy to make time for a quiet interview with each of the delegates. Then I talked to her in the evening to pick up what she'd found.

'She said she couldn't find anyone who admitted to knowing Donald before the conference, apart from the two other actors in their drama group who were also at the event. And no-one had seen him leave.'

'Are you sure that's not because Joy herself was involved?'

Frances looked shocked. 'That'd never crossed my mind. I mean, Joy's a lovely, caring woman – and she's a vicar. I suppose you're thinking, like Agatha Christie, that the least likely person in a story is really the best bet to be the murderer?'

George shook her head. 'I was just asking the question, I thought that was what you wanted. I've no idea – as far as I know I've never met her. Let's assume the post-mortem that you've engineered supports your suspicions. Have you any ideas on why the murder might have happened – assuming one did?'

Frances took a spoonful of cheesecake and ate it slowly.

She felt a little drowsy. That gave her a few seconds to think but it didn't give her any answers.

'To be honest, George, I have no idea. I mean, Joy had dealt with Donald over a few weeks as they wrote the drama and then rehearsed it. She told me he seemed a lovely man, content in his retirement. But of course none of us ever displays our whole selves. That'd make police work far too easy.'

George gave a smile. It was good to see her friend being self-critical. 'OK. So here's another question. It'll probably be the sort of thing your boss asks when you tell him the whole story.'

Frances forced herself to sit forwards. This was what she needed. Tim Barwell was an excellent junior foil, but what she really needed was hard-nosed peer pressure. Not too hard, mind, she was starting to feel very tired . . .

'Go on.'

'Let's assume that the murderer came to Donald's house then went off with both the wine bottle and the keys. Well, we can guess why the wine bottle might go – if he'd been poisoned it might still contain some of the poison. But why on earth would they bother with Donald's keys?'

Frances tried to answer but suddenly felt the ripple of tiredness turn into an overwhelming wave.

She gave a big yawn. 'I've had a really busy few days, George. It's a good question but I'm not sure if I can think clearly enough to tell you at this stage of the evening.'

George was starting to feel tired too. It was, she told herself, the end of a busy working week. 'OK, it'll wait. Let's at least finish our cheesecake. Then, for both of us, an early night might be in order.'

CHAPTER 9

George Gilbert awoke parched and with a massive headache. For a few seconds she had no idea where she was. It certainly wasn't her own bedroom in Treknow; and it wasn't the Premier Inn guestroom where she'd recently been staying in Truro. The room was in pitch darkness but there was a crack of light in the doorway.

Slowly, gingerly, she sat up. She seemed to be in some sort of bed, or to be precise, on top of the bed. There was a duvet underneath her. And, bizarrely, she was still fully clothed.

But her tummy was aching. She had to take action. Carefully she reached sideways until she came across a bedside light. After a struggle she managed to turn it on.

Now she could see where she was. She'd been here several times before, this was Frances Cober's spare bedroom. Memories started to flood back. Yes, that was right, they'd had a meal together the evening before. But they must have eaten something questionable. Both had felt unexpectedly tired. She'd tottered off to the bedroom as soon as she'd finished the cheesecake – must have collapsed on the bed and gone straight to sleep.

Slightly more awake now, George squinted at her watch. It was half past six – presumably that was in the morning? She hoped she hadn't slept for twenty-four hours, through to Sunday evening. But now she needed to move. Inch by inch she manoeuvred herself out of bed and towards the fractionally open door. She was badly in need of the toilet.

Half an hour later, after putting on some fresh clothes and splashing her face several times with icy cold water, George was feeling a little more alert. Her stomach still ached but at least it wasn't getting worse. She made her way down the corridor to the kitchen diner and switched on the kettle. She was still very thirsty. A mug of tea was desperately needed.

As she waited for it to boil, she glanced round the room. Frances must have retired almost as soon as she had. She hadn't even cleared the table. George noticed that the wine was still unfinished. As well as a half-empty bottle, there was plenty left in their glasses. Ah, so had that been the culprit?

George picked up the wine bottle. The label was pastel green with an outline of some cathedral or other, she couldn't be sure it was Truro. The rest of the label was fairly anodyne – nothing suspicious, anyway.

As the kettle boiled it occurred to her that if Frances had suffered the same stomach upset that she had, she might also be very thirsty. Perhaps she too would be glad of a mug of tea?

An hour later the two women were having the lightest of breakfasts, with drinks of strong coffee to wash down their cereal and toast.

'That wasn't normal tiredness. We must have eaten something that disagreed with us,' said Frances.

Cautiously, moving her head slowly to avoid it falling off, she glanced round the kitchen.

'I doubt it was the beef. I'd only just picked it up from

Sainsbury's and it was well inside its sell-by date – I always check that carefully. And the same goes for the roast potatoes and the cheesecake – and the cream.'

'What about the wine?'

'I got that at Diocese House.' It occurred to her that George wouldn't know where she meant. 'That's a building next to the Cathedral; it's the place where we were having the conference. They sell all sorts of drinks in the common room.' She reached for the bottle. 'From somewhere as respectable as that, the wine must be alright, surely?'

There was a moment of silence. Then a memory associated with the location triggered a horrible thought.

'Hey George, could Donald have bought the same stuff from the same bar on Wednesday evening? And suffered a far worse version of whatever it was that we did.'

George pondered. She knew her friend was prone to dramatic extremes. 'I suppose it's just about possible. We didn't drink very much of it, you know. He might well have drunk a lot more than we did.'

'Stuff the volume, George. Donald had a heart condition. My constable who went to his house told me he had boxes of medication by his bedside. Donald was under active medical treatment. If there's something wrong with that wine, even one glass of it might have been enough to finish him off.'

The police officer frowned. 'You know, this could be far more serious than I'd realised. We'd better give it some fresh thought.'

The similarity of their reactions to what could have happened to Donald gave the women's alertness a fresh boost. They could think more incisively now than they'd managed the night before.

'The thing is, George, I've been wracking my brain for some reason – any reason – why Donald might have been killed. He didn't seem a likely murder victim. But if several of those bottles are suspect, he might just have been really unlucky.'

George still saw a need to offer restraint. 'But even if that's what happened to him, it doesn't explain everything. For example, if he'd also bought a bottle of this wine, what happened to that?'

Silence. It seemed there must have been someone else with him. The trouble was they had no idea who, or what they'd been doing.

Then George saw a wider angle. Maybe her friend's concern was justified. 'Frances, d'you think only the two bottles were doctored? Might there be others as well?'

She paused, then continued the thought. 'To put it another way, are any other delegates affected? Might the wine have been bought as a gift, say, or a bargain? Did you see anyone else buying the stuff?'

Frances thought for a moment and then shook her head. 'No-one I can remember. But that doesn't mean anything. I wasn't watching the bar all the time. I wasn't always there.'

'Mm.' It was inconclusive. But now George could see other lines of enquiry. 'At least we've still got most of your bottle left for testing. Forensics should be able to tell what's been added. Presumably that's easy to organise?'

Frances nodded. 'I'll take it in tomorrow. We have access to a forensic lab from Helston. But let's assume for a moment that something has been added and it's not just an accident. What might that tell us?'

There was a longer silence. This was a much bigger question. Frances stood up to make some more coffee while George took the chance to move to a more comfortable chair. Her head was still aching.

'D'you know much about this wine?' asked George, once she'd had her mug replenished. 'Was it very expensive? Was it a church special? I noticed a cathedral outline on the label.'

'Well, it was sweeter than I was expecting,' replied the police officer. 'Maybe that's why we didn't drink as much as we might with the main course? It didn't go as well as I'd hoped with the beef stew.'

'Of course,' she continued, 'that might also have been why it was chosen – say if the sweetness helped to disguise the taste of whatever was added.'

George was more convinced now that something was wrong. That made her impatient. She was used to seeking out vital data, whatever the source and whatever the difficulty. It happened all the time in her work. Who else might know anything about this wine? Then a name Frances had mentioned came to her.

'Is there any chance the Revd Joy Tregorran might know?' she asked. 'She was in overall charge, you said. Perhaps she was the one to suggest Diocese House should stock this brand for her conference?'

'Good idea, George. I think somewhere in the material they gave me I was given her direct phone number. Hold on, I'll have a look.'

Fifteen minutes later, the half-empty wine bottle carefully packed inside a padded rucksack and strapped to the back seat – it would be a calamity if it was broken – Frances and George were driving across the Lizard to Joy's vicarage in Gunwalloe.

'It's only a few miles,' said Frances, 'and the roads are always quiet, early on Sunday morning.'

George hoped so. Their road was narrow and her friend was driving alarmingly fast, gripped by some deep-rooted sense of urgency.

Joy had been intrigued by Frances' call, had suggested that they came to her at once as she was due to preach later that morning.

'As I recall, Joy's vicarage is not exactly warm,' Frances had warned. 'You'll need an extra jumper – or maybe two.'

When they got there Joy didn't seem fazed by their appearance. She was obviously used to welcoming relative strangers to her door and was quick to offer them coffee.

Frances hastily declined. They'd already had plenty to drink and she was in a hurry. She explained briefly what had happened the night before and handed over the wine bottle. 'The thing that worried George and I was, firstly, if it had been doctored and, secondly, if any others might have been affected as well. D'you happen to know where it came from?'

A visit from the police was unusual and Joy sensed potential problems for Diocese House. But she wanted to help if she could. She examined the bottle carefully.

'I'm not going to risk drinking any of it but could I smell the aroma?'

Frances nodded permission. Joy removed the cap and gave the contents a cautious sniff. Then she quickly screwed it back

63

on and sat back, looking very concerned.

'I took no interest in what the bar was selling,' she said. 'As conference leader I wasn't there for the alcohol. I had plenty of other things to think about. So I can't answer your question for certain.

'But I have a horrible feeling that I know what that wine is. Look at the caption. It looks and smells a lot like the one they use in the Cathedral to administer Holy Communion.'

CHAPTER 10

F rances Cober was not a regular churchgoer. It took her a moment to register the possible implications of what Joy Tregorran had just told her. Startled, she started to voice her concerns.

'You mean, Joy, that bottles of wine like this, that did for me and George last night, from essentially the same location, are regularly drunk by members of the Cathedral congregation?'

Her pitch was rising as the consequences started to unfold. Dealing with any form of activist protest was not usually part of her brief. She recalled hearing on the news about occasional attacks on churches in other parts of the world. Surely that couldn't be happening, here in Truro?

This was a nightmare. The police officer swallowed hard, forced herself to slow down. It wouldn't help to gabble. 'So we might have stumbled on a deliberate attempt to harm dozens of Truro worshippers, to poison them as they attend Sunday morning worship?'

Frances' words came to a halt; she was hardly able to believe what she was saying. But despite the shocking nature of her words she saw that Joy had remained calm.

'Aren't you worried too, Joy? What's the matter – have I got this all wrong?'

Joy was far from laughing but she wasn't in tears either.

The vicar had a deeper perspective on church matters.

'We need to think about it, Frances, talk it through and maybe make further enquiries. But there are one or two things I know that perhaps you don't. Firstly, when Anglican churchgoers take communion, they only ever have the tiniest sip of wine from a common chalice. That's offered by the priest who is taking the sacrament to the people as they line up for communion, one at a time. They get far less than a teaspoonful, nowhere near a wine glass. So unless the whole bottle was filled with something toxic, say like cyanide, it can't have that much impact, can it?'

Frances was silent, listening hard as Joy continued. 'That's one thing. Secondly, I happen to know the regular service times at the Cathedral. The only Holy Communion scheduled for today has already taken place. It happened at eight am. But if there had been some sort of attack, it would surely have made the nine o'clock news. I was listening to that before you got here; there were no reports of trouble of any kind.

'They don't always have weekday communions. There won't be another in the Cathedral until later in the week. That gives us a day or two to look into the question before it becomes a serious issue, even if one were to arise.'

It was sound logic, reassuring. And a relief that Joy was not panicking, thought George. But maybe she'd also better intervene. Frances needed time to calm down. She was relieved to see that at least her friend had stopped gabbling.

Suddenly it occurred to George that she'd been given a chance to talk directly to a key witness about Donald's death. She might as well make the most of it.

'Frances was telling me that someone at your conference

had passed away very suddenly, Joy, on the first evening. It occurred to us this morning that he might also have consumed some of this wine, another bottle from the same stock. That's really what made us so worried. It wasn't just a matter of us having a few hours unplanned extra sleep.'

Joy mused for a moment. 'It's not my field,' she observed, 'but I used to be a science teacher so I know how labs work. You've got suspected links between a man who has died, two of you falling into a deep sleep and a dodgy wine bottle. Surely the first thing the lab needs to do is to see what else is in the wine, and if the same stuff was also found inside the dead man?'

'That's right,' said George, keen to keep Joy onside. 'I understand that's what the police will set in motion tomorrow.'

'Good,' said the vicar. 'Then you'll also need to know if the wine that's sold in Diocese House comes from the same supplier as that used in the Cathedral. There's no-one there now but I'll find that out for you tomorrow – I've got to go over to tidy a few things up. If it isn't, the main threat you've been worrying about – of poisoned communicants in Truro – will fade away.'

George was equally persistent. 'But even if the Cathedral isn't affected, Joy, there's still a question over how many other Diocese bottles were sold. Someone else at your conference might have a heart condition and have drunk too much.'

Joy mused for a moment. 'So is there any way to tell how the bottle you two drank from might have been doctored?'

Frances had been looking at the top of the wine bottle during the recent exchange. Now she spoke.

'It's a screw cap and as you can see, there's no hole

punched in the top. The easiest thing to do would be to unscrew it, pour out some of the wine and then replace that with something more toxic. Then screw the top tightly back on until the notches matched. Unless the second drinker examined it minutely they'd never notice it had already been opened. I mean, I opened this bottle last night and didn't notice anything.'

George, glancing at the bottle, could see what she meant. 'But in that case, it should be easy enough to see if any of the other bottles in Diocese House have been tampered with.'

'Or any of the bottles in the Cathedral's own store, down in the Crypt,' added Joy. She sounded relieved, thankful that there was some sort of response emerging.

'But that still leaves the question of how many more bottles of wine were sold to delegates,' said George. 'Someone will need to check the bar's sales record during the conference – assuming they can separate it out. But they might not have sold any. In that case there'd be no further problem at all.'

The plan for George's visit had been that on Sunday morning she and Frances would go for a sharp but not too long walk along the Lizard's rugged coastline. After that, George would treat the pair to a Sunday roast in the famous Ship Inn at Mawgan – a village in central Lizard, not far from Gweek.

It was George who had had the spark of insight to suggest inviting Joy Tregorran to join them, once she'd completed her ministry in Gunwalloe Church. Joy had nothing else on that afternoon, was delighted to accept – though she knew the conversation was bound to continue focussed around the recent Assisted Dying conference.

After they'd left Joy to get ready for her morning service, the two had driven down to the car park in Church Cove, then had a breezy walk northward, up the narrow and rather muddy coastal footpath.

Frances had pointed out the adjacent bay. 'That's Dollar Cove. A Spanish vessel was shipwrecked there in the seventeen hundreds and gold coins have been found here ever since. I've painted it more than once.'

They'd continued round the headland to the village of Gunwalloe, with a view up as far as Porthleven. Then they'd walked back. The views in the opposite direction were equally stark but dramatically different, including Mullion and Mullion Island.

They'd reached Joy's ancient church, nestled under the headland, at twelve thirty, just as the service finished and the congregation was emerging. It turned out that Joy usually walked (or jogged) the mile to the church from her vicarage. She was happy to accept a lift home, and also an invitation to lunch.

George kept the conversation general as Frances drove over to Mawgan. She quickly learned of Joy's previous career as a science teacher in Penzance. She was able to match that with an outline of her own life as an industrial mathematician.

'So what's your current project?' asked Joy.

'Well, I can't tell you any details but the broad task isn't that confidential. Have you ever heard about the projected space station at Newquay?' It turned out that given her scientific background Joy kept up with technical hopes for Cornwall.

'They're hoping to launch rocket-powered planes,' said Joy,

'that will go to a high altitude, as far as inner space, out over the Atlantic. Some say they'll be ego-trips for super-rich millionaires.'

'That's right. But do you know how they'll be monitored?'

Joy frowned. 'Through the Earth Station at Goonhilly, I think. That's here on the Lizard, it's in my parish. I must say, it sounds very twenty-first century. So where does your work come in?'

'It's made people question the links between Newquay Airport and Goonhilly. I mean, if these were severed while Goonhilly was monitoring a flight, even for just a few seconds, that could lead to disaster. So as part of the space flight project they're prepared to spend a lot of money to eliminate the risk. The question is how and where to spend it.'

'Mm. I thought the internet was a cable network, with lots of alternative routes?'

'That's true. But links do fail from time to time. Say, if there's a flood along a road that carries a cable. Or a major traffic accident that tears up the road. Or even road works dug in the wrong place. So the question is, what are the chances of each of these incidents and where's the best line for an alternative route? That's what I'm working on and it's a real headache.'

'Don't want to interrupt you, George, but we've reached the Ship,' said Frances.

'I'll tell you a bit more later,' whispered George.

'I get an allowance for the time I spend away from home,' said George to her fellow-diners, 'so we can have this meal on me.'

Frances and Joy didn't object. They ordered roast beef and

Yorkshire pudding, George settled for roast lamb. Even outside the holiday season the Ship was fairly busy. But the three women were in no hurry, the wait gave them longer to talk.

'There are some obvious enquiries that the police can make, which I'll pursue tomorrow,' said Frances. 'But I think we're all concerned that something is going on, even if we don't know quite what.' Joy and George both nodded. 'One angle that it would be good to go into while we've got Joy with us is the question of motive: why on earth should anyone want to do any harm in this location?'

'It may have nothing to do with the conference,' cautioned George. 'Donald might have had some other dubious project on the go. For instance, what if he picked someone up on the way home which ended with an argument at his bungalow? But let's leave that for now – that wouldn't fit if he'd been poisoned with wine from Diocese House, anyway.'

'Let's take it that Donald, like us, was an accidental target. But both attacks could relate to Cathedral premises. I can think of two possible types of motive,' said Frances. 'The first is that it's something to do with the conference. But even though I attended the whole thing, I know very little about how it came about. Joy, could you give us some background, please.'

Joy took a moment to arrange her thoughts. 'The first thing I need to say,' she began, 'is that though I was the convenor, it wasn't my idea. It all began with the new Bishop of Truro, you see. He could see that after Brexit there was a big need to encourage people in Cornwall to relate to one another again. Having very different world views shouldn't – mustn't – stop us being fellow citizens. His idea was to arrange conferences on controversial subjects, where different groups would meet one another and start new friendships across a number of divides. Assisted Dying just happened to be the first one we tried.'

'So how did you come to be leading it?' asked George.

'Our new Bishop arrived eighteen months ago. Once he'd met his clergy and taken stock, he decided that if the church wasn't to go into terminal decline it needed a much bigger impact on the younger generation. One side of that was giving more space to the younger vicars – and also to women. He had a couple of dozen women like me to a workshop last February; his choice of me for this first one came out of that. But there are plenty of others lined up to lead later conferences.'

'You say the subject was controversial,' said Frances. 'Is there any chance that the topic chosen was so divisive that it could have led to someone wanting to . . . well, to sabotage it?'

It was a big question. Fortunately, their roast dinners arrived at that moment, giving Joy a few moments to ponder. Once they had all settled to eat, she started her reply.

'Assisted dying is a topic with advocates on all sides. On the one hand there are those who believe in the sanctity of life: that mankind is never entitled to kill. In other words, assisted dying is always wrong. That's a logical position. But if you accept it then there are many consequences: you ought never to believe in war, for instance, since that will always end up with people being killed, even if you don't know who they are.'

Frances and George nodded. That was a logical conundrum.

'But it's not always easy to uphold an abstract moral position,' she went on, 'however clear, when you have personal reasons for believing something else. So in our conference drama, for example, there was a man in great pain who was desperate to die. The pragmatist might ask, what is actually achieved by prolonging his life?'

'And you could take that further. If you accept suicide is permissible in certain circumstances, are there any limits on that? What about patients with dementia, who can no longer make the choice for themselves? Do the opinions which they held much earlier in life still apply? Could the choice be fudged or made to appear more acceptable? Should we let, or even force, doctors to make choices on their behalf? And finally, if you do that, what safeguards are needed to stop the process going too far?'

Joy stopped. These were deep, emotional questions with no easy answers.

'Have your lunch, Joy,' said George. 'Frances and I can muse over what you've just told us for a few minutes. That roast beef is very tasty. It'd be a shame to let it go cold.'

They ate in companionable silence for a few minutes.

'It's hard to see anyone with a pure position against killing being prepared to take a life to sustain that view,' said Frances.

'No,' replied George. 'But someone with personal reasons in favour of assisted dying might be driven so frantic by their circumstances that they'd do anything to register a protest. Anything at all.'

There was a pause as they finished their main courses and negotiated desserts.

As these arrived, George recalled the earlier conversation. 'You said you could envisage two sorts of motive, Frances. What's the other one?'

Frances had to finish a mouthful of trifle before replying. 'If something is going on, the conference and the emotions it can arouse might just be incidental. There might be something else altogether. Something focussed on the Cathedral itself?'

'I'm afraid I know very little about Truro Cathedral,' said George. 'It doesn't come up very often in my conversations.'

She looked across to Joy, who was just starting her Eton Mess. 'Joy, is there anything in Truro Cathedral's history that might invite some sort of hostility or revenge?'

Joy thought for a moment. 'I'm a bit of an outsider there, remember, but I've never heard anything along those lines. I know of nothing that would make anyone seriously antagonistic. I found it all peaceful and friendly. But if there is, there's someone I know who might – or at least they might have subtle ways of finding out. Give me a few days and I'll let you know.'

CHAPTER 11

Harry Jennings sat in his flat in Exeter, reflecting on life after finishing his solitary lunch. He would leave the washing up for now. He was quite pleased with the progress of ECHO so far. The group had evolved a weekly pattern of working which, as far as he could judge, they would be well-pleased to continue.

On one day each week his students would take turns to give an informal lecture to the rest of the team, on their most recent findings. He hadn't insisted on them providing a formal paper but had been pleased to see that each one turned up with an extensive, typed summary of the material they would be presenting. He'd brought the folder holding those back with him.

It had been agreed that these lectures would be open to question and challenge from the rest of the group. Often these responses had led on to wider discussion. Each of his team had told him privately that the interactions they had received had sparked many fresh ideas and topics for further lines of research.

On another day he would give his team a seminar on broadly related historical topics, now mostly from other parts of the world. He had added his own backup material and notes, freshly compiled, to the pile.

Most recently he had been unpacking issues which arose from the Napoleonic Wars. These had happened at the turn of the nineteenth century, close to the time frames that two of his students were investigating.

The folder of material would be useful for his forthcoming meeting with the ECHO Trustees. Harry flipped back through the pages and refreshed his memory.

The first lecture in the folder had been given by Ben Williams. He had been attempting to fill some of the gaps in the story of the black musician, Joseph Emidy.

'The early history,' Ben began, 'how Emidy came to learn the violin whilst being held a slave somewhere in South America, is hard to get hold of. I've spent ages in the archives of the Royal Cornwall Museum, but they haven't got much material on that – not that I've found, anyway. I'd wondered, for example, about Emidy's family background in Conakry – that was and still is the capital of Portuguese Guinea in West Africa. Did anyone in his family have any sort of musical background, for example?'

'They'd probably have had a strong tradition on rhythm,' suggested Bill Towers. 'After I graduated, I spent a year in Nigeria with Voluntary Service Overseas. In the training week before we went, we had a wonderful lecture by an old man who'd studied African music for years and years. He said Europeans might be centuries ahead of Africans in terms of subtle tunes and complex harmonies; but the Africans were equally far ahead in terms of rhythm – could produce simultaneous, different but matching beats with each hand, for example.'

Harry recalled that Bill's remarks had led to fifteen minutes discussion from the group. Music was something they all had views on.

'Anyway,' Ben went on, when he thought he'd been interrupted for long enough, 'I decided it would be easier to begin with the later part of the story that happened in Cornwall. There must be more known about that, I thought, than on the African's wanderings in the South Atlantic. It's known that Emidy was put ashore at Falmouth in 1799; but how on earth did he land up in Truro?

'There was almost nothing solid that I could start from. For example, did the man speak any English? Was he penniless when he was cast ashore? Had he got anywhere to live? Could he even read music? I assumed that, on the story we'd been told, he would never have been to England before. So, in that case, if he'd got to Falmouth, why would he want to move on to Truro?'

Ben had stopped to see if anyone could give an answer. But, at short notice, no-one had much idea.

'Well, as Harry has said to us repeatedly, when there's no direct information on something that you know happened, the good historian will try to work out which other parties might have had some reason to keep track of the same data. And in this case, I recalled – after a while – that Emidy landed up with the Truro Philharmonic Orchestra. So I decided to find out how they operated in the early nineteenth century; was there, by chance, any written record?'

'I find it pretty amazing that Truro had any sort of orchestra at all back then,' said Ellie Masters. 'I mean, it was only a small Cornish town – it wasn't a big place, like Birmingham or

Cardiff.'

'The thing is, there weren't so many alternative forms of entertainment in those days,' observed Dr Jennings. 'I mean, we're told that John Wesley could stand up in Boscawen Street here in Truro and gather huge crowds for hours. I guess there wasn't that much else to do.'

Another wide-ranging discussion had erupted for a few moments. Fashions in entertainment were a big topic, in the past and in the present. Finally Ben took charge once more.

'It turns out that the Truro Philharmonic Orchestra was well organised, it had monthly meetings of what we would call a management team, with written and approved minutes of each meeting. And wonder of wonders, the Museum here in Truro has copies of them all.

'I looked back at all the management meetings around the turn of the century – the nineteenth century, I mean. Then, in May 1799, I found the critical entry. Someone or other mentioned the arrival of Joseph Emidy at Falmouth. New musical talent was rare and after some discussion it was decided that Truro needed to send someone to meet him, at least to welcome him to England. If all went well they might even be able to persuade him to play his instrument. Was he a showman or a serious musician?'

'But even if he was serious, how might they persuade him to move to Truro?' asked Bill.

'Well, from some of the other entries in the minutes, I gathered that Falmouth had nothing at all that could match the Truro Philharmonic Orchestra. So if it turned out that he was any good, Truro would be his best chance of finding paid employment.'

'So it was a shot in the dark that someone was sent. Who made up the deputation to Falmouth?' asked Ellie.

'It turned out that the Secretary of the Truro Philharmonic, the day-to-day organiser, was a woman called Mrs Eleanor Kempthorne. She'd been with them for years. She was a forceful woman, a widow, wasn't easily pushed around, and she also had a musical ear. And for some reason, Emidy's background – his years as a slave – seemed to catch her interest. So she was deputed to go and investigate.'

There had been a moment's pause in the ECHO Chamber, as the Portakabin was now affectionately known. 'Do the minutes record what she found?' asked Bill.

'At first I thought they hadn't,' admitted Ben. 'I ploughed through every page of the record for one month ahead and then for two, but there was no mention of her. In fact Eleanor seemed to have vanished. There were even questions raised about her absence: Falmouth was known to be a rough area.

'Then I got to the record three months on and there she was again, holding forth once more. "It took me ages to find him," she reported. "In the end I came across him living in a rough shelter at the far end of a dark alley. Terribly cold and hungry – he couldn't afford to buy food. It was his violin-playing that gave him away; I heard the sound echoing hauntingly up the passage."'

'So he really could play?' Bill sounded surprised.

'He certainly could,' replied Ben. '"Joseph Emidy played like an angel," Eleanor reported. "He wasn't just good: he was brilliant, out of this world. His touch was magical. His repertoire was a bit limited – I guess he only had a few scores of classical music to work on – but on these pieces I've never heard the violin played better," she said, "even by the most famous players that we've ever had visit us in Truro."

'That led to a wide-ranging discussion,' reported Ben. 'Some said that a black man couldn't possibly be paid as much as local Cornishmen. But others argued that music wasn't a white man's preserve, it was a universal talent. "We have a responsibility to pay the rate for the job," they said. "In this case, for this man, the rate must be the best that we can afford."'

'There's certainly scope for more research on these questions,' said Harry. 'Of course, this was all before Parliament voted to abolish slavery – only a few years, mind. But it's one thing to discuss this in the abstract, something else to bring in a black man and pay him the top rate in the orchestra. Especially someone who not long ago had been a slave.'

Ben concluded, 'In the end Eleanor won the day. As I say, she seems to have been a forceful woman – an early feminist,' he hazarded, glancing at Ellie. 'She was determined that they accepted the black virtuoso and in the end that's what happened. Joseph Emidy came to Truro and remained here for thirty-five years. Today you can still see his grave up in Kenwyn.'

Harry had been pleased with Ben's progress and thought it would go down well with the Trust. He would make himself a pot of tea then review what else the first two months of ECHO had brought forth.

CHAPTER 12

The recovery of a fresh angle on the story of Joseph Emidy was promising, Harry decided. If the research went well, and with backing from the Trustees, it might even form the basis of a film. Someone in the ensuing discussion had mentioned "Twelve Years a Slave": with the right producer this could make a powerful sequel. There had been other promising starts, too. He recalled that Simon had made a decent beginning on the real, no holds barred, history of Truro Cathedral.

But the most unusual and distinctive contribution so far had come four weeks after Ben's Emidy story, from Ellie Masters. Harry flipped through the file until he came to her contribution. He recalled her demeanour: she had seemed buoyant, looked like she had plenty to say.

'As I said at the start, I'm interested in the history of early feminism in Cornwall,' Ellie had begun. 'I want to root that history in individual women and their particular stories. So I was really struck by Ben's tale of Eleanor Kempthorne. A female, organising a man's orchestra in eighteen hundred, sounded like a woman well ahead of her time. It was as good a place as any to start.

'I went back to the Royal Cornwall Museum to see if they had anything written by the woman herself. And after a long search in their archives, I found that they had. They had her own personal diary.'

'It's all handwritten, of course – no typewriters in those days – and handwriting was rather different two hundred years ago. Much more flowery and harder to read. But I've forced myself to work through it, line by line and page by page and transcribe it. Then I've had a go at rewriting it as a memoir in present-day English. When you do that it's a really good story – as far as I've got, anyway.'

'D'you think it'll help you understand eighteenth century feminism in Cornwall?' asked Simon. He felt slightly envious. His topic was the growth of Truro cathedral and lessons for new Cornish investments today. Right now that didn't sound half as interesting as Ellie's project.

'Don't know yet. I need the whole story before I can develop the lines to pursue. Anyway, would you like to hear what I've found so far?'

The group had sat back in their easy chairs. The story of a real person, a woman who had lived most of her life in or close to Truro, sounded more gripping than most of the items that they'd been wrestling with.

'Take it away, Ellie,' Harry had said.

'This is a memoir based on the diary of a Truro woman, birth name Eleanor Sandys, born around 1745 and brought up on the Lizard. Her only special gift that I can make out was an interest in music but that didn't take her far in those days: not in Cornwall, anyway. Eleanor married a local sea captain called James Kempthorne around 1775 and they started a family a few years later.

'It seems it was while she was stuck at home with her child that she started keeping this diary – I've searched their files but I can't find anything in the Museum by her that was written any earlier. But she was a determined woman and she kept it going, with occasional gaps for reasons that will become clear, for many years.'

'A lengthy narrative, written by an author just for her own satisfaction, with no hope of publication, is a valuable source,' Harry had commented. 'Part of the impact in your research will be setting her story into a wider context. And of course these were interesting times. The English had not long lost their American colonies, while the French were about to have their Revolution.'

Ellie had nodded. 'The first years are very mundane. Bringing up children was no easier in those days than it is today – they'd no television or even radio to act as entertainment, for example. And she was doing it on her own; her husband was mostly out to sea. But it got more interesting in the 1780s, as you will see.'

Ellie had seized her tablet and started to read.

'It was John Wesley that had started the real adventure for me. Or at least his preaching, proclaimed for hours in Boscawen Street in the middle of Truro, that freezing January afternoon.

I'd never thought about slavery in those terms. Of course I'd heard of it, but it didn't have much local impact and hadn't been any sort of issue of conscience. It hadn't affected my life as a wife and mother, helping to promote music and bringing up my children in the town as my husband captained his ship for the good of his country on the far side of the Atlantic.

Boscawen St, still in the centre of Truro today

The trouble was, Wesley painted such a harrowing picture of life for those slaves. And he left his audience in no doubt that it affected the women as much as the men. That was a new idea to me.

"It's the great evil of our time," he said. "God would have no pity, could have no mercy on any one nation that exploited others in this way. The recent loss of our American Colonies was not just a diplomatic disaster," the preacher declared, "not just a monumental political failure. It was the judgement

84

of God on a wicked system that was the shameful financial bedrock of our Empire."

I tried not to think about his words too much. After all, I could pray for those poor Africans, men and women, taken across to the West Indies to work in those plantations. But the more I thought about it, the more I had to pray. I was driven to my knees, day after day.

I tried to console myself. Perhaps it wasn't as bad as he implied: what did he know of life so far away? Maybe regular labour, harvesting abundant crops in the warm sun, would give their lives more meaning? After all, Europe was now awash with coffee and spices and sugar from all over those same West Indian islands.

But I'll say this for Wesley: he was a canny preacher. He wasn't content for people just to listen and enjoy his diction. Or his jokes – there weren't many of them, anyway. He would stir folk up, wring them inside out, make them feel they had to take action.

As senior history lecturer and mentor, Harry had wanted to make sure his students learned all they could from this tale. 'John Wesley spent a long time in Cornwall,' he began.

'Perhaps he was into surfing,' suggested Simon.

Harry had given him a hard glance. 'There's a lot to be said about the effect of Wesley in slowing the impact of the Church of England,' he replied. 'That's one reason for the late development of Truro Cathedral. You'll need to look into it at some point.'

But Ellie hadn't wanted a diversion. Before Simon could

make any response, she had seized her tablet again and was reading on.

'It was two months later that I got the official-looking letter from the Navy. They'd never written to me before and I feared the worst. They regretted to inform me that my husband, Captain James Kempthorne, "had led his ship in a valiant battle with a French vessel. He had fought courageously to the end. Unfortunately the end had not been the one our country desired. His ship had capsized and sunk in a place I'd never heard of, called Samana Bay. There was no record of any British survivors."

For a long time I was heartbroken with grief. James and I had been married in St Keverne, on the Lizard, twelve years earlier in 1775. He was in his late thirties and I was a mere twenty nine but the age difference was no problem to either of us – no problem at all. We were deeply in love. James was tall, dark and handsome, making his way purposefully in a tangled world.

But these were tough times. Life was hard and often did not last that long. It was little surprise that his end had come, it seemed, in conflict with the French.

There were reports of much strife on the other side of the English Channel – indeed talk of a revolution – and the turmoil there was reaching everywhere in Europe.

'So I was a widow in my early forties. It was fortunate that I had not moved far from my place of early upbringing on the Lizard. A year ago I had managed to secure a job as secretary and performance organiser for the recently formed Truro

Philharmonic Orchestra. It wasn't well paid – indeed it was but a pittance – but it gave me some funds of my own. I had a pair of aunts who had been helping me regularly with childcare as I worked; they were doughty champions of feminine independence and in the new situation where I found myself were ready to do even more.

My oldest boy, John, was by now eleven and said by his teachers to be "extremely bright". I arranged to see the Revd Cardew, Headmaster of Truro Grammar School and told him my sad tale.

In retrospect I had the impression that Cardew was less impressed by my account of my husband's valour and more by the chance of acquiring a bright student at an early age. Though its buildings in the middle of Truro, just along from St Mary's Parish Church, were small and rather shabby, the Grammar School was renowned for scholarship; it was already over two hundred and fifty years old.

Cardew was said to be an outstanding teacher of mathematics and it was clear to both of us that the subject was my boy's special passion. I didn't yet realise how far he would go.

But even though my life was more settled I was still bothered by Wesley's words on the slave trade. My aunts, who had also heard the sermon, were almost equally indignant.

"But if your complaint on Mr Wesley is that he is speaking here at one remove, should you not go and see for yourself?" asked Aunt Jemima.

"After all, my dear, you no longer have a husband that will expect to find you here on his return," added her sister, Esmeralda.

87

"*We are capable of minding your younger children for a few months,*" *concluded Jemima.* "*We can all see that John is very clever. I'm sure he will settle in to the Grammar School and be no trouble to anyone.*"

It had never occurred to me that I could take such drastic action – women didn't do that sort of thing – but once the words had been spoken my conscience and the words of Mr Wesley gave me no peace. Eventually I could find no good excuse to stay. I could see, too, that I might have a more useful role in supporting the abolition of slavery in Britain if I had seen its rigours for myself.

As you can imagine, it took some time to arrange. Truro, though, was a seaport and had a few ships trading to Africa. On advice from Aunt Jemima, I took time to find a ship where I already knew the captain and he knew my late husband. 'You need to be able to trust him, my dear,' she warned.

It wasn't so much that I trusted him – I mean, I've lived in the world, Truro is hardly genteel. I know the drives of men, especially men on their own and far from home – but Horatio was old, at least in his sixties. There was some risk for a single woman but for a man of his age it seemed small – and by now I was unstoppable.

I'd been in small boats up and down the Carrick Roads from Falmouth but never been far out to sea in a large boat. So we set out. But we were barely out of sight of land before I was violently seasick. I had hired a tiny cabin of my own in the stern and stayed inside for many days. Eventually, weak and wobbly, I ventured outside in search of food.

This part of the voyage did not involve slaves. The ship was carrying items for sale in those parts of Africa where the slaves would be found. The crew, though, would stay with the vessel for the whole voyage to Africa, across to the West Indies (carrying the slaves that had been bought) and then back to Europe, loaded with plantation produce.

And eventually, many days later, we came to a port called Conakry. I staggered ashore for my first and I hope only trip to Africa.'

It was clear that this was by no means the end of the story. Ellie was less than halfway, there was plenty more still to come.

But at that moment Harry's phone started to ring.

CHAPTER 13

' Hello, Harry,' said the voice down the phone.

'Joy. What a pleasant surprise. I wasn't expecting to hear from you today. Aren't you still busy with your conference?'

Harry and Joy were close friends but they both had separate professional lives that needed careful management. They had agreed not to bother one another this weekend because of Joy's work on Assisted Dying.

Joy's infectious giggle came down the line, sending a shiver down his spine. 'That finished last night, Harry. I'm back in Gunwalloe now, I preached this morning in Church Cove and I'm helping a colleague in Mullion this evening. But the conference has left a lot of loose ends to tidy up.'

'Anything I can help with?'

'Well, there is actually. But it's too complicated to explain over the phone. Is there any chance we could meet up in the next couple of days?'

'I'm always in Truro on Mondays. Is there any time . . .?'

'I'm afraid I'll be busy in the Cathedral for most of the day.'

'It'll have to be later, then.' He mused for a second. 'Well, Joy, would you let me buy you a post-conference dinner at that little cocktail bar just down St Mary's Street?'

Harry and Joy had an unspoken agreement in their relationship. If Harry was going to pay, which he did much of the time, then he also had first choice of venue. Joy had never been to the cocktail bar he'd mentioned but she had passed it often enough in her walks around the Cathedral.

'That's quiet enough, Harry. And close to the Cathedral. What I need help on is highly confidential but I'm sure we can find a table at the back where we won't be overheard.'

A time was agreed and a few minutes later Joy rang off.

Harry scowled at the phone. This semi-detached relationship was all very well, he thought, but if it was going anywhere he wanted it to get there much, much faster.

But for now he might as well continue to read Ellie's modernised memoir. That couldn't possibly have anything to do with Joy's problem, whatever that turned out to be.

'Conakry was hot and sweltering, with the sun beating down. The light was intense – dazzling – and the place was full of noise and bustle. I certainly didn't want to get lost, had no plans to go beyond the battered jetty where our vessel had been moored. I was just after a place that was stationary – I'd had enough of being buffeted to and fro by ferocious ocean waves. And where I might find something to eat. Days and days of being seasick had left me very hungry indeed, feeling extremely weak.

Fruit was my best hope, I decided. There were many Africans on the jetty, most with baskets full of items that were the same shape and size as oranges, except that, bizarrely, they were green. I might as well start with these.

I had managed to acquire some local currency. Captain Horatio had "sold" me some local coins in exchange for an English shilling before I had ventured ashore.

I offered the first stall-holder one of these coins and pointed at the "oranges". The owner nodded and gave me a dozen for my coin. I had no idea if I was being swindled or being offered a bargain but I was in no position to argue anyway.

Of course, he could provide no bags to hold them but I managed to bundle them down the front of my dress. Already I was feeling faint in the steaming tropical heat. I decided I would return to my boat and try eating them at once in my tiny cabin. And they were delicious – far better than any I had ever eaten in England.

Next Harry came across a note from Ellie. 'I found pages and pages of description of Eleanor's life in Conakry. She must have been there for a month – she got beyond oranges and onto fried sweet corn and plantain. On one horrific occasion, she wrote, Captain Horatio took her to the slave market. 'A long description followed. It was all very brutal, on a par with the worst I've read about in my lifetime. I decided that for the time being I wouldn't transcribe the detail at all.'

'Finally, four weeks later, the captain had sold all the tools, clothes and other items he had brought from Europe and the bartering at the market was concluded.

A hundred native Guineans, mostly young and almost half of them women, came limping reluctantly, without hope in their eyes, along the jetty, up the gang plank and onto my boat. They limped, I saw, because each pair had been chained at the ankle. For some reason Captain Horatio wasn't around. Instead the First Mate, a man of a bullying nature, who I had noticed eyeing me voraciously, even licking his lips when the captain wasn't to hand, took charge.

Because I had been preoccupied on the earlier voyage with my severe bouts of seasickness, I hadn't thought much about where the slaves would actually be held during their passage across the Atlantic. When I eventually found out I was horrified.

The men were pushed onto the boat's low-ceilinged middle deck, crammed together like the pilchards I'd often seen brought ashore at Truro. Once they had all been squashed in, their ankle chains were threaded round the boat's vertical pillars. Each man could move a little, probably just enough to dip his hands into one of the water barrels or troughs of food, but not far. They might fight among themselves but they certainly wouldn't cause much trouble for the ship's crew.

Once the men were fastened in, the First Mate brought the women down to the deck below. The ceiling here was even lower and there were no portholes to allow access to daylight. The women, too, were chained to the boat's pillars. But there was something different about the way they were held. They were not laid as tightly together, had slightly more space between them.

It did not occur to me till later, after we had set sail, why the arrangement for the African women might be so different to that of the men.

For some reason my simple diet in Conakry had taken care of my seasickness. Perhaps there was no more left inside me to come out. But whatever the reason I no longer had to cower in my cabin, it was time to explore the boat properly. In particular I wanted to see my friend Captain Horatio in full control on the bridge, to make sure he was alright.

The trouble was, I couldn't find him. I searched high and low without effect. I even started asking members of the crew that I encountered. No-one admitted to having seen him.

In the end I took courage and asked the First Mate directly. "Horatio?" he asked. "He was taken ill on our final trip to the bar, too far gone to travel. We had to leave him in Conakry. I'm captain for the rest of this voyage." Then a thought came to him. "Maybe from now on, Eleanor, you should eat at the Captain's table?"

There was nothing I would like less. But I dare not say so. Horatio had agreed to be my protector for the voyage. Without him I needed to be very cunning indeed.

I kept my eyes wide open for the rest of the voyage. I told myself that I was in no position to openly challenge the treatment of the slaves during the journey itself, whatever distress they suffered. If I spoke out, that would be bound to arouse the First Mate to fury. I did not know what form that anger would take but I didn't want to find out.

I was a single, vulnerable woman, far out in the Atlantic Ocean. I did not want to be thrown overboard.

But I could still record what I saw within my private diary, I decided, as long as I kept it well hidden. Fortunately I had brought a lock for my casket: it would be safe there. I hung the key next to my skin, around my neck.

At this point in the file, Harry came across another note from Ellie. 'The next pages of her diary were unbearable. I couldn't bring myself to transcribe them in detail. Eleanor discovered that the slave women were regarded by the entire male crew as being available for their pleasure – hence the way they were positioned in the darkened hold. The First Mate did nothing to hold back his men's assaults; indeed, on many nights he would lead the way.

'Two of the women, perhaps the two strongest, tried to resist. The first was heaved overboard by the frustrated crewman in the dead of night, in a fit of incandescent rage. Eleanor had gathered what happened from the chatter which she overheard amongst the crew but, safe in her cabin, could pretend she knew nothing about it.

'The second woman, though, was "keel hauled" in broad daylight.' Ellie admitted that she'd had to do extra research to find out what this entailed. 'It's horrendous,' she'd recalled. 'Two ropes were arranged so they ran amidships, right under the boat, from one side to the other.

'Next the recalcitrant slave woman was stripped naked and lay on the deck, sobbing in fear. Each of her arms was tied to the first of the ropes, then both ankles to the other.

'Finally, the off-duty members of the crew grabbed hold of both ropes and the woman was slowly lowered down the ship's side. She continued to whimper but the sound was lost in the surges of the sea.

'As she reached the level of the waves, the First Mate, watching from the side, gave a signal. Now the ropes on the other side were heaved in by the crew, as fiercely and as fast as possible. The woman was pulled tightly against the barnacled hull as she was dragged under the keel. Finally, two minutes later, she emerged from the water. She was pulled up the other side and heaved, limply, back onto the deck.

'But surely that was far, far too late to save the poor woman's life?'

Harry recalled the live conversation which had taken place at that point in the reading. 'But guys, that wasn't the end,' said Ellie, her green eyes shining. 'For Eleanor had seen what had happened, couldn't just pretend to be ignorant this time. She had taught her boy John to swim back in Cornwall, knew a little about resuscitation. She'd heard it said that a rescuer might sometimes be able to blow air into a collapsed person's lungs until they revived.

'I looked that up, too,' said Ellie. 'A Scottish doctor had proposed the idea half a century earlier. So Eleanor rushed onto the deck and started treating the slave woman. And by some miracle – maybe 'cos she'd started the process so quickly – it actually worked. The woman coughed and spluttered, then she revived.'

'I bet that didn't go down too well with the First Mate,' Harry had remarked.

'It certainly didn't. But Eleanor had succeeded in restoring life, and that was miraculous – gave her almost magical powers in the eyes of the crew. From now on the First Mate daren't touch her. In the end Eleanor insisted on sharing her cabin with the woman, so she could continue to care for her for the rest of the voyage.'

It was turning into a remarkable story, and it was far from over. But it seemed that this was as far as Ellie had got in her transcription. Harry, like the others, would have to wait another week for the next instalment.

CHAPTER 14

Frances Cober was into Helston Police Station early on Monday morning. She wanted to get the suspect wine bottle off to Forensics, over in Plymouth, as soon as possible. She was almost certain that it was the immediate cause of her hangover, but she didn't know what was in the mixture. It wasn't clear what other steps she could take until that was known.

Frances had been out of the office since Wednesday and there were various colleagues she had to talk with and tasks to catch up on. But half an hour later she was interrupted by an outside call. It was Joy Tregorran.

'Hi Frances. I've been into the Chapter House, found out a few details on the communion wine they use at the Cathedral. They get it from Falmouth, a firm called "Anglican Alms". They bottle it for most of the diocese, I think.' Joy added an address and phone number.

'Thanks, Joy. I'll try and see them straight away. I'll let you know how I get on.'

Frances was an officer who preferred action to deskwork. She rang Anglican Alms and got an appointment with the Managing Director for half past ten.

She looked up. Tim Barwell had only just got into the office; punctuality was not his strong point. 'Tim, we need to go to a bottling plant. I'll explain why as we go.'

Anglican Alms was on an industrial estate on the edge of Falmouth. It was only a small plant but there was a steady hum of activity as the police officers walked in. The lady on reception quickly led them to her boss's office.

'Good morning, sergeant. I'm Trevor Jones, the MD here. Please have a seat.'

The two officers sat and Frances introduced herself and Tim Barwell.

'Thank you for seeing us at such short notice, sir,' she continued. 'This is the early stage of an investigation into the communion wine that I believe you supply to the Cathedral in Truro.'

'That's right. What's the problem?'

'I don't want to get into too much detail at this stage,' Frances replied, 'but the Cathedral has had issues with one or two bottles of the wine, so I'm just trying to understand the full picture.'

Trevor Jones looked a little puzzled. 'Well, what can I tell you? We've supplied the Cathedral for forty five years and we've never had any complaints.'

'Do you supply many churches, sir?'

'A hundred and twenty seven at the last count, I believe. Of course, most of them are fairly small.'

'How often d'you have new orders?'

'It varies. The Cathedral's order comes to us monthly. The amount varies slightly from month to month – more at Easter, for example. We're due to send our delivery lorry there again this week, in fact.'

'There's been a problem, I'm told, with a couple of bottles. Is there any chance at all that someone could have tampered with them at this end?'

Jones pondered for a moment. 'I don't think so. The process is all automated, you see. The wine has to be fortified if it's going to be used for Communion. It needs to be 20% proof. So we deal in big batches at a time, in huge containers, two or three times a week.'

'And is that tamper-proof?'

'Well. It might be possible for a supervisor to add something to the whole batch but you couldn't do anything to an individual bottle. It's a production line, you see.'

'How many bottles are filled in each batch?' asked Tim.

'Two hundred and fifty.'

'So if a lot of churches complained you could make some sense of it, but not problems with individual bottles?'

'That's right.'

'Have you ever had any complaints at all, sir?'

Jones reflected for a moment. 'Not in my time. There were plenty, though, in 1976. That was the year after we started production. That was the drought year, of course: water shortages everywhere, even in Cornwall. It turned out, afterwards, that the bottle washing equipment had run dry. Lots of churches complained, I think. It took several years' hard work to restore our reputation.'

There was silence for a moment.

'You talked about your delivery lorry, sir,' said Tim. 'Could anyone break into that and doctor or steal just a few bottles?'

'Our drivers have all been here for years. In any case, the

bottles are put into sealed boxes before they leave the works. And we have various measures to make sure none of the boxes disappear on the rounds. I reckon the whole thing is pretty secure.'

Once more there was silence.

'I could get my foreman to give you a tour of the plant if you like?' offered Jones. 'The next batch will be starting to run in half an hour.'

Tim was keen to take up the offer but Frances was satisfied with the account they'd been given.

'I think we've taken up enough of your time, sir,' she said. 'Thank you very much indeed. It seems clear to me that if there's a problem just affecting one or two bottles at a single site, it must have happened after delivery. I think we'll continue the investigation at the other end of the chain.'

CHAPTER 15

Monday afternoon. Police Inspector Kevin Marsh scowled as his internal phone rang and he was told that Sergeant Frances Cober had just grabbed the last free diary slot of the day. He muttered impatiently under his breath. He'd been hoping to catch up with his paperwork. His bosses had been making noises recently about taking a firmer grip on activist threats and terrorist activity.

Marsh was a tall, burly man, fit enough, well over fifty. Once upon a time that would have meant an approaching retirement but these days he still had some years to go.

Even so he had plenty to do. His primary task was to translate the whims of senior Devon and Cornwall police officers over in Exeter into practical actions for his steady-paced but slowly-reducing workforce, spread thinly across the towns of Cornwall. Only the seasonality of the crime workload, as the many summer visitors came and went, made the task remotely possible.

Frances Cober was one of his brightest sergeants. On the whole that was a good thing – intelligence was a virtue, even in police work. He had had several brushes with her, though, over suspected "crimes" which had turned out not to exist at all, except in his sergeant's vivid imagination. He had no idea what she was coming to see him about this time, but he could only hope it wasn't too serious.

Maybe she just wanted to report back on Assisted Dying? He recalled he'd passed on the invitation.

'Afternoon, sir,' she began. 'Thank you for seeing me at short notice.'

Marsh was immediately on his guard: Frances was not normally so polite. What yarn was she going to spin him this time?

His secretary brought in a tray of coffee, with biscuits, confirming his worst fears. Frances must have fixed that beforehand. But maybe whatever she had to say was important. He switched off his computer as a silent signal that he was giving her his full attention.

'I went to that Cathedral Assisted Dying conference,' she began. 'It had some interesting moments. But also a real death on the first evening.'

Here we go, thought Marsh. Cober was always suspicious of death, could hardly credit that people did sometimes die without human intervention. He nodded for her to continue.

'The oddest thing was that the person who died had been playing a part earlier in the evening, a short drama in which he had been poisoned by his wife.' The sergeant went on to outline some of the key features, though she didn't mention the visit of her own officer, Tim Barwell.

Marsh stole a quick glance at his in-tray, which was practically overflowing. He did his best to look interested in the tale he was being told. Presumably Frances would soon come to the nub: why ever might this death be considered a crime?

'Anyway,' she went on, 'I rang up the doctor who had

attended the death. She was having second thoughts, so the body was sent for a post-mortem, which I attended late this morning.'

'Right. And what came out of that?'

'The pathologist, Dr Emily Barton, agreed it might just have been natural death. The man – he was called Donald McKay, by the way – had some sort of heart condition that might have given way at any time. But if that had happened, she said, she would have expected him to thrash about more than he had. So she took blood, stomach and urine samples and sent them off to the labs, asking for urgent analysis. She should get the results later this week.'

'So this might be . . . some sort of poisoning?' Marsh asked. He was far from convinced but he knew he had to play safe, keep his officer onside.

'That's not all, sir. I bought a bottle of Cathedral wine at the conference and had a small drink when I got home on Saturday evening. I had a friend with me and she had some of it too. It had a dramatic effect on us both.' Frances went on to outline the effect and the conversation next morning with Revd Joy Tregorran, the conference convenor.

'Hm. I presume that bottle is now with Forensics?'

'Yes, sir. I'm expecting that result tomorrow. And the key question is, will it be the same substance?'

'If it is, then?'

'In that case, sir, we have two similar assaults relating to the Cathedral and its activities, such as the conference on Assisted Dying, at almost exactly the same time.'

Marsh hadn't been told all the possible linkages but suddenly recalled the latest edict from Exeter, sent on from the

Home Office and relating to activist and terrorist alerts. There had been warnings that future attacks might spread out from the major cities. 'I don't suppose the contents of this bottle could have been intended to damage the Cathedral itself?'

He'd expected the idea to be dismissed out of hand but to his surprise his sergeant took it seriously. 'I'm not sure, sir. I'm waiting to hear from Joy Tregorran. She thought this wine could be the regular communion wine used at the Cathedral.'

The possibility, however remote and far-fetched, of some sort of attack on the Cathedral finally pulled Marsh off his fence.

'Right, Sergeant. Thank you for informing me about all this so promptly. You must make this your top priority – at least to talk to the Dean and check out security at the Cathedral. In fact, if he wants, I could look for extra resources to help with ongoing security. Not a policeman, you understand. A real security expert.'

The sergeant's reporting session had not been a waste of time after all. Marsh felt pleased that this crime (if indeed it was a crime) could perhaps be tied in with some higher-level action on security. That would make his bosses very happy indeed.

CHAPTER 16

Frances Cober had picked up her coat and was making her way out of Truro Police Station, planning to go back to her office in Helston, when the call came through from Joy Tregorran.

'Hi, Frances. I've learned more about the wine bottles they sell in Diocese House. I could tell you over the phone but it's slightly complicated. Or I could write you a report. But if you're anywhere close it might be easier to show you in person.'

Truro is a compact city and the Police Station only a few minutes walk from the Cathedral. 'I'll come right over,' replied Frances. 'Be with you in ten minutes.'

When the police officer got to Diocese House she had expected that it would be empty, unless another conference on some topic or another had already started. But it wasn't, it was full of church administrators, occupying most desks on the first two floors.

Joy was waiting at the entrance foyer and led her up the stairs to the common room and bar on the third floor.

Frances noted that the room was locked when they arrived but Joy had a key. 'Is that the one you had for the Assisted Dying conference, or one that you've acquired for today?'

'It's the one the authorities lent me a week ago. The room is normally locked, I'm told – it certainly was today when I got here. But I decided I wouldn't hand it back until we were both sure there was nothing else to look at.'

'Good move, Joy. Right, what've you found?'

'Various details, but it's not as clear as I'd hoped. First of all, the bad news, this bar obtains its red wine directly from the Cathedral store, down in the Crypt. We can go down and look at that if you like, trouble is we won't be able to get in until tomorrow morning.'

Frances said nothing but wrote the details in her notebook.

'Secondly,' Joy went on, 'they keep a record, in this folder here, of the number of wine bottles to be collected, the date they were ordered and the total behind the counter at that point.'

'What about payment?'

'Oh, there's no payment, Frances, it's all deemed to be part of Cathedral overheads. Like stocks of tea and coffee.'

'Right. So can we see the folder, please.'

Joy reached behind the bar and seized a red file. The details were hand-written on successive A4 pages, with dates, initialled, down the left hand column. Frances took it from her and found the latest entries.

'So they sent for another delivery just in time for the Assisted Dying conference. Half a dozen more bottles of Cathedral Red – they must have expected the conference to drive some of us to drink. Which would bring their total supplies to eight. So how many have they got now?'

'I've had a good look, Frances, gone through every cupboard. But I can only find five.'

'In other words, Joy, they sold three bottles of red wine to one delegate or another during the conference. I had one, probably Donald had another, so that leaves just one more that we have to account for.'

Frances gave a sigh. 'Well, it could have been a lot worse.'

Joy was following her logic and had already reached the same conclusion. 'I've examined all the bottles that are here on the back shelf, Frances. In my opinion none of them have been opened at all. But maybe you ought to check for yourself?'

Frances was keen to do so. She slipped behind the bar and scrutinised the top on each bottle in turn. She could see that in each case the ten or so tiny threads of metal, which secured the top to the rest of the bottle, had not been broken. She couldn't see any way that the liquid inside could have been tampered with. 'No, I reckon all these bottles are fine.'

Frances turned to her companion. 'So that leaves the question, Frances, were the two (or maybe three) tampered bottles dealt with here, in the bar; or earlier on, down in the Crypt? And if that was the case, are there any more stored down there which are still a potential risk?'

That question couldn't be answered until tomorrow. But Joy was still concerned about the third wine bottle, potentially lethal and sold to persons unknown, during the conference she had led.

'Frances, I'm trying to remember who was serving behind the bar in the evenings last week. I was putting all my energy into talking to delegates; I don't really remember who that was. But it must have been someone from the Cathedral staff.'

The police officer picked up the red folder and glanced through the entries again. 'Well, look. It's almost always the same initials when the new wine is ordered. Looks like "P T". Does that help?'

Joy mused for a few seconds. 'Hey, that's right. When I came here a couple of weeks ago, there was a catering woman I talked to called Trish Townsend. That could have been short for Patricia.'

'Was she on the staff at Diocese House? Could we see her now?' Frances was impatient to learn more.

'No. She was on loan from the Chapter House. She won't be there this late, they stop serving at 4.30. She's only part-time in any case: I think she told me that she doesn't often work on Mondays or Tuesdays – got some sort of caring role at home. But we could probably catch her tomorrow morning.'

Joy had exhausted her store of information on the Diocese House catering officer. In any case, she was losing interest in the finer details of detection. She had her date with Harry Jennings coming up shortly.

CHAPTER 17

By half past six, Truro's Monday evening rush hour, such as it was in the depths of autumn, had subsided. Harry Jennings had been looking forward all day to meeting his friend, Joy Tregorran, once again. He made his way from the ECHO Chamber down the hill to the Cocktail Bar and restaurant in St Mary's Street with anticipation in his mind and a glow in his heart.

He recalled there was some reason why they were to meet: Joy wanted to mine his expertise or ask his advice about something or other. But he didn't take that too seriously: Joy often overestimated his wisdom. The breakthrough, to his mind, was that she had asked to see him.

When he got to the Cocktail Bar, set back a few yards from the pavement, Harry saw that Joy had already claimed a table at the back of the main eating area. She stood to greet him and they gave one another a discreet hug.

'Great to see you again,' Harry enthused. 'Can I get you a drink to start with or shall we order food straight away?'

'We're in no hurry,' she replied. 'Let's wait for the waitress.'

Glancing round, Harry saw that the restaurant was hardly overflowing. He peeled off his cagoule, hung it over his chair and sat down. The light was subdued (deliberately, he thought:

not just reducing the electricity bill via low-wattage lighting). Some sort of choral music was playing quietly in the background.

The place was discreet enough, anyway. It would have been a good place for a spy rendezvous.

'You said you had some issue or other that came up at your conference. D'you want to start with that straight away?'

'If you don't mind, Harry. I'm afraid it might take us some time.'

'Joy, most of my time these days is being some sort of Mentor to my PhD students. Since September, my listening skills have improved no end. Please, tell me the tale from the beginning.'

'Well, can I say first, Harry, that all this is highly confidential. It's not made the public domain and I'm only telling you the story on that basis.'

Harry nodded. He had assumed this would be the case, anyway. Not many people sought out media attention.

So Joy told him all that she knew of the sad tale of Donald McKay: retired engineer, occasional actor and conference delegate. 'He offered one example of assisted dying to an audience in the Cathedral Crypt and he's now a corpse in the local hospital.'

The waitress appeared as Joy reached the end of her narrative. There was a pause while they both ordered their meals: grilled steak and chips for Harry and lasagne for his companion. Harry also asked for a pint of Doom Bar bitter and Joy a half of berry cider. The interruption also gave the historian a welcome few moments to take stock.

'Right, Joy, that's a very clear account of the background. I

111

can see it's been a traumatic few days, thank you for sharing it. Now we move onto the next stage: whatever has all this to do with me? And how is any of this an ongoing issue for you?'

Joy took a moment before she answered. 'So far, Harry, I haven't mentioned the police. As it happened there was one off-duty police officer present at the conference as a delegate, a woman called Frances Cober . . .'

For the first time since she had started, Harry broke into her narrative. 'Hey, Joy, I know that name. Frances was the one who helped me in that dreadful business that brought you and I together last January. Well, you couldn't do better, I would say, if you wanted professional help. She's very thorough, also very bright. So how did she get involved?'

At this point the waitress returned with their meals and drinks. A couple of minutes were taken to sort out condiments and sauces. When she had left them, Joy took a deep breath and responded.

'This is the bit that really is confidential.' Joy took a mouthful of her lasagne. Then, as she continued to eat, she outlined the events over the weekend, starting with Frances and a friend arriving at the Gunwalloe vicarage at half past nine on Sunday morning.

Finally, she summarised the conversation she'd had with the pair over lunch in Mawgan. 'It was after that that I decided I needed your help,' she concluded.

'You'd better stop talking for a few moments while you finish your lasagne, Joy. It'd be a shame if it got cold.' The ensuing silence also gave Harry time to think. The problem was starting to take a rough shape in his mind.

He waited until Joy had finished eating. Then the historian

leant forwards.

'So the whole thing rests, really, on the forensics. Are the death of Donald, followed by the doctoring of the policewoman's wine, two independent incidents – or are they part of the same assault?'

'That's right. But I don't think they've had the results back yet – or if they know, they've not told me. No reason, of course, why they should.'

'It would be a remarkable coincidence, though, if two distinct acts of aggression, both apparently linked to poisoning, took place at much the same time in almost the same context. I can see why the police might fear the worst. So let's assume for now, Joy, that the forensics will eventually link the two assaults together. Right: so what's the question; where I might be able to contribute?'

Before Joy had time to answer, the waitress appeared once more. In truth, this early in the evening, there were not many other diners to catch her attention. A dessert menu was offered and two items were chosen, profiteroles with cream for Joy and chocolate brownies for Harry. The pair also ordered coffee.

'It's the two attacks together that are telling, Harry. The identities of the victims might just have been random; the aim might have been primarily to attack the Cathedral. The question the police asked me, where I was really stuck for an answer, was about the Cathedral itself. In terms of motive for crime, they asked, is there anything in its history which could conceivably stir up aggression today?'

There was a pause. Joy feared that Harry might not know that much about the building's history. But in fact that wasn't the case. By pure chance, Harry had spent the morning listening to Simon as he outlined the Cathedral's development. The trouble was, the presentation hadn't been made with this question in mind. Some mental reordering was needed.

Fortunately their desserts appeared as he pondered, giving him a couple of minutes leeway.

'As you know, Joy, the Cathedral here is scarcely a century old,' the historian began. 'There was much debate over where a new cathedral should be built but eventually Truro was chosen. That it was built in the centre of Truro and completed in less than thirty years was due mainly to the combined efforts of two strong characters who generally worked together well.'

'Who was that?'

'One was the newly appointed Bishop of Truro, Edward White Benson. He'd studied at Cambridge then rose to be headmaster of Wellington College before being appointed a Bishop. He was a driven, well-organised man. Indeed, he went on to become Archbishop of Canterbury.'

'And the other?'

'That was the architect, a man called John Loughborough Pearson. He'd designed church buildings all over the place – even done one in Australia.'

Joy had been listening with a purpose. 'You said that these two generally agreed – was there something they fell out over?'

'Well, there was one question which arose early on, where should the Cathedral be located? Both wanted it in the centre of Truro. Trouble was, there was a building here already: the Parish Church of St Mary's. It wasn't an architectural masterpiece by any means, but it had been here since the thirteen hundreds.'

'Ah.' As a vicar, Joy could understand the dynamics that would come into play. 'The Bishop wanted to keep the old, while the architect wanted to demolish it and develop something new.'

Harry smiled. 'Oddly enough, it was the other way round. The Bishop was all for starting afresh, whereas the architect wanted to merge old and new. In the end, for reasons my researcher is now looking into, the architect won. Most of the old Parish church was knocked down but its south aisle was preserved and later made part of the cathedral. It's been beautifully done, though. The casual visitor might never notice where they join.'

Joy nodded. 'That's true. Now you mention it, I know where you mean. I've had to walk around the Cathedral a lot in the last week. It never occurred to me that I'd wandered into an older section. So you think the argument between Bishop and architect might have repercussions today?'

'Not exactly, Joy. That was a hundred years ago. But there might be something more recent – which could incite a response today. Now you've raised the question I'll give it my top attention. Maybe I'll start with a tour of the Cathedral. My student tells me there are free tours, put on by volunteers on most weekday mornings.'

For the time being, Harry had responded to Joy's anxiety and now she was happy for the talk to turn to more personal matters. It was the first time they'd met since her conference and she intrigued him with thumbnail sketches of some of the delegates. In turn he outlined the latest twists of local history turned up by his students.

By nine o'clock Joy was feeling tired. She'd had a busy day and had to drive back to Gunwalloe. Harry, too, had to leave soon if he was to catch the last sensible train back to Exeter.

As they walked out of the restaurant Harry noticed a plaque beside the door. It claimed that the place where they had just eaten had once been home to Truro Grammar School. For some reason the name rang a bell. Had the place had been mentioned by one of his students?

As the two came out, they saw the southeast corner of the Cathedral, fifty yards along the road. 'Have a proper look in daylight,' said Joy. 'You'll be able to make out the old Parish Church, or at least its remaining aisle, on this corner.'

At the time Harry had no idea that the links might be anything more than geographical.

CHAPTER 18

Frances was at her desk in Helston Police Station bright and alert by half past eight on Tuesday morning. She was expecting to hear from Forensics about the contents of the wine bottle which had induced deep slumber for her and George the previous weekend. She was slightly surprised, though, when the news came through so swiftly – and directly on her phone.

'Hi there, Frances.' She recognised the lilt of the cheerful Scottish scientist who had somehow found his way from Thurso down into the Plymouth laboratory that also serviced Cornwall. The two had hardly ever met, but had a longstanding working relationship.

'Hi, Angus. What've you got for me?'

'Ye were verra lucky on the wine,' he asserted, 'verra lucky. If you'd drunk that bottle at any speed, and if you'd been on your own, you'd probably not be takin' this call. Or any other calls ever again.'

'That sounds ominous. So you know what it was – I mean, apart from Cathedral wine?'

'Och, aye. It was a verra large dose of methadone. You're supposed to take it by the teaspoon but with that bottle you might have taken it by the bucket. It's addictive, you see, could easily ha' been fatal.'

'Right.' Frances had half expected to hear something of the sort but the words still shocked her. She'd had a lucky escape.

'Is methadone easy to get hold of, Angus?'

'You or I couldn't just buy it over the counter at a chemist. It's known to be dangerous. One of the drugs often prescribed by doctors to reduce pain, say in the later stages of cancer. So I guess it wouldn't be that hard to find, if you had the connections and knew where to look.'

Frances paused for a minute, wondering if there was anything else she needed to know at this point. There were plenty of facts still missing, but none would come from Forensics. 'Right, thank you, Angus. I presume I'll get a formal report on this in due course?'

'Och, aye. Couple of days. But I thought you might want to know as soon as possible. I would if it had happened to me. I'm so glad, lassie, that you're OK.'

His good wishes sounded very sincere. Frances thanked him, put down the phone and took a deep breath. She wondered what time Inspector Marsh would be in his office. And how soon she might hear from pathologist Emily Barton.

Frances didn't have to wait that long. A few moments later her internet chuntered into life and there was a copy for her of the email that had been sent to Dr Barton by the laboratory staff at Truro Hospital.

It was the usual medical gobbledygook. Frances, though, was used to reading between the lines on such reports and getting to the core message. Down towards the bottom of the screen she spotted the crucial line.

"The dead man – Donald McKay – had a striking excess of

methadone in his blood stream."

So the reason for the trouble, in both cases, had been methadone. Last week's two peculiar events coming out of the same conference – Donald's death and her poisoning – must almost certainly be linked.

A few minutes later she was on the phone to Inspector Marsh. But for the moment he was unavailable. His secretary told her he was in a meeting with "someone senior from Exeter", though she couldn't (or wouldn't) give a name. Slightly frustrated, Frances booked a meeting with her boss for later in the morning. There were other things she could usefully do in the meantime. For a start, she could go with Joy Tregorran to check the wine store in the Cathedral Crypt.

Joy was working for the day in Diocese House, tidying up loose ends from the Assisted Dying conference. One of her tasks was to write a concluding report from the convenor's viewpoint, to help leaders of later Encounter Conferences. She assumed that, perhaps after a delay, these would still take place. In most respects she would rate her event as a success.

One phone call later the meeting with Joy had been arranged. Frances parked her car at Truro Police Station and walked up St Mary's Street to the Cathedral. The usual buskers were playing on the cobbled forecourt. She went in at the West End, along the quiet, almost-empty Nave, under the central tower and through to the Crypt entrance, alongside the Quire. She was glad to see Joy was already waiting.

Strictly speaking, both lab reports which Frances had received that morning were confidential to the police. However, she was bursting to tell someone; and found it almost impossible not to share them, in confidence, with Joy. After all, Joy had been the leader of the conference where all the trouble began and already knew most of the background.

Also, the news was relevant to their search of the wine store. It moved that from a theoretical study to a life and death investigation. Her visit to the bottling plant the day before had made it clear that any bottle-doctoring must have taken place at the Cathedral end. If two bottles of wine from this store had been tampered with, there might indeed be others. Both women needed to be fully alert to the possibilities.

The Crypt was locked but once again Joy had a key. 'I was loaned it a few weeks ago, once we'd decided that was the best place to put on the drama. I thought I'd better hang onto it until the McKay investigation was over.'

Frances had a quick look at the key. It was nothing special, would be easy enough to copy if someone was inclined to do so. Security within the Cathedral was indeed a little flaky.

Frances had been in the Crypt before, of course, on the first evening of the conference. But that had been at night, with the Cathedral mostly unlit or with limited lighting – even less once the drama began. Then the police officer had been off duty, having no cause to think of it as a possible crime scene.

Seen in the daytime it wasn't particularly sinister. The whole Cathedral was fairly modern and the Crypt had been constructed at the same time. It was basically a large lower-level storage area, not an ancient place of prayer from centuries earlier.

Frances noted that the stage used last week must have been a temporary construct, made up of six feet square by one foot thick wooden platform blocks. The audience, after all, was modest. The blocks were now stacked on the far side. Round the vacant area in the centre were a number of doors.

'The drama group used these as dressing rooms,' explained Joy. 'Donald was fussy, for some reason. He insisted on having his own – that one.' She pointed to the room on the far end.

'Are any locked?' asked Frances. In her mind's eye she could see a security audit heading for the Cathedral. It would be best to prepare for it as much as she could.

'Nothing is locked in here,' replied Joy. 'There's no point is there, as long as the Crypt itself is kept locked when not in use?'

Frances elected not to respond. 'Which one stores the wine?'

'This cupboard over here,' replied Joy. She led the way over to it and opened the door. Inside were several shelves of Cathedral red wine, perhaps thirty bottles in all.

'The ones on the left are for sale in the Diocese bar or Chapter House. On the right is the Communion wine.'

Frances frowned. 'But there's no labelling, Joy. The bottles look identical. It would be easy for anyone in a hurry to muddle the two. Perhaps that happened before the conference?'

'I hadn't thought of that, but yes, you're right.'

'Do they have records here, like we saw in Diocese House?'

'Mm. It doesn't look like it. I guess someone must order more when there's only one shelf left. Or perhaps they have a regular monthly delivery direct from Anglican Alms.'

'Anyway,' said Frances, 'let's check that these bottles haven't been tampered with.'

Once they'd got started it didn't take long. There was no sign at all that any bottle, of either type, had been modified.

'So there's no immediate risk to communicants,' concluded Joy. 'That's a relief, I guess.'

Frances saw there was still over an hour before her appointment with her boss. Then she remembered Joy had mentioned a chat with the bar manager. 'Doesn't Patricia Townsend work around the corner? Could we see her?'

'We might as well try.'

The two women went to the refectory, now in full swing. Clearly many Truronians appreciated the mid-morning coffee and cakes on sale there. After a brief enquiry, a rather fierce-looking woman emerged from the kitchen and addressed herself to Joy. 'Someone said you wanted to see me?'

'That's right. But could we go somewhere more quiet?'

There were plenty of nooks around the Cathedral. Joy introduced Frances – 'one of the delegates from last week's conference' – but carefully made no mention of her police association.

'I bought a bottle of red wine from the Diocese House bar to take home,' explained Frances. 'But when a friend and I had a little, it made us very drowsy.'

'When I heard this, I checked the record behind the bar,' added Joy. 'I reckon that you sold another bottle or two during the conference. Is there any chance you can remember who you sold to? I'd like to contact them, check they've not had any trouble.'

Frances and Joy had concocted this edited version of events as they walked round to the Chapter House. With a bit of luck

Trish would not be too inquisitive and would simply answer their question.

They were partially successful. Trish did not challenge the effect of her wine – maybe she daren't. But she couldn't remember who else had bought any. 'I'm selling beverages all the time, Joy. In Diocese House or the refectory. You can't expect me to remember who bought what. For goodness sake, you're talking about last week.'

Frances was used to seeing witnesses interrogated. She had seen the whole gamut, from the person who could do nothing but tell lies, to the ones that tried, but struggled to remember the whole truth.

On this occasion she was pretty sure the woman was doing her best to tell the truth. Another bottle or two of wine might have been bought by a conference delegate at some point. But there was no easy way to work out who that might have been.

CHAPTER 19

Frances was just about on time for her scheduled meeting with Inspector Kevin Marsh. But for once he was slightly late; he'd been delayed by his extended encounter with the Exeter bigwig.

Often Frances had seen such situations lead to irritation with his subordinates, as Marsh took all his unspoken frustration with the man above him out onto the man or woman below. But for some reason Frances sensed that, this time, he was almost pleased to see her. Maybe he saw her as someone who, whatever her shortcomings, belonged to his own West Cornwall tribe?

Whatever the explanation, Marsh's secretary had seen the emotional lie of the land. She appeared with a tray of coffee and a plate of biscuits, almost as soon as their meeting commenced.

Frances decided it would be best to start speaking whilst the going was good. 'I wanted to tell you as soon as I could, sir. I've heard this morning both from our Forensics and the hospital laboratory. It was the same stuff in my wine and also inside the dead man – methadone. It's a prescription drug for the later stages of cancer and the like – but you're only meant to take it in very small quantities. So I'd say that means it's almost certain that Donald McKay's death was deliberate.'

124

Marsh reflected for a few seconds and then nodded. But he had seen another angle that bothered him just as much.

'Forget McKay for a moment, Frances. If he was murdered then what should I make of what happened to you?'

'How d'you mean, sir?'

'I mean, Frances, have you narrowly escaped from an accidental death or were you also intended to be killed?'

Marsh had never shown concern for her before. Was he getting soft in his old age? 'It must have been an accident, sir. No-one at the conference knew that I had anything to do with the police. I checked: there was no mention of rank or employer on the material that was circulated to the other delegates.'

'They might not have read anything, Frances. They might know already. Say, they could have seen you supervising one of those endless Brexit marches we had earlier this year. Or, I don't know. . . dealing with a traffic accident?'

'If I was in uniform, sir, they'd probably register a female police officer but they'd never remember what I looked like.'

'OK. But might you have mentioned your job in all innocence, say when you first arrived?'

'These days I'm very careful, sir, when I'm off duty, not to give any clue that I belong to the police. Otherwise you spend the whole time listening to complaints of one sort or another.'

'Actually, Frances, that used to happen to me, too. But what about after you heard of McKay's death? Your crime instinct was aroused – correctly, as it turns out. What if you asked too many questions too early?'

'I did my best to avoid that, sir, I asked the Revd Joy Tregorran, that's the convenor, to have chats with everyone

125

over the next day – and to disguise these as checks on their wellbeing.'

'Good, good. It's not easy to be an undercover officer at a crime scene; sounds like you handled it well. But what about when the news of the death first broke? Did you perhaps take too much interest then?'

'I don't think so, sir.'

'But when this Joy was interviewing on your behalf, might she have given you away?'

'I can't be certain, sir, I wasn't there. But as it happens, I've met Joy before and I know that she's a very sensible woman. I would be amazed if anything leaked.'

Finally it seemed Marsh was convinced. It was pretty unlikely that Frances had aroused any attention at the conference as a police officer. For now he was content to treat her near-poisoning as some sort of accident.

'Alright then, Frances, you'd better concentrate on McKay. Get your team to do all the usual checks, see if there's anything odd about him which might provide a motive for murder. After that you'll need to follow your famous feminine intuition.'

The Inspector paused for a moment, glanced at the calm Sergeant once more. Then he decided it was right to trust her with his own concerns, raised by his previous meeting and by the context in which McKay's death had occurred.

'What you told me about the conference at the Cathedral, Frances, overlapped with concerns that have been expressed to me by the senior team in Exeter. They all relate to security. Can we discuss that for a few minutes, please?'

Frances certainly wasn't going to turn her boss down if he

wanted, for the first time she could remember, to treat her as a colleague. The question of security within the Cathedral had already been exercising her thoughts.

'You haven't been told any intelligence suggesting the Cathedral might be attacked, have you, sir?'

'Good gracious, no. That'd be far too much to hope for from our security colleagues. Why, have you seen anything?'

Frances went through the provenance of the tampered wine bottle that had been sold to her, and how it had come from the wine store in the Crypt. 'That's where the Cathedral stores the wine which they administer in Communion every week, sir.'

Marsh went pale. 'So you might be onto an activist attack of some sort already?'

Frances hastened to reassure him. 'Joy Tregorran and I went through the wine store this morning sir, both the retail red and the Communion wine. We checked the cap on every bottle. There's no sign that any have been tampered with.'

Marsh breathed a sigh of relief. But Frances wasn't giving him too much respite.

'So I'd say, sir, there's no risk down that route at present. But it's one way for an activist to attack the Cathedral if they really wanted to. In fact, I reckon security in there is pretty lax.'

'Hm. So we ought to be worried?'

'The trouble is, sir, neither of us – or anyone else round here – is a trained security expert. What the Cathedral needs is a professional to give it rigorous analysis. There might be various defence mechanisms that could be installed without costing very much at all.'

Marsh had spent the morning being told this sort of thing in a high-flown language. Hearing it from his own staff was even more convincing.

'OK then. We need to start by seeing the Dean, or whoever's in charge of the Cathedral, for a general chat. If you'd come with me that would be good. We could move from generalities that he (or she?) is bound to agree with to specifics that you could provide. Are they keen to protect the place at any cost – or more worried by the message that excess protection might give?'

This case seemed to have grown legs since it emerged this morning, thought Frances. But if she was being given a hearing then she needed to make sure she had something to say. Even if it meant being a little unorthodox in where she went for advice.

CHAPTER 20

'Hi, George.'

George Gilbert looked at her phone in surprise. It wasn't that unusual to hear directly from Frances Cober, but she didn't often call in the middle of the working day.

'Hi, Frances. Is something the matter?'

'Can you spare me a few minutes? Or at least suggest when might be a good time to chat?'

'Well, I'm fairly busy right now. I'm over in Newquay. We have a weekly meeting every Tuesday for the team working on Airport Security issues. I haven't done my bit yet but it's due next, after the coffee break. And it could take a couple of hours. Could you wait till tomorrow? I'll be over in Truro then – we could have a meal out somewhere if you liked.'

In fact, Frances told herself, tomorrow would do fine. All she really needed was a background chat, before she met the Cathedral Dean. A location to meet was arranged and she rang off.

She wrinkled her nose. There was nothing for it now but to get back to Helston Police Station, to start making the most of her slender resources.

Frances was glad to see her team was working away steadily. Tim Barwell was beavering away in the corner. She had a moment's indecision: who should she talk to first? Then she realised her protégé was due some quality time, anyway.

Mind, he seemed cheerful enough. 'Hi, boss,' he greeted her. 'So have you seen off the Inspector?'

Frances' sometimes turbulent relationship with Kevin Marsh was of course well known in the Helston Police Station, though usually only openly discussed behind her back.

'Last seen cowering behind the desk,' she told him with a grin. 'Right, I'll get us both some coffee from the Fizzo Wizzo downstairs. Then come into my office and I'll bring you up to date on the case of Donald McKay.'

Frances had already phoned Tim to tell him the core of the new evidence reported that morning, but there'd been no time to discuss it. He'd obviously been giving the matter some thought.

'So the two events are evidentially connected?' he began, once they'd sat down and taken their coffees.

'Seems that way, Tim. Trouble is, it's not obvious why. The most likely link, I suppose, is someone fearing what I might have uncovered about Donald. Perhaps they wanted to deal with me before I'd had time to report my ideas to anyone else?'

'But,' she continued, 'Marsh quizzed me pretty hard. We couldn't see any way I might have given away my full identity. I certainly hadn't intended to. But if that's not why I got the tampered bottle, then goodness knows what is – it might just be pure bad luck.'

There was silence. Tim had no idea either.

'At least Marsh now accepts there's a case for us to investigate,' said the sergeant. 'Though that's been helped along, I think, by the possibility that it might be linked to a security alert – something to do with the Cathedral. Top brass in Exeter are bothered by that sort of thing at present.'

'Maybe that's a ripple from the latest London outrage,' suggested Tim. 'If you were a terrorist, boss, wouldn't you want to do something different next time, away from the capital and all its famous bridges, just to shake up the general public? I would.'

But he sensed that he'd said enough – maybe sounded too enthusiastic. 'Anyway, boss, where do we start, on the case of Donald McKay?'

Frances paused. 'At this early stage, Tim, we need to keep all options open. Leave aside any connection with me, and even any direct link to the Cathedral conference. So what motives can we think of for a retired man, living on his own, to incur a sudden death?'

'Well, what do we really know about Donald McKay, boss? Can we be sure he wasn't leading some sort of double life? He might not be living in Shortlanesend all the time. For example, do we even know where he goes on holiday?'

Frances considered. 'Well, I didn't hear him mention holidays at the conference, the only time I was on his table. One thing we could do, that might help, would be to talk to his bank. Given his sudden death they should be happy to give us access to all his recent statements.'

Frances started to enumerate some of the questions. 'Does Donald have a credit card? Is he solvent or in debt? Is he the recipient of odd cash donations – or paying regular amounts out? If he'd paid for any big holidays in the past year, you'd probably find them there too.'

Tim nodded. 'I'd be happy to do that, boss. I'll go back to Shortlanesend and find out which bank he uses. Then contact them, arrange to see the manager as soon as possible.' He gave a sigh of regret. 'Maybe I should have done all that last time.'

'It wasn't a crime at that point, Tim. But right now chasing his finances would be a really useful step forward.'

Frances saw the need to take her protégé's thinking further. 'It'd be worth hanging onto that key to Donald's bungalow, by the way, the neighbour won't need it now. And also – maybe on a later visit – to go round the Close and chat with the other residents. See what they can tell us about Donald's habits: how often he's seen about, regular companions and so on.'

'Right, boss. I'll give it my best shot. What'll you be doing?'

Frances could have told him he didn't need to know but to her mentoring often meant sharing. 'I've got a unique position, Tim, from being a conference delegate. Over the next few days I want to go round the other delegates, see if they heard anything that could help us. Maybe find someone else who bought wine.

'I've also got a meeting lined up tomorrow with someone who knows about security. She's currently working on something linked to Newquay airport. Inspector Marsh wants me to go with him to talk about security to the Cathedral Dean later this week. But if that's going to work, at least one of us needs to know something about it.'

CHAPTER 21

It was Wednesday lunch time. 'So you see, George, I'm not the only one to worry about possible threats to the Cathedral. In fact, my boss and I are going to see the Dean about it tomorrow. That's why I need all the help you can give me about security in general and what a safety zealot might be looking for in this case.'

Frances Cober and George Gilbert were seated in a secluded alcove on the first floor of Charlotte's Teashop, looking down on Boscawen Street in the centre of Truro. They had already

put in their orders for a light lunch. Mercifully, though, the waitress was in no hurry to deliver it.

George gave a grin. At least her friend wasn't in any trouble.

'I don't know all that much,' the analyst began. 'I'll tell you what I've picked up over the years, but you mustn't think that's everything that can be said. This is a massive topic. You need a real expert to turn my generalities into hard specifics. And, of course, to tell you about the latest equipment and what it might cost. It's forever being updated, I'm afraid that's bound to shove up the price.'

Frances nodded. 'OK, George. I accept your limitations. You don't know everything. But, please, tell me what you can.'

George paused for a moment to collect her thoughts.

'There are all kinds of threats that might be made in today's world, from all sorts of people. And they each call for different types of response.

'First of all, perhaps worst of the lot, there are threats to people, whether famous or unknown – often folk just going innocently about their daily business. Like we've seen recently, with those poor Londoners stabbed to death on London Bridge.

'Secondly, there are threats to specific buildings which are deemed to be of lasting value, whether full or empty. Here in Truro the Cathedral would be one such place, perhaps the only one that would fit that description.'

George paused to make sure Frances was giving proper weight to her words, then continued. 'Causing visible damage to a place like the Cathedral would certainly make the television national news and have a wide impact across society. That could include damaging the building itself – in the last resort, I suppose, with some sort of bomb. On a less grand scale it might include threatening some routine activity that goes on there – for example, taking of Holy Communion.

'Finally,' George concluded, 'there are also all sorts of intermediate steps. Say trying to steal something valuable – or at least that's of perceived value to the owner. One aim in practically every case, you see, will be to achieve publicity for the attacker's cause.'

George noticed Frances was busy, scribbling all this down in her notebook. She stopped talking to give her a chance to catch up.

As it happened their lunch arrived at that point. Just as well to pause, George thought, we don't want the waitress overhearing too much and starting a rumour – or even a major panic.

Once they were on their own again, George went on with some of these themes.

'To be honest, protecting visitors from random attacks is almost impossible to do discreetly. Imagine that the Prince of Wales – the Duke of Cornwall – was coming for a visit to the Cathedral. He'd need round the clock protection from patrolling police officers with rapid access to armed backup. If it was an event shared with the general public, they'd probably also insist on security arches on the doors at the West End, you know, like they have at major airports.'

'That's to make sure no-one could smuggle in a weapon, like a knife or a machete?'

'That's right. Now all that might be OK for a major visitor like the Prime Minister or the Prince of Wales. But such a system would never happen in Truro for ordinary churchgoers. At least, not until there'd been similar attacks at other cathedrals in the UK.'

Frances reflected for a moment and then nodded. 'Right. So you're saying there's some "principle of proportionality" in what an expert could propose. But there must be other things a security man could do?'

'One manageable goal, almost certainly worthwhile, would be to make it much harder to get into the Cathedral when it's supposed to be locked. At night, for instance. And also to keep each section separately locked, so getting into one bit wouldn't necessarily help with any of the others.'

'You mean key management?'

'Well, that'd be a start. I'd want a designated security manager, with tight control on spare keys and security numbers.'

Frances considered, remembering odd comments from Joy. 'I suspect even that would be a big step forward for Truro.'

George nodded. 'But that would only be a start. Once that was in place I'd say that for somewhere as large as the Cathedral you'd need systems to check that the place was really empty when it was supposed to be.'

She saw Frances was looking slightly puzzled.

'For example, CCTV cameras and motion detectors to put on floodlights if they sensed movement – or maybe even detected body heat. With microphones for unexpected sounds. But if you'd got that, you'd need someone to keep an eye on it all, maybe to wander round and make occasional inspections.'

'That's all starting to sound rather expensive.' Her friend was looking doubtful, maybe pondering the challenge of relaying this tomorrow to the Cathedral Dean.

'Well, security is expensive, Frances. But can you afford to be without it? Do they have much in the way of valuables in the Cathedral?'

'To be honest, George, I've no idea. Remember, this isn't really my patch, I'm supposed to be in Helston, looking after the Lizard. I suppose I could ask our clerical companion, Joy Tregorran. She must have some idea. But the Cathedral is modern – only a hundred years old – so it might not have had time to accumulate much in the way of earthly wealth.'

George thought for a moment. 'You could always pop into the Cathedral shop and buy yourself a guide book. Then at least the Dean could see that you'd tried to do your homework.'

CHAPTER 22

Given that the meeting had been preceded in the Truro Police Station by an awkward difference of opinion with her boss, Frances thought the main event was starting well.

It was late Thursday morning. They were in the Dean's office, an elegantly furnished room in a smart, stone building overlooking the West End of the Cathedral. The Dean, Peter Kennedy, was wearing a grey suit, offset by a flamboyant tie, with no sign of a clerical collar: though Frances had looked him up and he was fully entitled to wear one. Obviously he was acting today as Cathedral manager rather than church minister.

In style the Dean reminded her slightly of Tony Blair in his heyday. He was impressive in his language and inclusive in his manner – aiming for a consensus but certainly no pushover. He would not take any action unless a strong case had been made in its favour.

Also in the room, to Frances' surprise, was the Revd Joy Tregorran. 'I thought it would be useful to have someone who has recently been doing a project here, inside the Cathedral,' the Dean remarked by way of explanation. 'Joy isn't on the staff, so she has something of an outsider's perspective. But if I end up needing someone to manage actions on a daily basis for a limited period, Joy has generously agreed to act as my right-hand woman.'

Frances wondered whose side Joy would be on if it came to a political tussle. Was she there to back up the status quo or to support the case for change? Or was she simply the elusive floating voter, whose gentle opinion would end up determining where the debate would go?

Frances noted, with private amusement, that neither the Dean nor Inspector Marsh seemed to realise that she and Joy already knew each other from a long way back, and had a good working understanding.

Coffee was served and introductions made. It was clear that today only first names would be needed.

Time to begin; the Dean turned to the senior policeman, sitting in the easy chair alongside him. 'Kevin, perhaps you could outline why you asked for this meeting with me at this point in time?'

The Inspector seemed caught off guard by the specific question, perhaps unsettled by his earlier conversation with Frances. He took a deep breath. Then he started with some general observations about security fears across the country, mentioning the recent terrorist assault on London Bridge. Finally he went on to expand on some of the recent fears expressed by the Chief Constable of Exeter.

The Dean did not interrupt. But Frances could see that he was becoming impatient, did not want to waste time on generalities. 'Kevin, we could have had this sort of discussion throughout our working lives,' he asserted. 'What's so special for Truro Cathedral today?'

It was clear to Frances that her input was needed to tether the conversation down to specifics.

'Perhaps I could start to answer that,' she began. 'There

was an unfortunate incident at Joy's recent Assisted Dying conference. I bought a bottle of Cathedral Red from the Diocese House bar to take home. When I had some – not much, just half a glass – with my evening meal, it caused me to drop into a deep sleep.

'This week I had the bottle analysed by Forensics. It had been tampered with – was strongly mixed with methadone. Now I can live with a few hours extra sleep, Peter. But the real worry was that Joy checked, these bottles came straight from the store in the Cathedral Crypt. They're in a cupboard alongside the regular supply for the weekly communion service.'

Frances stopped. There was plenty more she could say but she wanted to hear the Dean's initial response. How seriously would he take her?

The Dean paused to take stock. 'Mm. That does sound a real problem. It's a good job you're a healthy woman, Frances, and that you hadn't drunk a lot more.'

He turned to Joy. 'Have we any idea how safe our Crypt is? Is the Cathedral wine cupboard always locked, for example? And assuming it is, do you know the official key holder? And how many copies of that key exist?'

Joy looked embarrassed. 'I'm sorry to say, Peter, that the wine cupboard isn't locked at all. The assumption seems to be that it's enough to keep the Crypt itself locked. But I've no idea how many spare keys there are for the Crypt.'

The vicar paused but could see more was expected. 'I was lent a Crypt key by one of the vergers. I needed regular access, you see, for my conference. I had to let the group in to rehearse the drama that would start the whole thing off. But now I think

140

about it, I didn't see the verger recording the loan and he hasn't asked for the key back.'

'Joy's experience suggests that security here is not altogether watertight,' added Frances. 'We've no idea why the wine bottle was doctored – whether it was intended to get at the Cathedral, or there was some other purpose – we're still working on that. But even if it was nothing to do with drugging communicants, it's a warning that such a thing is possible: next time it could easily happen, unless we tighten up security.'

Kevin Marsh was feeling out of the loop. As a senior policeman he didn't like to be marginalised and needed to say something.

'There are several reasons why someone might want access to the Cathedral,' he observed. 'Harming communicants, having them doze off by the row, would obviously be bad publicity. Especially if the local press was given advance warning and pictures appeared in their paper. But there might be other forms of assault that you'd find far more costly.'

He turned to the Dean. 'Peter, what sorts of valuables are held within the Cathedral building?'

The Dean gave a sigh. 'I expected this might come up so, since the meeting was fixed, I've been seeking that information from older staff. I've only been in post for a couple of years, you see. I'm afraid I found a lot of things here hard to get to grips with. In my innocence I'd assumed that all the main valuables here would be listed, photographed and insured.'

He didn't say it but he'd obviously been disappointed.

'The thing is,' he went on, 'this Cathedral is really not very old, not by comparison with many others. It hasn't had long to build up a collection of rare antiquities or generous bequests.

141

We don't have valuable oil paintings, for example, left to us by an Old Master – or even a famous modern work like the Graham Sutherland they have at Coventry.'

He paused to gather his thoughts. 'What we do have are all sorts of oddities that are precious to our community here – they are part of the fabric of the Cathedral – but which would be hard to sell on to anyone else.'

'I'm afraid I don't know the Cathedral that well, Peter,' said Kevin (the understatement of the year, thought Frances). 'Can you give us some examples?'

The Dean thought through what he had gleaned. 'Well, there's the terracotta montage of the Way to the Cross, with the figure of Jesus carrying the wooden cross he would be crucified on. Every face in the crowd is different and quite a few are famous. One of them is the man who would become King Edward the Seventh. He laid the Cathedral Foundation Stone in 1880.'

'There's also a full-sized black mahogany statue of the Virgin Mary, cuddling her Child,' added Joy, seeing the need to add to the list. 'That came from Italy. I'm told it was found gathering dust in a corner of the Crypt. It was lifted into the open and dragged halfway down the Nave, a few paces a day, by two of the Cathedral guides.'

'And we mustn't forget the model of the Cathedral, made out of thousands of matchsticks,' continued the Dean. 'That's probably not worth very much – I mean, it's only wood, not silver or anything – but it's rather striking. A lot of people would miss it if it ever disappeared.'

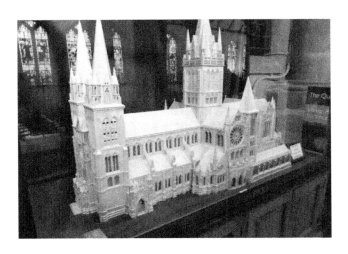

Kevin Marsh was starting to wish he'd never asked. 'But you must have a few conventional valuables: silver chalices and the like?'

'Oh, yes,' said the Dean, looking relieved. 'I checked on those when I first came. They are locked away. There's a safe in the Crypt that I'm told only has got the one key. It only needs to be opened, you see, for the time the vessels are in use.'

'That's good,' said Marsh, magnanimously. 'Well done, Peter. But we're still agreed, are we, that security here is hardly top notch: something could usefully be done?'

143

'I think so,' the Dean replied, cautiously. 'I'd certainly be interested in having an expert check things over and advise us on what else needs to be done. It'd be easier for me to enforce any changes needed if there was an outside authority behind them.'

A further thought came to him. 'But we'd need to be very careful not to arouse the media,' he mused. 'That could make things worse, could even provoke activists to come down and disrupt us.

'If we were already under assault it'd be different, of course. But until that happens – and I hope it never will – I'd want to keep any security checkup well under wraps. We certainly don't need a man in a hi-vis jacket tramping around the Cathedral, claiming to be "security".'

By now Kevin Marsh had achieved the result he was after. He'd got an opening from a fairly willing volunteer: Exeter would be happy. Now he would ask them to pursue the provision of a suitable security assessor from the Metropolitan Police or possibly the Home Office.

To the Inspector, the details of what they actually did once they arrived were of less concern. That could no doubt be handled by his sergeant and the lively vicar from Gunwalloe.

CHAPTER 23

For days Harry Jennings had been itching to hear more of the tale of Eleanor Kempthorne. Whatever would happen next? Then, at their weekly tutorial, Ellie told him she had completed more transcription of the diary and was ready to share it with the group. As a consequence, an ECHO session had been arranged, slightly out of sequence, for Friday afternoon.

Ellie took the memoir based on Eleanor's diary in her hand and glanced round the room. Her fellow students were all there, happily content, almost eager for her to continue. A human interest story would always beat bare-boned factual recital. Harry gave a nod and she began.

'I had no idea where we were supposed to land in America, or even how long it should take us to get there. But the Trade Winds were blowing and we were certainly moving along at speed. I could only trust the First Mate, who seemed to know where he was heading. After all, he'd been to these parts many times before.

My fruit-based diet seemed to keep the seasickness at bay. Or maybe it was that I now had a job that kept my brain exercised. I continued to tend the keel-hauled slave girl who lay bruised and bleeding in my cabin, slowly recovering her strength.

Finally, after many days as I stood in the cabin doorway, I heard a shout from the lookout, perched atop the forward mast. 'Land ahoy.' How did I understand him? Well, the crew spoke mainly English, though I had now been told that Conakry was run by the Portuguese. The slaves spoke an indecipherable language all of their own, but then they didn't need to speak much at all. The voyage was hardly a pleasure trip for their benefit.

I learned from one of the crew that we had arrived at the port of Saint-Domingue, on the large Caribbean island of Hispaniola. Only many months later had I much idea where the island lay.

What mattered for now was that I was in one of the major West Indian ports. This was where the African slaves that had survived the crossing were received, bought and sold, and then assigned to their plantations. Disturbed by the savage words of John Wesley in central Truro, this was what I had come all this way to see. I needed to give it my full attention.

After some argument about landing rights with the locals, our ship was fastened to a rickety pier that stretched out a short way from the quayside. Safe enough, I guessed, unless there was a tropical storm. How often did these happen? I had no idea.

The First Mate disappeared for the best part of a day. I feared he had headed off to sample the local rum that I'd heard the crew speak so highly of, but it turned out that for all of them the drinking would come later. The First Mate's task today was to find a local buyer for his hundred or so slaves. There were less than a hundred left now, of course, almost a dozen had died on the voyage.

It came as a shock to me to realise how lightly I had made that calculation. What had happened to me? After pondering for a while, I concluded that when individual people – men or women – are reduced to being measured in mere numbers, their value seems to crumble.

It might have been different if I had known some of my fellow-passengers' names; but apart from Mapinga, as I had come to call my nursing charge, I knew not one. Was that not shameful, I rebuked myself. But there were mitigating circumstances. I remembered the cruelty that I had seen from the crew towards the slaves, and how fortunate I had been to keep out of its power.

Late in the afternoon, the sun still beating down as fiercely as ever, the First Mate reappeared with another man, who I think was speaking a form of French – I had picked up a little on my musical work in Truro. He was the better dressed of the two and I guessed ran one of the many plantations that spread across the island.

I was watching from a sheltered spot on the deck, along with Mapinga. The two men didn't see me as they headed to inspect the slaves filling the two decks below. Some time elapsed and I presumed that counting was now taking place. I surmised that negotiations over price were under way between the two men.

Finally the two reappeared, both looking satisfied. The First Mate looked especially pleased; no doubt he had driven a hard bargain.

All might have been well for me, and maybe even Mapinga, except that the plantation owner spotted the African and me as

147

he glanced round the top deck before making his departure.

The owner pointed at the two of us and made a questioning comment, in French. But the First Mate was not going to lose his precious agreement for the sake of two women, especially if the alternative would be taking us back all the way across the Atlantic. With scarcely a pause he nodded in agreement.

And so, with no chance to protest or argue, my fate was sealed. I had declared that I wanted to see the reality of the slave trade. Now I was to see it at first hand. For I was now a part of the ship's slave cargo that would be put ashore in Saint-Domingue the following morning.

CHAPTER 24

Harry Jennings had called a halt at that point. 'Guys, we'll take a short coffee break. But we won't discuss any of the wider issues at this stage. Ellie has too much still to tell us. But even she could use a pause for a few minutes.'

Harry could see that the narrator was upset as she had retold what had happened. History at its best, history in the raw, could sometimes do that to a sensitive being.

Twenty minutes later Ellie had composed herself. Her reading of Eleanor Kempthorne's shocking memoir resumed.

'For a while the shock of what was happening to me also stopped me noting the details. Much of the next few days, as recorded in my diary, was only written down in arrears. But the overall impact was only too clear.

I had stated my intention to see the slave-handling process for myself. John Wesley had declared the slave life to be "harrowing" and the "great evil of our time". What I had seen, first in Conakry and then on the voyage of the slave-vessel to Saint-Domingue, had underlined his comments: I could add a heartfelt "Amen". I had witnessed at least something of the evil he had described.

In truth, though, if I had returned to England at that point, I would have shared some of Wesley's knowledge in my mind but it still would not have penetrated my heart. It was hard to see at the time, but the personal disaster of being included in the slave owner's deal and, I now realised, losing my paid-for journey home would have some long-term benefits.

Each of the slaves held below deck had first to be released from their ankle chains, before being let out, hobbling and blinking in the bright sunlight, onto the jetty.

I thought at first this was an act of kindness by the plantation owner who had bought them. He must be concerned for their welfare. But then we started the long, long walk to his plantation. It was clear now that the journey would have been impossible for a bunch of slaves still chained at the ankle.

By comparison with my fellow slaves I was a fit woman. I used to walk long distances around Truro: Aunt Jemima had told me the effort would do me good. I'd had the chance to exercise regularly on board the ship and, best of all, I had not been chained. I had also eaten a steady diet of fruit of all kinds.

My only disadvantage, in fact, was that I was still gripping the small locked casket which contained my diary. But I was determined that at any cost I would not part with that: it held my most precious memories.

Mapinga walked beside me. She'd had an easier voyage than those held below deck, although she'd also suffered that gruelling keel hauling. But she seemed to be on the mend. If we'd had a common language, we might even have become friends.

Even so, I was exhausted long before we reached the plantation which I knew would be our long-term home. It must have been a dozen miles away and, as we struggled along, the sun burned down on us as strongly as ever.

The plantation owner would not let us dawdle. I was horrified to see that he had armed himself with a wicked-looking whip, which he cracked on the ground behind anyone whom he judged to be lagging. I was grateful that my relative fitness spared me from the treatment. Perhaps, also, he was wary of applying the whip to a white woman? Every other person in the party, except he and I, was charcoal black.

At long last we reached the plantation. It was guarded by a high wooden fence that I judged would run all the way round, to offer the owner protection from outsiders. Later I realised that it wasn't that at all, it was there to keep his slaves in. He had no intention of losing any of his workers, except by their death.

The men and the women of the plantation were housed in a series of separate circular huts, each with thick, baked-mud walls and straw roofs. Our beds were on the floor: further bundles of straw and leaves, laid along the hut's spokes, with the head rests close to the wall.

I was the only white woman in the place. I let Mapinga explain about me to the rest of my hut in her native tongue. I guess she shared her story, made much of my powers to assist recovery after her near drowning. When she had finished the rest of the hut seemed to regard me with a sense of awe.

I placed my casket at the head of my bed, next to the wall. Then I made sure by use of my hands that every woman understood: this was my possession and was precious to me. Mapinga gave a further diatribe on the subject, maybe referencing some African magic. I could only hope it would have the desired effect.

151

By now it was practically dark. I had learned over the last few weeks that in the tropics dusk did not last for long. There were many sounds of insects flying around. I wrapped my flimsy dress around me, fearful they would regard a white woman's flesh as a special treat. Then, completely worn out, I lay down and did my best to gain some sleep.

Next morning our work as slaves began soon after dawn. A guard appeared, another African, this one armed with a heavy stick. We were called out of the hut and put into a rough line. Then we were marched along a narrow path through high-standing fields until we reached the working heart of the plantation.

Of course, my women – the women in my hut – were all new to this. I saw massive rows of high, leafy bushes, teeming with coffee beans. At least I could recognise them. There was a smart restaurant in Truro where my beloved James and I had once gone on our wedding anniversary. In there, beans much like these were roasted, ground down and finally mixed to make a hot drink. It tasted delicious, though it was far too expensive to enjoy on a regular basis. The thought made me sad but I was given some succour by the memory.

Now, though, I could see the full cost of that drink. Our hut's occupants were set to work, each of us armed with a large basket, to pick the shiny dark beans before us and put them into the baskets.

At that time, first thing in the morning, it was bearably cool, almost pleasant. But it would soon become dreadfully hot. Even so our guard gave us no respite from the heat. We worked on and on, picking away at the beans. My back was hideously painful with the repeated stretching and stooping.

It was late afternoon before we were escorted by the guard back to our hut. I was absolutely exhausted; and also famished. Outside the hut – my new home – I saw a bucket of what I later learned was groundnut stew, also some bowls and a handful of spoons. That was our meal of the day and I forced myself to eat the portion I'd been given. There was not much chatter between the women in any language. We were all far too exhausted. It was not long before I was lying down, trying once more to sleep.

That was the day of an African slave. And it went on, day after draining day. I could have coped for a couple of days, taken a pride in the authentic slave experience. But for the rest of my life? How long would I last in this hell hole? Would I ever again see my home back in England and my family?

I knew I had to look strong. In the daytime I would put on a pretence but every night I cried myself to sleep.

Ellie's voice had cracked as she read the last sentence. Harry could see she was close to tears. 'Should we stop there?' he murmured.

'No. Something else happened. I have to read that today or we'll all end up with miserable weekends.'

She swallowed hard and then picked up her notes once more.

'A month of this relentless torment went by. Oddly, my fitness seemed to increase: physical work was evidently good for me! But I hardly dared think how it was all going to end.

We had the same guard day after day and we got used to

one another. He no longer saw a need to see us right back to our hut. One day we must have started the journey home slightly early: it was still light as we arrived.

As we drew close to our hut, we saw a man creeping out. Worst of all, he was carrying my casket. I gave a cry of alarm.

Mapinga saw the problem and reacted at once. She raced forward and hurled herself onto the intruder, thrusting him and the casket to the ground. Then the rest of us reached him. With hindsight it was barbaric, but we were living in a land with no laws. Every one of us gave him a good kicking, over and over again. One of those kicks must have been fatal.

Eventually, worn out, we stopped and realised what we had done. In the fading light we peered at the man: it was one of the guards.

In a moment of clarity, I decided to check his pockets. And there they were: a set of keys to the plantation.

Until that moment I had never considered the possibility of escape. But for some reason the keys changed everything. By now it was dark and, as it happened, there was no moon. There was a fair chance I could move to the gate without being spotted. And if the worst came to the worst and I was caught, what did I have to lose? Even a slow, gruesome execution would be no worse than spending the rest of my life in this slave camp.

I gave Mapinga a farewell hug. I took time for one last look around the circle of my fellow slaves. Then I grabbed my casket and headed silently for the plantation entrance.

CHAPTER 25

On Friday afternoon Sergeant Frances Cober called an end-of-week review in the main meeting room at Helston Police Station. She had the white progress boards moved out of her office and lined up at the front. There were several pictures of Donald on the first, alive in the drama and later dead in Shortlanesend, but the second board, intended to display suspects, was so far empty.

The only other person present was her fellow-worker on the McKay case, Tim Barwell. She consoled herself with the thought that quality was sometimes more useful than quantity.

It was nine days since McKay had died, three days since the forensic evidence had emerged, and time now for frantic police probing to give way to quiet reflection. And also exchanging notes on progress. The two hadn't had time to leave more than scribbled messages for days.

Frances began by outlining Thursday's meeting at the Cathedral between herself, her boss and the Dean.

'So what will happen next?' asked Tim, once she'd completed her account.

'Inspector Marsh is like a dog with two tails. After the meeting he pressed Exeter for a security expert to join us and that's been approved. The Home Office have got someone, apparently, who is happy to come to Cornwall. He should be down early next week. Initially he'll be here for a fortnight.

Joy Tregorran and I will do our best to manage him. Let's hope he'll bring us some fresh ideas.'

'Of course, security might have nothing at all to do with McKay's death,' warned her colleague.

'That's true,' Frances agreed. 'But it should teach us more about the Cathedral and its foibles. I'd say there must be some sort of connection.' She gave a sigh. 'Right, Tim. That's me. What've you got on McKay from your interviews and finance checks?'

The constable outlined his latest visits to Shortlanesend and to the bank in Truro. 'McKay was financially sound: a regular pension and modest outgoings. Nothing to induce suicide.

'I've spent this morning sifting through his bank statements, line by line. I can't see anything odd in them. No big sums moving in either direction. The man's last two holidays were both bird watching: Northumberland in the spring and Norfolk in the autumn.'

'What about how he spends his time?'

'I haven't got far yet. He pays an annual subscription to a local reading group – '

'– is that in the village?'

'Well, the convenor's address is, I expect it's a local activity. He must have known quite a few villagers – the better-read ones, anyway. Someone, I can't remember who, told me he'd lived there for years.'

'What about those house-to-house visits round the Close?'

'I had one go yesterday. But it wasn't very successful. Most were out and those I talked to could tell me nothing. Not one had even been inside his bungalow. I'll try again go next week.'

'Keep trying. If he's lived there that long, someone in the village must know something. What about his bungalow?'

'Well, I've had one more look round. One thing I did wonder was, what had happened to his laptop? I couldn't see one anywhere. But he's a retired engineer: surely he'd have had one?'

Frances pondered. 'That's very interesting. But had anyone seen it – that neighbour, for instance? If they had, they might know where he'd bought it. If we could prove one had been stolen, we could contact internet broadband suppliers. It'd be a long battle but I suppose we might one day get to his email history.'

After a pause she added, 'But I'd be amazed if we got that sort of help. It goes along with the missing bunch of keys. Suggests that someone took away the things that, if a death came to be suspected and then investigated, might give away too much.'

Tim remembered his earlier thoughts. 'Right. I can see the computer might give us his email history and photos. Either might be useful, I suppose – there might be pictures of his associates. But what on earth is suspicious about his keys?'

There was a moment's silence.

'If every key on the bunch was for his bungalow or car,' Frances said slowly, 'that wouldn't tell us anything. So I'd say that there must have been extra keys on that ring. Keys that, if we got hold of, might tell us something vital.'

'Probably similar to his front door key: that's a Yale. The killer would be in a hurry, once Donald had taken the poison and was dead or dying. They wouldn't want to take the house key off the ring and leave the wrong one behind, so they'd swipe the lot.'

'Not for long, though. They're probably inside a sock stuffed inside a tin, chucked on a local rubbish tip.'

Tim shook his head. 'Not just one tin, boss. They'd split them up, put them in separate locations. I'd say our chance of finding them is zero.'

Further silence, both thinking hard.

'Wind back, Tim. What if Donald had one extra key that he used so regularly he added it to his key ring. What door might it have unlocked?'

Tim shrugged. 'Could be anywhere. A boat house say, or another garage?' He grinned. 'His secret lover's cottage?'

Frances grinned in response. 'Possibly. But what if it was linked to the drama at the Cathedral? Joy told me that was where they did their writing and rehearsals. So that's one place he went to regularly. Could it have been a key to the Crypt?'

Tim mused. 'If it was, you might have recognised it – or Joy Tregorran, if she was shown the whole bunch. So if the killer was playing safe, that would be a good reason for removing it. But what's peculiar about that Crypt?'

It was far from obvious. They had several pieces of jigsaw, but it wasn't clear they were from the same puzzle, or where this line of enquiry might land up.

After a pause Frances decided to move the review on.

'We're not leaving this room today, Tim, without at least something on that Suspects Board,' stated Frances. 'So go on, give us a first entry.'

There was a pause. Tim selected his best idea from a limited field. 'Well. Let's take it that McKay was poisoned in his own home, late on Wednesday evening. No signs of forced entry, so it must have been someone he knew and was happy to let in. My Option One is that it was someone he brought back with him, that he'd met in Truro.'

'Right. But they'd need a bottle of tampered wine already with them. The attack must have been deliberate – not just chance, say, or the result of a quarrel. And what about motive?'

Tim gave a shrug. 'No idea, boss. McKay could have been involved in something shady that we've not yet got hold of. It's been deeply hidden. But . . .' He paused, not quite sure where to go next. Frances though had a vital fact.

'A second red wine bottle, containing the same poison, was sold to me two days later from the Diocese House bar. It's beyond belief that the two events aren't linked. So the killer must have had some connection with the conference. Go on, then: what's Option Two?'

Tim paused to order his ideas. 'Option Two is that the killer came with McKay from the conference, bringing some wine from the bar, to which he'd added poison. Maybe that was someone else from the drama group?'

'Barry? He knew where McKay lived, certainly. But Joy was talking to him in the post-drama social. He's got an alibi.'

'The thing is, boss, the post-mortem didn't give the exact time of death. If Barry had gone on to McKay's after the social, he could be there by, what? ten fifteen or ten twenty. That's not too late for McKay to let in someone he knew, especially someone he'd just been working with.'

Frances nodded. 'OK. Then Barry could propose a drink, "I've brought us a drink to celebrate." He would open the bottle but make sure McKay took the major share, say by drinking his own glass extremely slowly.'

'Perhaps McKay's a secret alcoholic, boss, desperate for a drink?'

Frances frowned. 'Possibly. . . or just glad of the company. Anyway, McKay glugged it down. It would quickly make him drowsy. Then the killer would propose a refill, "One for the road" or something. After that he'd just wait.'

'And once he could see McKay was dead, he'd take his keys and laptop and head back to the conference. Arrive back late but gamble that no-one would see him.'

There was silence as they assessed their reconstruction.

'The thing is, Tim, we've put Barry in that role because we know that he knew Donald. But the logic would work for anyone at the conference who happened to know Donald from an earlier time.'

'Not just "happened" boss. Remember, this killing was deliberate. But that person could have learned by chance that McKay was attending this conference, looked into it and decided to come as well. So until we can narrow it down, the suspects list should include every delegate at the conference.'

All of a sudden the Suspects Board had gone from being empty to being heavily populated. Frances wasn't sure how she could possibly know who had known McKay earlier and who hadn't. Unless a delegate gave something away at interview, that could only come from a detailed understanding of McKay's life and contacts.

Frances started to feel overwhelmed. There was a great deal more needing to be done.

CHAPTER 26

Harry Jennings was feeling pleased with himself. With some trepidation he had broached the topic of staying for the weekend with Joy Tregorran in her vicarage in Gunwalloe and for once she had agreed.

'Harry, we've both been so busy these last few weeks,' she said, 'you with launching ECHO and me with Assisted Dying. Spending a bit of time together would help us both unwind. And there's no problem with transport. I've got my car here in Truro so I can give you a lift. Mind, I'm afraid there's a sermon I have to write at some point tomorrow.'

'Don't worry, Joy, there's plenty of stuff I can bring to do while you're doing that,' he replied cheerfully. 'Next week I'm supposed to be putting on some background history lectures for ECHO, to back up my team's research. We're halfway through a dramatic tale of a Truro woman who went to see the slave trade at first hand. I need to mug up on the Napoleonic Wars. They happened around that time, so might have some relevance.'

Elsewhere a similar phone conversation would take place a day later, between George Gilbert and Frances Cober.

'Frances, I've to work overtime today at Goonhilly and I'm due there again on Monday.'

'Dare you risk another weekend with me? I've got plenty to

do during the day but you'd be welcome early evening. I've no more Cathedral wine but you'd be welcome to join me - maybe to help me eat a Sainsbury's Chinese banquet?'

'Thank you very much. Then I'll treat us to lunch again somewhere, after our Sunday stroll. Hey, you can tell me what came out of your security conference, if you're allowed.'

When George got to Frances' old fisherman's cottage in Gweek, she observed it was less tidy than usual. Frances had been using the place to eat and sleep and little else. The case of Donald McKay and the poisoned wine was obviously taking all her energies. George felt for her friend, resolved to do whatever she could to help move the case along.

'I bought us a bottle of Sauvignon,' Frances said as they sat down to eat. 'Not from the front, got this one from behind. Don't worry, I checked the top, it's not been opened. And the sell-by isn't till late next year.'

This sounded excessive. Last week's experience with the poisoned wine must have rattled Frances more than she'd wanted to admit.

'Well done,' said George. 'I'll drink it, anyway. Frances, you look shattered.'

'It's been a hard week,' her friend responded. 'Above the usual stress levels, anyway. I'm not used to being the victim as well as the investigator, you see. Not just being put into a deep sleep: that was manageable. I also had to receive the post-mortem on Donald and the forensics on the wine.'

Frances scowled. 'Trouble is, the consequences are getting more serious. Next week I've got a Home Office man coming down to take stock of Cathedral security. Goodness knows

162

how, but I'm supposed to manage him.'

George smiled. 'You never know. He might turn out to be tall, dark and handsome. At least give him a chance.'

But at this point Frances needed to sound off about the week just gone. Maybe she had no-one else of similar age to share with? It would be best for the time being to offer supportive empathy.

'The Dean gave his approval then?'

'After a bit of a tussle. But he didn't want any publicity. I think he feared we'd have the Daily Mail taking pictures, claiming the Cathedral was under threat from Russian spies.'

'Well, they did know Salisbury Cathedral was 123 metres tall. Maybe Russians like tall buildings?' George grinned as she spoke, trying to diffuse the tension. 'Nerve agent would be far worse than our poison: that, in small doses, just sends people to sleep.'

After a moment's thought, Frances grinned back. 'OK. I do need to keep it all in perspective. We're both alive. And this wine is delicious.'

As they worked their way through the banquet, course by course, Frances went through the previous day's review of the case. She wouldn't normally share her police work with anyone but George was a fellow-victim. She was also a wise friend who could distinguish common gossip from a highly confidential debriefing.

George listened hard but felt there was little she could add.

'Where are we going for our Sunday stroll?' asked George as the pair enjoyed a leisurely breakfast next morning.

Frances had been out interviewing all day Saturday. But

George knew no-one could work all the time. Today she was determined to make sure her friend took a full day off.

The morning had started well. This time there'd been no after-effects on either of them from the previous evening's wine – and between them, slightly to their surprise, they'd consumed the whole bottle.

Frances grabbed her much-thumbed map of the Lizard from the sideboard. 'We could do another bit of the Coast Path. Maybe start along the Loe, walk to the coast and then south over the cliffs? That should get us to the Halzaphron Inn in Gunwalloe for lunch time. We don't need to book at this time of year.'

'That sounds fine to me, Frances. I really don't care where we eat. All these out-of-the-way places do good roast lunches. And then?'

'Well, depends how much energy we had left. If we'd done enough we could simply walk back to the car. If we wanted more we could come back inland, go right round the Loe.'

It was a wild day, grey skies and plenty of strong wind, but at least there was no rain. They drove in George's yellow Mini-Cooper that she'd had for years. Frances navigated them round Helston and out towards Porthleven. Then they turned off down a narrow lane which led through the National Trust estate at Penrose. A few minutes later they'd parked and were off.

'Over the centuries boats were wrecked all along this coastline,' observed Frances cheerfully as they reached the beach beside the Loe and started to climb the cliffs beyond. 'It's the rip tides, you see. The route into the beach looks safe enough but you can get swept along when you'd expected to come straight in. And there are serious rocks further down. That's where we were last week.'

She pointed a couple of miles further along and George could see the fierce headland beyond which, she remembered, was Dollar Cove. It was hard enough battling into the wind on foot, she thought, without being tossed about by the waves in a boat.

Just after one o'clock they arrived at the Halzaphron Inn. There was a choice of roast dinners on the menu: beef, lamb and pork, all with associated roast vegetables. There were still a couple of empty tables. Frances picked the one closest to the roaring fire: after their walk into the wind some heat would be welcome.

A few minutes later the door of the Inn opened. Joy and Harry appeared, also in search of food and warmth. Harry had sat attentively through Joy's sermon in Church Cove, then they'd discussed it forensically as they walked back to Gunwalloe. Harry had been in student mentor mode, more searching than usual. Now he was looking forward to some non-work time alone with his friend.

 But that would not happen yet.

'Hey, you two, come and join us,' said Frances, waving to Joy as she spotted them. All four knew one another but had they enough in common to sustain a whole meal? In fact there was no problem, although George didn't know Joy well, and her friendship with Harry had only been vibrant in Cambridge, decades earlier. Even so, the mutual attraction between the pair was not extinct.

Fresh introductions were made as food and drinks were ordered. Harry sketched out the role of ECHO. George explained that she was currently working at the nearby Goonhilly Earth Station. Frances realised she shouldn't be surprised to meet Joy here: it was, after all, the vicar's nearest place to eat out. Which in turn accounted for Harry; presumably he was staying for the weekend. In a way it was Frances, with her office back in Helston, who had the most distant link.

The main topics in which the four had a common interest soon emerged as Donald McKay's death, poisoned Cathedral wine and possible links to the Cathedral.

Frances had no desire to discuss police work in a public place. But she was interested to discover that the fresh source on Cathedral history, which Joy had offered to tap the previous Sunday, was in fact Harry. That made it easier to include him in the discussion, although she wasn't going to disclose any case details.

It would be alright, though to seek Harry's perspective on recent events as a historian. Would that give her some fresh insights?

Food and drinks arrived at that point and enhanced their conviviality.

'You're the least involved in this, Harry,' said Frances, as they started on their food. 'What d'you make of it all?'

Joy feared they were expecting too much. 'Hey, guys, this is Sunday lunch, not a history tutorial.' But Harry liked being asked questions, especially on the wider view: he relished the challenge.

'One question from the past,' he began, 'is to decide

whether or not two events from the same time are in fact linked. And if so, how? Is one the cause of the other; if so, which came first? Or do both stem from something else that happened even earlier?'

He paused to order his thoughts. 'In this case, as I understand it, the sudden death preceded the poison but, crucially, it was the same poison both times. There must be a link. Mercifully, for two ladies – as it happens, both of you here – the effect was short-term. But for the other victim it was permanent.

'To account for his death on its own you'd need to know something special about his life. But for the events taken together you have to find a common cause. And the only link that makes sense so far is the location they both started in, which is the Cathedral itself, or possibly the Assisted Dying conference.

'So I'd say the primary cause was something that happened a lot earlier and could well be something to do with the Cathedral.

'Joy asked me about the history of the Cathedral last week. Since then I've been doing a little digging. How could a hundred-year-old building possibly trigger a crime today? It's an interesting question.'

Harry paused for another mouthful of his roast beef. 'I had various ideas. Firstly, is there a building debt still unpaid, with a lender who's increasingly desperate? Well, the building was finished a hundred years ago. One of my students is looking into how it was paid for but so far he's not found anything remotely suspicious.'

He paused for a further mouthful. 'A second possibility is

167

some issue of design that still rankles today. For example, the building has a six foot bend over its length. Once you notice, it's impossible to forget. But the design has been settled for a long time. It's hard to imagine any concern big enough to engender a crime today.

'A more remote possibility is if the building sparked a quarrel that still rumbles on. For example, there was a row in the 1870s over whether the Cathedral build should begin by flattening the old church that was on the spot, or merge it in. But since one of the participants later became Archbishop of Canterbury, I'd say that one's been settled.'

Harry smiled. 'Finally, scraping the barrel, is there some sort of treasure hidden within the building? It's unlikely but, if there was, the search for it might rouse strong emotions. These could be as strong today as when the item was first hidden. Mind, I have absolutely no idea what that might be.'

At this point Harry stopped talking to finish his roast beef. The others seized the opportunity to respond. There was a lot of discussion but no strong conclusions. Frances still felt grateful: her perspective was growing a little wider.

'There's one more thing,' Harry concluded. 'Most actions for historians are long in the past. But this is something that, for whatever reason, has only just happened. One further question that I'd have is this: has this crime sequence now reached its end – or is there more still to come?'

CHAPTER 27

When Harry Jennings got to the ECHO Chamber on Monday morning he could see that Ellie had been busy over the weekend with her memoir based on Eleanor Kempthorne's diary. It must have been an exciting process, for she was eager, almost desperate, to share the results.

Harry consulted the rest of his team. They had no other urgent deadlines and were also keen to know the next turn of events in this remarkable drama. Eleanor had last been heard of heading for the plantation gate. Whatever happened next?

The ECHO schedule was designed to be flexible. History could not be regimented. By eleven o'clock the team was gathered in the meeting room, mugs of coffee in their hands, and Ellie could begin.

'I was thankful that my dress was a dingy dark blue and I had long, chestnut-brown hair. But the fair skin on my arms and face would still be easily seen in the dark. Then, to my relief, I came across a pool of slimy mud. I quickly scraped plenty of it over both.

The plantation was settling down for the night now, not many people were out in the open. Most were inside, talking or getting ready to sleep. It took a while to find my way to the entrance but I took great care, hiding behind one hut and then another, and mercifully was not spotted on the way.

As you might guess, the plantation entrance had a guard. But the owner was no more generous in the numbers assigned to this than to anywhere else. There was only one man in the cubicle beside the gateway; I could hear his snores from twenty yards. The keys that I'd taken from the guard, the one we'd kicked to death, would be the vital factor.

I took a deep breath then sidled up to the gate, keys in hand. The snoring continued. I examined the gate and spotted the keyhole. Slowly, carefully, I tried the largest key: it fitted! I gave it a twist and felt the gate starting to open.

A moment later, casket in hand, I was through and out into the lane. I even managed to lock the gate behind me. Which was the best way to go – towards the port of Saint-Domingue or away and across the island?

At this point I had a lurch of realism. True, I was out of the hated plantation but that was only the first step on the long journey back to England. I hadn't even thought what would happen next.

By morning my escape would no doubt be discovered. One missing black woman among hundreds might not matter, but the only white woman working in the whole plantation couldn't possibly just go absent.

At best this might not be linked with the missing guide whom my hut women and I had kicked to death. But at worst . . . suddenly I realised to my horror just what danger I had left behind.

I had no idea what form execution usually took on Hispaniola but it certainly wouldn't be pleasant.

And that led back to my decision. It wouldn't be enough for the owner to execute my hut-mates. He would certainly want to find and punish me as well, no doubt horribly slowly and as painfully as possible.

There was no way, therefore, that I would choose to head back towards the port and make it easy for him to find me.

So now, utterly downcast, I turned and headed away from the port – away from the only place on the island where I could possibly find a boat to go home.

An hour or so later I was struggling along the lane to nowhere. The night sky was clear, so the wide coverage of stars had some effect; and by now my eyes had got used to the dark. The overall result was that I could see the sides of the lane, but not a lot more.

There were also the persistent sounds of a tropical night: fireflies and frogs, insects and bats, making whispers and clicks, croaks and groans. I did my best to ignore them all.

Then I heard another sound, one that was much more frightening. For it sounded like a fast-moving horse and cart. My disappearance had been noted and I was being pursued.

I was in despair. I could never outrun a horse. The chance of escape was nil. But could I hide by slipping off the lane?

It might have worked, but there wasn't enough time between me hearing the clip-clopping horse and it catching me up. Worse still, the animal had a lamp mounted over its head. So as it reached me I was blinded, trapped in the lane side.

Then, out of the darkness, a voice spoke. And for the first time, I felt a sliver of hope. For the rider, whoever it was, spoke in English.

'Hey there, lady,' he began. 'What are you doing in the middle of the night?'

I had no idea what he was after. But it was unlikely that the owner of the plantation, who after all had spoken French even to the First Mate, would have someone who spoke English to chase after me. This man must therefore be different, some sort of passing traveller. My only chance was to throw myself on his mercy.

'Sire, I am fleeing from the last coffee plantation down this road. Please can you help me?'

There was a pause as my words were analysed. Then the man spoke again. 'Madam, I am no friend of any plantation owner. Come, you may travel with me.'

In the gloom I could now see that the vehicle in which the man sat wasn't just a farm cart, like they used to take coffee beans to the port, but a proper trap. I couldn't make out his face, though I sensed he had a massive beard, but I'd made my decision and for better or worse clambered in beside him. My precious casket was stowed behind.

The driver tugged on the reins and we set off.

'Are you travelling far, sire?' I asked.

'Many miles, I fear. My home is on the far side of the island of Hispaniola. But this lane goes from one side to the other and I do the journey regularly.'

There was a pause. There was hope here. The "far side of the island" would be a long way for the plantation owner to come and find me.

'But it must be hard for you to travel at night?' I persisted.

'For my own reasons I dare not travel by day. This island is no place for Englishmen – or Englishwomen, if I hear your voice aright.'

His voice sounded so friendly. It was over a month since I had heard a word of English spoken. Never had it sounded so sweet. It reminded me of everyday conversations back home in Truro.

'I am from Cornwall,' I confessed, 'brought up on the Lizard.'

'Well I never,' he replied, 'I come from the Lizard too.'

He also was Cornish – he couldn't be an enemy. I wanted to ask him more about himself but feared he would not feel free to answer. So I decided to tell him a little about myself.

'I came this way to see a slave plantation in action,' I began. 'You've 'eard of John Wesley, no doubt? He preached one time in Truro, said slavery was evil. My aunt – she's looking after my son – urged me to come and see for myself. But it all went wrong at the port – very wrong. I ended up being sold as a slave myself.'

' 'Tis a sorry tale you tell,' he responded. 'And your husband, does he not worry for you?'

'My husband is dead, sire. He fought one battle too many for the English Navy. Took on a French vessel in Samana Bay, wherever that be, and lost. I had an official letter to tell me. But that wuz years ago.'

As I spoke to a self-confessed Cornishman I heard my voice tinged with sadness as my accent became ever more pronounced.

'What about you, sire? Does ee have a wife?'

The man was silent for some time. I told myself that I should never have asked. He was probably doing secret work of some kind, could never tell me. And my question was a gross intrusion. But something told me I had to ask.

Then he spoke. 'I believe I still have a wife. I love her

dearly and one day, God willing, I will see her again. And also my son, John. He is a bright lad, good at mathematics, so I am told. But for now, due to forces beyond my control, I must serve my country in this God-forsaken land.'

I considered his answer in silence for some time. He also had a son called John who was good at mathematics. There was far too much in what he was saying that matched only too well with my own situation. It was unreal – well, either unreal or true.

'What is your wife's name?' I whispered. I almost sensed the answer but dare not yet believe it.

'My wife? She is called Eleanor. Eleanor Kempthorne.'

Now I thought about it, the voice had sounded eerily familiar all the way along. 'And you are James Kempthorne,' I replied. 'My husband – still alive, despite what our manipulative Navy told me.'

'Eleanor!' He gave a great big gulp and pulled the trap fiercely to a halt.

Then he turned towards me, put his arms around me and gave me a huge kiss.

'Mind,' he said, many minutes later, when our first embrace was over, 'you could do with some better makeup, m'dear. What you've got covering your face right now smells . . . well, it smells like mud.'

CHAPTER 28

'For some reason there was a gap in Eleanor's diary at this point,' said Ellie.

'I shouldn't worry,' advised Ben. 'Any document hand-written two hundred years ago on the far side of the Atlantic is likely to have bits missing. It's amazing you've got as much as you have.'

'No, Ben, it wasn't that pages had got lost. I think life was simply too full for Eleanor to be bothered to write anything down. But eventually life settled down and she started recording again. The next big chunk was to say what she'd gleaned had happened to husband James, after he lost his sea battle in Samana Bay.'

'We're itching to know, Ellie,' said Harry. 'Please, read on.' So she did.

'It took a while to make any sense of James' story. It was meant to be a state secret, you see. I had to promise I would never tell it to anyone. But it's an exciting tale and does need to be told; and recording it in my own words, in my private diary, is surely not telling anyone else at all?

'Captain James Kempthorne stumbled ashore, more dead than alive, from the wreck of HMS London. He'd been shipwrecked on remote Samana Bay, on the northern side of Hispaniola. He was far from any of the coffee and sugar

plantations that spread across the south. But he soon found to his cost that the area was far from deserted.

James was too exhausted to flee as a gang of bearded brigands, armed with knives and cutlasses, appeared from the jungle. They must have been watching the naval battle and hoping to gain something from the residue. The men spoke only what he judged to be Spanish – though he doubted they'd ever been to Spain. He thought he was destined for an early grave, but protesting in English turned out to be his salvation – it showed them that he was far from being a hated Frenchman.

France and Spain had battled for years for control of the island of Hispaniola. So James and the brigands had a common enemy. He quickly made himself part of their group and in time, speaking a passable form of pidgin Spanish, became their acknowledged leader.

These brigands had established a base on the northern coast of Hispaniola in a small town with a natural harbour, facing towards America. James managed to take over a colonial-type dwelling near there, with shuttered windows, a wide veranda and an enclosed courtyard. It had been built for use by their previous leader, before he'd been killed in a skirmish with the hated French.

One day there was excitement as a small boat came into the harbour. There was fear that it was French but it turned out to belong to the English Navy. They had heard rumours, you see, that James Kempthorne was still alive. They wanted to see for themselves if the story was true.

The captain and crew were royally entertained for a couple of days in the town. Then came an invitation to James' residence, where they were welcomed with a magnificent banquet. French wine, which had been brought back on every trip across the island from Saint-Domingue, flowed freely. When they awoke next morning, the crew were badly hung over, not in any state where they could conduct a serious assessment.

Somehow or other a deal was struck. James Kempthorne was to remain here until further notice, aided by his Spanish brigands. But he would also undertake monitoring duties on behalf of the English Navy, on any French vessels or personnel who visited the harbour.

'But James, that's not fair,' I protested. 'You are a Captain in the English Navy. They should have shown you respect, taken you away with them. By now you could even have returned to England.'

'Life isn't always fair, Eleanor,' he replied. 'You see, somehow or other the crew had learned that this port was used by the French who had captured parts of southern America, the area around Louisiana, to communicate with their political masters in France.'

I had not even heard of the French in America before this, but I resolved to research it when I could.

'Once they were on Hispaniola, they only had to make their way to Saint-Domingue to demand passage on a boat taking goods from a plantation back to Europe. They saw that, with my big house, I was someone who could be a staging point on the way, with a remit to find out what messages were being sent back and forth.'

I laughed. He made it sound so simple. But I was suspicious of naval motives. 'Was that an option they offered you or an order they imposed?'

James hesitated. 'Strictly speaking it was neither. But they told me there was a threat that could be withheld, as long as I cooperated with them.'

I looked at him in amazement. He went on, 'You see, any Captain who loses his ship to the French, if he survives, faces a Court Martial. So if I refused the challenge, they would take me back to Trinidad and put me through that process. After all, I had lost my ship. I would be found guilty and dismissed from the Navy in disgrace.'

'Whereas . . .'

'If I accepted the challenge, a Court Martial would still happen. But this time the case made would be lenient: I would not need to be present and the judgment would be "Not guilty". I could leave the affair behind with full honours.'

I pondered his words for a few moments. As James' innocent wife in Truro I would have accepted his "bargain" with no questions asked. But my experiences in reaching Hispaniola had hardened me, made me realise that life was always to be challenged, not just accepted.

'So with this deal you are still a senior officer in the English Navy?'

James considered for a moment. 'I suppose that I am.'

'And you are being paid wages for that job each month?'

James gave a snort of derision. 'Would that I were.'

Finally, under persistent questioning, he had agreed that he was being exploited. I set myself to find a way to correct this, but I knew it might take some time.

James and I had a good time together in his colonial mansion, especially making up for lost years in the bedroom, but both of us knew it could not last. I started to miss our children in and around Truro. Getting back to them, though, would not be easy.

'The only boats from this island to Europe go from the south,' he said. 'The trouble is, Eleanor, that if you go anywhere near Saint-Domingue on your own you'll be arrested. The plantation owner you left behind has been humiliated. He was the only man on the island with a white worker and now he's lost her. Even though it happened months ago it won't have been forgotten. He will want public revenge.'

'Couldn't you find me a disguise?'

'What do you suggest, Eleanor? That I cut off your locks and paint you black from head to foot, then take you along as my servant? Or maybe that I should seal you inside a barrel of pitch?'

It wasn't easy. We went round and round but could find no good answer.

Then, out of the blue, an idea came.

The boat arrived, unannounced, in the harbour. Rumour quickly decided that, whatever the flag, it was here on French business.

There had been other French boats calling since I arrived. Most had been working vessels, quickly passing in and out. A couple had taken on board passengers and their parcels, travelling away from the island to who knows where.

This boat, though, was rather different.

James put on his best clothes and went down to greet the key passenger, an elegant man in a French style of clothing.

The newcomer was also clutching a heavy leather document bag.

The two shook hands. 'My name is James Kempthorne. Would you care to stay with me this night?' James asked. 'Tomorrow my servants will prepare my horse and trap, to take you across to Saint-Domingue.'

'Je m'appelle Pierre. Merci beaucoup,' the man replied. 'Aussi un grand repas et du vin?' It looked like dialogue at this meal could be limited to a mimed appreciation of James' wine.

It was as the pair walked up from the harbour, James told me, that the idea came. Pierre was clearly a man of importance. His heavy document bag looked to be vital, so his journey must be urgent. No-one would dream of getting in his way in Saint-Domingue. And the same would apply to anyone travelling with him.

I was horrified a little later when James broached the idea. Yes, I was pretty desperate to go home but this was ridiculous. 'You want me to travel all the way to Europe, as the intimate partner for this Frenchman? Non! Ce n'est pas possible.'

James looked surprised. Was it that I had said no or that I had spoken in French? The enormity of his proposal – and its impact on me – hadn't yet sunk in. But, slowly, it started to do so.

'Eleanor, my love, I see your fears, but I am begging you to do this for me – whatever it takes. It matters so much to me that you reach England once again. Tell them that I am still alive. Our children would demand it. I promise I will join you when I can.'

If it hadn't been for our French visitor we would have continued to argue the case for hours, but his presence stifled our debate – though it certainly didn't quell my feelings. What was I being asked to do?

That evening I was invited to the banquet and my limited French allowed some conversation to take place. In fact, given that he spoke no English and James no French, Pierre and I did most of the talking. The trouble was, the more we interacted the more stupid my refusal started to feel.

I was increasingly struck by Pierre's suave looks and crisp manners: he was a man of authority. Between ourselves, dear reader, if a woman was ever to be unfaithful to her husband on his direct orders, this was the man to be with.

I sensed that Pierre also did not find the idea abhorrent. Maybe he had a wife back in Paris and had missed her for many months? As a good hostess I saw him to his room at the end of the evening and we gave one another a polite kiss, followed, at his insistence, by a passionate embrace. He would have gone further had I not eased gently away.

'Tonight,' I declared, 'I have to say a proper farewell to my husband.' The nights that would follow I left to his imagination.

It was looking as though the journey home might be even more eventful than the journey here.

CHAPTER 29

Following on from the previous week's case review, Monday was a busy day for Frances Cober and her small team as they investigated the death of Donald McKay.

First she had to go in to Helston to check on her Station team and their more regular tasks; these seemed to be in hand. There was also the usual weekly flurry of reports to deal with, fortunately mostly routine.

Then she liaised with Tim Barwell. They both had jobs in and around Truro but would take separate cars: they would likely be coming home at different times.

Tim's first assignment was to check the traffic cameras covering Truro on the previous Wednesday evening. These were sprinkled across the town's main roads and official car parks. Tim already knew the make of McKay's car, a grubby, olive green, five-year-old Golf; and he'd made a note of its registration. Neighbour Jim had pointed it out as they had first crossed the road outside his bungalow in Cranfield Close.

'The first task, Tim,' said Frances, 'is to look for his car, heading in for central Truro, early on Wednesday evening. The conference started with an informal welcome at seven; he might have been a bit earlier or later. The road he comes in on might show the car park he'd be using. We could do with that as well.

'The most crucial thing, though, is any sightings of McKay's return journey. I was watching him perform until 8.45 and then he had to take off his makeup, so he wouldn't leave before nine on Wednesday evening. Our key question: is he travelling alone or does he have a passenger? That's the crux of the case and will affect what we do next. Did he take someone home with him; or did he and his killer reach there separately?'

Tim nodded. But he had a further question. 'Once I've found McKay, boss, if he's on his own, shouldn't I also check for any of our suspects driving out after him? And then coming back to the conference, later in the evening?'

'Not yet, Tim. I'm still working my way through the delegate interviews. That's giving me registration numbers and parking spots for anyone that drove here. But there will be quite a few of those and I haven't got them all yet. And of course, the killer, if he's local, will be aware of the Truro camera locations: there aren't that many. Trouble is, it'd be easy to take a route out to Shortlanesend that dodges them all.'

Once Tim was settled for the morning with the Truro traffic control team, Frances assembled her own list of questions for delegates. It would be best to do all these interviews herself, she decided. They would all know her and be comfortable with her from the conference.

She began by printing off hard copies of the application forms from Joy Tregorran, which she'd copied onto her phone in Diocese House. She was glad that Joy had, in her wisdom, asked for photographs from each applicant. She recognised most, though one or two had sent in self-deluding photos from when they were much younger.

Frances arranged the forms in increasing order of home-address distance from Truro. That gave a priority on whom to see first; after all, she and Tim had agreed they needed to focus on those who already knew Donald McKay. That would most likely be those nearest to Truro. She also added in the drama group members who had not attended the conference.

Next she planned the interviews. How had they travelled in and what was their car registration? Had they met anyone from the drama team before the conference (particularly McKay)? Had they talked to him on that first evening? If so, what did they recall of the encounter? Was McKay upset or troubled? How quickly had they left the Crypt once the drama was over? When had they retired to their room on the first evening? Which guests were still around at that point? Finally, when was their first inkling that McKay was missing?

Frances reckoned that each interview would take half an hour, once she'd got hold of the delegate. It was going to be a slog. She shrugged, it would be best to make a start; she might get three or four done this morning. This afternoon was already spoken for as she was to welcome the new security expert from London.

In the end Frances completed six interviews, all with delegates who worked in Truro. But she didn't learn much that was unexpected or revealing. She had a light lunch in the Cocktail Bar that was once Truro Grammar School, then headed for the Cathedral. Her first challenge was to identify the security expert.

When Frances crept through the double door into the Nave she saw that the Cathedral was relatively empty. Not like the summer when there were always crowds of visitors. But that made it easier to identify her quarry.

She soon saw a rather bedraggled, bearded character, unobtrusively dressed and a few years older than herself. He had a small rucksack and was seated near the back, looking up and around him. He seemed to recognise her almost at once and stood to greet her. With a little trepidation she walked over and shook his hand.

'Hi, I'm Police Sergeant Frances Cober.'

'Great. I'm Marcus Tredwell, from Home Security. They gave me your name and an up-to-date picture. I'm very glad to meet you.'

'Right. Would you prefer to chat over a cup of tea here in the refectory, or to go somewhere offsite?'

'Whatever you think, Frances. Maybe we should start away from the place, where we won't be overheard? I had a short interview before I accepted the posting but to all intents and purposes you can take it that I know nothing.'

Frances was relieved that this London expert was not pretending to know everything. That would have been hard to take. 'OK, let's go and find a café with a quiet corner. Then I'll do my best to bring you up to speed.'

Ten minutes later they were in Charlotte's Teashop, seated in an alcove looking down on Boscawen Street. 'Hey, have you had any lunch?' asked Frances as she studied the menu. 'They do Cornish cheese and salad; and look, they've got some tasty looking home-baked cakes under that counter.'

'I'm afraid I have dietary problems, Frances. A pot of

English tea would suit me fine.'

In this traditional teashop a pot of tea could be made to last a long time. The café was not overcrowded, and their waitress made no attempt to hurry them. For the next hour Frances did her best to explain how the issues in the Cathedral had arisen.

It was hard to know how much detail was needed and she found herself saying more than was strictly necessary. But Marcus didn't seem to mind, lapped up everything she had to tell him.

'It's the mixture of a conference delegate being poisoned and then my friend and I getting a small dose from the Cathedral wine,' she concluded. 'Plus the realisation that a similar wine, also stored in the Crypt, is used for Communion. That was what alerted my boss and then worried the Dean. Before all this I don't think anyone had given security much thought.'

There was a pause. 'Would you like another pot of tea, Marcus?' asked the police officer.

'We got three cups each out of the last one, Frances. I don't think I could take any more at present. In fact, if you'd excuse me, I need the toilet.'

He stood up to go on his search. When he returned he said, 'Why don't we go for a stroll, once I've paid, and have a first look round the Cathedral. It won't be closed yet, will it?'

Frances was surprised to find how much she was enjoying Marcus's company as they walked back over Truro's cobbled streets and narrow cut-throughs. She had expected an austere man, bossy, obsessed with minute security details. Instead she found someone who was warm and likeable. He was interested in her, not just her technical conundrums.

'The West End is the main way in,' Frances observed, as they entered the Cathedral through the double door arrangement, located under the twin western towers. 'There's also a door at the far end, next to the Chapter House refectory. That's mainly a short cut for their customers. They do a good trade, you see, on their cooked breakfasts. There might be other routes too but I don't know them. You'd have to nose around – or ask the Revd Joy Tregorran. She's your other nominated contact. But I'm afraid she's not here today – her church is on the Lizard.'

'The place has a lovely calm feel,' he remarked as they continued round. 'You'd want any security here to be low key.' Frances felt sure the Dean would be encouraged by that viewpoint. Maybe Marcus's contribution would turn out to be helpful after all?

'Like any tall stone building it's intrinsically safe,' he observed. 'I mean, there are hardly any windows at ground level for thieves to have a go at. And not many doors. How can I find out about the key-handling regime, by the way?'

'You'd best start with our liaison vicar, Joy, I think. If she didn't know herself she could guide you to someone who would.'

They wandered into the aisle that ran around the Quire and Frances pointed out the entrance to the Crypt. Then she wondered how much explanation the man needed. 'Does that make sense, Marcus? Have you dealt with Cathedral security elsewhere?'

'Er, to be honest I'm not sure,' he replied.

An odd reply but Frances assumed that for some reason

Marcus wanted to keep his earlier life private. That was his business. But if they spent much more time together she resolved she'd winkle it out of him.

'So what's your plan for your time here?' she asked.

'I'd like to spend a bit longer inside first, taking it all in. On my own, if you don't mind. Then this evening, after dinner, I'll come back and wander round the place on the outside. I assume you can get right round? I'd like to know the noise and light levels round about for a start. Imagine what I'd have to do if I was trying to break in. Tomorrow I'll start the detailed work – keys and so on – with Joy Tregorran and her contacts.'

'Right. I'll come over in the afternoon. But you've got my number if you need me any earlier. It'd be good for us to work closely together.'

CHAPTER 30

Harry Jennings sat in his office within the ECHO Portakabin, thinking hard.

He had just come back from a light lunch with his students. The morning session with Ellie had drawn to a close an hour earlier, ending with a big disappointment. It turned out that, this time, she had come to the end of Eleanor's diary. Whatever happened to the feisty woman next was almost entirely a matter of speculation.

Harry had secretly been hoping that somehow or other there might be a link between Eleanor's return to Truro and his conjecture of a secret item, now hidden in the Cathedral, which he had mused on yesterday to Joy, Frances and George.

Of course, he had not voiced this thought to his ECHO students. He knew – Joy and Frances had both made it clear – that all details of the sad case of Donald McKay were closely confidential. But he was itching to take the idea further.

For a start, it seemed that Eleanor had come back to Truro, directly or indirectly, in the company of the elegant French diplomat – Pierre. She must have done, for he recalled Ben's earlier work on Eleanor as the secretary of Truro Philharmonic. She'd certainly been back in this country well before 1799.

Harry was slightly hazy on exactly when her visit to the West Indies, as recounted in her diary, had taken place, but it must have been around 1791 or 1792.

What might Pierre have been doing at that time? Was there some urgent diplomatic message that needed taking from the French part of America across the Atlantic to the leaders in France? If so, whatever might that be?

Harry smiled to himself. If he had asked the question for 1803 he knew what the answer would have been. He'd been studying it only the other day: it was one intriguing element of the Napoleonic Wars. He stood up and reached for the research file on the shelf behind him to check the details.

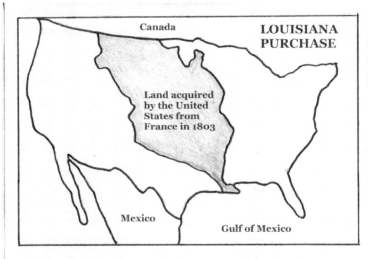

He flipped the file pages and there it was: the Louisiana Purchase. The most striking transaction ever to be agreed between two sovereign nations. It was a deal between Napoleon Bonaparte, now Emperor of France, and Thomas Jefferson, newly elected President of the United States.

Bonaparte was desperate for funds to continue his war against Britain and the rest of Europe. So desperate, in fact, that he was willing to sell all his French colonies in America to the newly independent United States, in order to acquire the cash needed.

The deal was confusingly titled, thought Harry. Louisiana sounded like a small area, somewhere along the southern American coast. Of no great consequence. Whereas in fact the area to be sold was the middle third of America – from the southern coast right up to beyond the border with Canada.

And what was so amazing about the deal was that it cost the Americans only $16 million, to increase their land holding by almost fifty percent.

This was before the era of international banking, of course. The required funds couldn't just be cabled across the Atlantic, or even transferred via a paper cheque. The only international currency in 1803 was ingots of gold.

Such deals didn't happen out of the blue, of course. There must have been years of discussion and negotiation. Suddenly a thought came to him: had by any chance Bonaparte and Jefferson met a few years earlier?

This was time for some fresh research. Harry consulted various internet sources, checked dates, cross-referenced to other sources and then sat back with a big smile.

Long before he became President of the United States, Thomas Jefferson had a leading role in France. He was the American Ambassador there from 1785 to 1789. Exactly the period in which Napoleon Bonaparte was emerging as the most successful, most imaginative, general in the French army. The two men of such renown would certainly know one another; probably the seeds of the Louisiana Purchase had been sown in those early days.

1789, of course, was the year of the French Revolution. Harry did some more checking. Yes, Jefferson had returned to America that year, just in time to avoid being trapped in the turmoil. But he'd want to maintain links into the future with Napoleon. Could those links – personal letters from one prospective leader to another – be what was carried by Diplomat Pierre?

Harry reflected on the idea. It made sense. The timings would work, anyway; and the relationships.

Then he remembered one more detail from Eleanor's diary. She had said, twice, that Pierre's diplomatic bag was extremely heavy. What if it contained not just letters from Jefferson to Bonaparte but also an advance: a token of good faith on the potential deal? Could that be . . . one or two ingots of gold?

Harry was excited now. He might be onto something. But then he stopped. How would the contents of the diplomatic bag have slipped away from Pierre and landed up with Eleanor Kempthorne?

He forced himself to stop and think. Her diary made it sound as though Eleanor would have a busy journey travelling home. For she would be depending entirely on the French diplomat for her protection: first as they hurried through the dangerous port of Saint-Domingue and then on the perilous crossing of the Atlantic. No doubt the crew of whatever boat they travelled with would be equally dissolute. To be kept safe she would have to do exactly what he said.

Harry didn't like to contemplate exactly what that might have involved but it could well have made Eleanor secretly bitter and hostile.

Then Harry remembered one other item from her diary.

Eleanor had discovered that James had been tricked into continuing to work for the Navy, but to do so without pay. She had pledged to reinstate him. What if, one time, she had looked inside the bag and seen the ingot? Might she have regarded that as a fair recompense for her husband's years of toiling as a Hispaniola secret agent?

And if so, would it have been beyond her to access Pierre's bag and to add the contents instead to her casket? Maybe to replace it with a bottle of wine or some other equivalent weight?

Harry dare not write any of this down. It had to remain a top secret. But he went through the steps again, deciding if they seemed likely and considering variations.

Finally, satisfied, he phoned Joy. He needed to share something with her. He had an idea which might help with the McKay inquiry. Could they meet for dinner again, one evening this week?

CHAPTER 31

Constable Tim Barwell was feeling frustrated. He'd spent the whole of Monday looking at traffic camera records, which it turned out were stills taken every twenty seconds in black and white and not of the crispest quality. It was a pity, he thought, that McKay had owned such a popular make of car: a Golf. If Tim hadn't had the car's registration number the task would have been impossible.

In the end he'd spotted the car's journeys, in both directions, that fateful Wednesday evening, at roughly the times expected. Only on one pair of cameras, though. And the pictures taken along the darkened road weren't good enough, even blown up, to be certain if McKay was carrying a passenger. The photos were taken from the rear and Tim couldn't distinguish occupants from their headrests. He wasn't even certain that the driver was McKay.

Tim needed new data to advance police thinking, so decided on Tuesday morning to make another visit to Shortlanesend.

The impression from everyone interviewed was that McKay was a blameless victim. It was a recurring image. But what if it wasn't true? It didn't seem likely that the man had traded in drugs or anything conspicuously evil. He wasn't on the National Crime database.

But there were plenty of other ways Tim could think of in which he might have incited assault on his person.

If he'd been a blackmailer, for example, that might have taken place alongside a genuine front as a long-standing Shortlanesend villager. It might have been small scale, say someone seen rather too often following children home from school. His victim might have been someone else in the village, for whom even a whisper of scandal would make their life intolerable. Cash to keep McKay quiet – say, a rolled-up bundle of notes – could have been transferred monthly, on quiet evenings in the Old Plough.

When he really thought about it, Tim could imagine dozens of ways that McKay could be running a scam. The man had a car and there were plenty of places within easy range of Truro: Falmouth, for example, or Helston. Threatening behaviour in any of these could lead on to a dispute that would eventually lead to him being eliminated.

At that point Tim realised that he still had the keys to McKay's bungalow. He resolved to start by giving the place one more search.

This time he'd not be looking for dangerous tools, like bottles to carry poison. He would be after anything that might give a clue on how the man spent his time. McKay was retired but he wasn't that old: he must spend his time doing something.

There was no-one in the Close when Tim arrived. The place was as quiet as a grave. Was this out of respect for the dead man or simply its normal weekday state? He didn't know. The policeman let himself into the fateful bungalow, poured himself a mug of coffee from his flask and then started his search.

All the cupboards in the kitchen held standard household items like food, tea-towels or crockery. He moved onto the main bedroom. There was a wardrobe full of clothes, some of which were a little unusual: perhaps these were costumes McKay had acquired during some drama sketch? He photographed them in case they came into a later conversation.

What about the bedside cabinet? It was frustrating: plenty of everyday items but nothing that might point to a hobby.

Once again, Tim decided, there was more to be learned from items that were missing than from those still present. There was a radio but no camera, for example, or smart phone. But either of those would be easy for someone present in the bungalow at the time of death to take away with them. Either might have contained images that revealed their identity.

The second bedroom was very small and seemed to be mainly a box room. The policeman peered inside various boxes littering the floor but again could spot nothing unusual. Then, glancing through the window, he saw a small garden shed. It was out of sight from the main bedroom or living room, which was why he had not seen it earlier.

A few minutes later he was giving it some attention. The door was locked but only needing the simplest of keys; it didn't take him long to open. Was this McKay's secret storehouse?

Having got in Tim was relieved to see at least a few signs of life. There was plenty of gardening gear, presumably tidied away now winter was approaching. Plus an electric lawn mower.

Also a set of golf clubs. Tim almost cheered, he'd found a

leisure activity. There was no clue, though, which course he played on. There was one public course on the far side of Truro: did he play there?

Tim stood in the middle of the shed and looked slowly around. Behind the door was an umpire's coat. Was McKay the umpire for the local cricket team; or maybe on some Truro-wide rota? It would keep him busy in the summer months, anyway.

Finally, Tim saw shelves holding do-it-yourself equipment, including paintbrushes and a set of woodwork tools. In the corner there was also a stepladder. Tim felt relieved. He could account for a significant chunk of McKay's time, anyway.

It was as he was making sure everything was tidy before heading back to Helston that Tim heard a loud knock at the front door. Who was that? Some sort of friend?

Carefully the policeman opened the door. A man stood there, medium height, sturdy and aged around sixty. He was carrying a large brief case and was dressed to cope with bad weather.

'Hello,' said Tim. 'Are you after Donald McKay?'

The man looked surprised. He obviously wasn't expecting to see a policeman behind the door. 'Has something happened?' he began.

'Why don't you come in, sir? It'd be easier for us to talk inside.'

The man followed him inside and the two sat down in the living room.

'What's your name?' began Tim.

'I'm Walter Wallace. I'm a friend of Donald's. Has

something happened to him?'

There was no hiding the fact. 'I'm afraid it has. Donald was found dead here on Thursday morning, the week before last. There's been no announcement yet: the police are still making inquiries. But I'm very happy to meet you. You're the first friend of his that we've come across.'

The man looked completely shocked. 'Donald and I go out painting, you see. We used to work together at Russell's Engineering, on the industrial estate on the road towards Redruth. Donald retired first, three years ago; I was offered early retirement early last year. We used to go painting together on Saturdays. Now we're retired we can go when we like, so we usually go in mid-week.'

At last Tim could credit McKay with a time-consuming hobby. And in Walter Wallace he'd been given a means to find out what that really meant.

'Why don't I get us both a mug of coffee,' he suggested. 'You sit here quietly and compose yourself. Then, if you don't mind, I'd like to know as much as you can tell me about Donald; and also about these painting trips.'

CHAPTER 32

At half past six on Tuesday evening Harry Jennings met Joy Tregorran at the restaurant and cocktail bar on St Mary's Street – the former site of Truro Grammar School. The meeting had to be early: Harry was still commuting from Exeter and sensible trains home later in the night were few and far between.

'So what's your new idea?' asked Joy, once they had placed their orders. It was fun being part of the creative process.

'I've found a plausible reason why something very valuable but necessarily secret might have been brought to Truro a long time ago. And there's quite a lot of evidence to back it up.'

'Ah. This follows up your suggestion on Sunday that a search for hidden treasure might lie behind the poisoned Communion wine and also McKay's killing?' Joy tried but found it hard to keep the cynicism out of her voice.

'That's right. It'll take me a while to tell it, though.'

'Fire away, Harry. I haven't much fresh to tell you. Apart from a stimulating meeting I had with the Cathedral's new security expert this morning. That's Marcus. He's tall, bearded and handsome – quite a catch for Frances or George, if they ever took him seriously. Also kind and considerate.'

Harry had no interest in security men, however handsome, and hastened on to his tale. It took him a while to tell Joy of Ellie's feminist ideals and then to give his friend the edited diary highlights of Eleanor Kempthorne's journey to the West

Indies in her research on slavery; her traumatic days as a slave; the escape and amazing reunion with her long-lost husband; and, lastly, her journey back to Europe as the companion of a French diplomat.

Their meal arrived at this point and the attentions of the waitress gave Joy a few minutes silence to evaluate Harry's story. The historian was notorious for his vivid imagination. She had to nail down how much of this was fully documented before she was drawn into any detail.

'And all of this is in Eleanor's diary?'

'Well. On its last page she's anticipating the trip back to Europe; we're not actually told that it happened. But something like it must have done, for we hear of her back here later on. She was the Secretary of the Truro Philharmonic for many years.'

This sounded relatively solid. So what was Harry's big idea?

He took a big mouthful of his newly arrived steak before he began. 'You need a bit more background. At this time – the late eighteenth century – England and France were mostly at war. France had huge armies and an outstanding general – Napoleon Bonaparte. England had its navy, led by Admiral Nelson.

'America had declared itself independent of England only a few years earlier. For a time France and America found themselves on the same side. That's why, a few years later, the French were able to sell their central territories in the land of America – a huge area – to the Americans. They wanted the money, you see, to pay for the continuing war with England. I'm certain that deal really happened – it's called the Louisiana

Purchase.'

'Right.' All this was new to Joy: her background was natural science. But she trusted Harry on historical facts.

'So is your idea that some of the payment on this Purchase – which I assume was vast – came to Truro by way of Eleanor?'

Harry laughed. 'That'd be great. The trouble is, the dates don't match. Eleanor returned in the 1790s and the Louisiana Purchase happened a few years later. But then I had a related idea.'

He paused to order his thoughts in a convincing manner.

'This deal would require a lot of imagination. It wouldn't just have come out of the blue. Now Thomas Jefferson, the author of the Declaration of Independence and later President of the United States, had been the US Ambassador in France at the time Napoleon emerged. I'm certain the two would have exchanged views: the deal could have first been talked about then. That dialogue would continue by letter when Jefferson returned home. With probably a few sweeteners – say gold ingots – along the way.'

'Maybe,' said Joy doubtfully. She was far from convinced and recalled being far too gullible to Harry in the past.

'When you get back to Gunwalloe, Joy, have a look at a map. The island Eleanor was being kept on, Hispaniola, was at the time a French colony and a natural staging post for someone travelling from the southern United States to France. Boats were travelling back from there all the time with plantation produce – coffee and so on.'

Harry paused to let Joy take the idea on board as he ate more of his steak. 'It's likely that the correspondence was what

201

the diplomat – he was called Pierre – was bringing back to Europe, when Eleanor became attached to his party. Crucially, her diary records that his diplomatic bag was extremely heavy.

'So it's not impossible, you see, that the woman arrived back in Truro carrying an ingot of gold. Those bars are typically 14 by 7 by 3 inches in old money, that's 36 by 18 by 8 in centimetres.'

Harry stopped talking to concentrate on his steak while Joy pondered the idea. It was a typical Harry construction, his imagination making up the missing details as the facts ran out.

Joy was just starting to admit to herself that it might possibly have some merit when, suddenly, she could see a problem.

'That's a great set of ideas, Harry, very entertaining.' She laughed. 'It might even be true. Except there's a massive snag.'

Her companion looked up from his meal, rather surprised. Joy was meant to like his ideas, not dismiss them. 'Oh yes. What's that?'

'Well, you say this happened in the 1790s. But Truro Cathedral didn't exist for another hundred years. It couldn't possibly have been used to hide the ingot: the building wasn't even there.'

For a few minutes Joy's observation seemed to knock the stuffing out of Harry. She took the chance to order them both a pudding. There was an uneasy silence until these arrived.

But Harry was a senior history lecturer. He knew that this was how historical ideas evolved. A gap emerged in a promising theory and then, after some effort, it was filled as the idea was refined.

'Right, then, Joy. Eleanor arrives back in Truro with her secret cargo sometime in the 1790s. Handwritten documents, perhaps, from a future President of the United States to Napoleon Bonaparte – plus an ingot of gold, maybe an advance on the Louisiana Purchase. She has to keep the whole thing secret, at least until her husband returns from Hispaniola. Where might she put it?'

'Wouldn't the obvious place be to bury it in her back garden?'

Harry nodded. 'The trouble with that would be if an undercover French agent came after it, once Pierre reported its disappearance. He might force Eleanor to divulge where she'd put it. I don't think she'd dare to have it anywhere around her home. So where else might she hide it?'

Joy frowned, a little irritated. Sometimes Harry seemed to forget that she was a vicar, not a professor of history. 'I have no idea, Harry. I don't know what the woman did for a living, or even where she lived.'

Then a thought came to her. 'Hey. Was there anything about her early life in her diary?'

Harry mused for a moment. There was something. He wished he'd brought his notes on Ellie's talks with him but he'd left them locked in the ECHO Chamber. Then it came to him. 'Yes, there was in fact. She had a very bright son called John, that she'd got into Truro Grammar School. So at the time she returned, he was almost certainly studying away in this building.'

Joy glanced around. It was hard to imagine the restaurant once being a schoolroom but that was what the plaque had said.

'If he was a bright teenager, Harry, that would be one way to hide it. Give it to her lad, ask him to put it somewhere really obscure. Maybe somewhere in this building? Trouble is, I doubt it would still be here.'

It was an advance but not the whole story. The two kicked ideas around for a long time but without much success. Then Harry suddenly noticed it was time to head for the railway station. His train to Exeter was due in fifteen minutes.

'Perhaps tomorrow, Joy, I'll make time for a guided tour of the Cathedral. You never know, the guide may give me something that takes this forward.

'It's a good theory,' he concluded. 'I'm not abandoning it just yet.'

Classroom of old Grammar School in St. Mary's Street, Truro.

Classroom of the Old Grammar School (c.1880)

CHAPTER 33

Wednesday morning. Tim Barwell had finally caught up with Frances Cober in Helston Police Station and was reporting back on his previous day in Shortlanesend.

'I'd done an extensive search of the bungalow, boss, looking for any clues on how McKay spent his days as a retired man. But there was nothing of interest. I was about to come home when there was a knock at the door. And there he was, a full-size, bona fide friend: Walter Wallace. So I invited him in and we had a long chat.'

'Well done Tim. That's how it works sometimes on an inquiry. You do a lot of work for no clear benefit at all and then, serendipity, a reward comes along anyway. So what did you learn?'

Tim peered at his notebook. 'Wallace hadn't heard about McKay's death till I told him and he was badly shocked. The two had worked together in a small Engineering Unit for many years. McKay retired a few years earlier and Wallace more recently. It turned out that their common interest was painting. Wallace had come to McKay's house, prepared for another outing.'

Frances was itching to ask questions but managed to restrain herself. She had to let Tim tell the story in his own way. So she just smiled and nodded and he continued with his account.

205

'What was really interesting was the type of painting they went in for. They were both engineers, you see, more fascinated by machinery than by landscapes. And of course Cornwall has plenty of both.

'As far as I could see, Wallace was the leader of the two. He lives halfway between Truro and St Agnes, that's on Cornwall's north coast. He'd managed to buy – or more probably lease – a small gallery in St Agnes. The two used that to store all their equipment and also to display and sell their finished products.'

Tim smiled at his boss. 'That was why there was nothing for us to find in Shortlanesend, boss. I don't really understand, though. Did McKay want to keep it secret till he'd made a success of it? Wasn't he keen to tell his friends in Truro all about it?'

'Maybe he wanted to keep the whole operation quiet to avoid paying Income Tax on his profits?' Frances saw a need to keep an open mind on McKay's honesty at this stage of the inquiry. Lack of honesty could make him vulnerable to blackmail.

Tim hadn't thought of this angle, had taken the painter at his word. 'Well, we'll be able to assess its profitability when we see the gallery, boss. Is it bursting with customers, coming out gleefully clutching their paintings, or is it empty for hours on end?'

He had a moment of doubt. 'I assume you want to come with me? Wallace said he was going straight home when we'd finished our chat. He seemed genuinely upset: he and McKay were very good friends, I think – as well as business partners. But I've booked a time to visit his gallery later this morning.

He said he'd be over there at any time after eleven.'

Frances had intended to work in the Station today but this was the nearest they'd had to a breakthrough and she had to make the most of it. A few routine office tasks were completed, then they set off just after ten.

Wallace's gallery was not easy to find. It wasn't in the centre of St Agnes and the address was rather vague. They found it eventually, a tiny shop in a row of slate houses, out on the road towards Perranporth. But the place wasn't dilapidated, it was a going concern. The shop windows had recently been repainted and a new sign above proclaiming its mission: the Wallace Gallery.

The shop was quiet when they went in, though a customer was just leaving, looking pleased and holding a large rectangular parcel. The place must make some profit.

Wallace immediately recognised that he was going to be interviewed as Tim introduced him to Frances – 'my boss'. He strode over to the doorway, locked the door and turned its sign to say 'Closed'.

'Can I offer you both a coffee?' he began. A few minutes later the interview was underway.

Frances began by outlining the main facts on how Donald McKay had spent his last hours. 'He was appearing in a short drama at a conference on Assisted Dying, at Truro Cathedral. He went home straight afterwards. Next morning one of the other actors went out to Shortlanesend to check he was alright and found him lying dead on the floor.'

Wallace looked very upset at this emotion-free account but said nothing.

'At this stage it's an unexplained death,' went on Frances. 'We're here to find out as much as possible about how Donald lived.'

Wallace had obviously been preparing for this question from the day before. He gave a lucid account of McKay's work life – 'he was well-respected and liked, been there for many years, no enemies' – and also sketched out his life in the world outside.

He mentioned drama – 'perhaps one event a year, it was just a sideline'. He went on to his monthly reading group in the village, his summer Saturdays as a cricket umpire, his love of gardening, his bird watching holidays, his plan to visit his son in Australia and finally his painting. When listed like that it sounded as if he'd have no spare time at all.

'Thank you, Mr Wallace,' said Frances. 'That's a clear summary. And it reinforces the things that we've learned from Donald's bank statements. But since we are here, can you tell us more, please, about his painting.'

Wallace took a moment to think. This was a key part of the life which he shared with his lost friend. He took a deep breath and then began.

'Donald and I both came from an engineering tradition. We always enjoyed seeing how things worked and appreciating the design. So when we started taking painting seriously, which was only a couple of years ago, we decided to learn and record as much as we could about any machinery that had captured our interest.'

He stopped to make sure the police officers were following.

'In particular,' he went on, 'here in Cornwall there are plenty of examples of old machines, like the gadgets in old mines and also in transport. After all, one of the first railways in the world was built here in Cornwall. So our painting came in two stages.'

Tim nodded; he'd already been told this the day before.

Wallace continued. 'First, we would do research on examples of old machines that we could get access to, here in West Cornwall. That was using the internet but also museums and other records.

'Then, secondly, we would visit and record them: first by photographs and then with acrylic and oil paints – even water colours. Finally, we'd take the best of our paintings and offer them for sale. Much to our surprise they found a market – not huge, but enough to cover our costs. Would you like to see one or two?'

'Yes, please,' said Frances. What quality of work would she be shown?

Wallace turned towards a large display board mounted on one wall. 'Our most recent outputs - or at least, the ones we've not yet sold. On the left are pistons and rods on the old steam engines from Levant Tin Mine. Next along are a few of the old mine shafts.'

Frances was amazed. The pictures made dazzling use of colour, despite being mostly pastel. With impressionist hints they conveyed both movement and structure. The officer had some insight into painting; she had recently taken up landscape painting as a hobby to make best use of her days off but was finding it hard work. Once the case was over, she resolved, she would come back here and buy one.

Wallace walked over to the opposite wall. 'These are bits of machinery from other places. One or two are the early

209

signalling devices from mines.'

'Do you sell everything you produce?' asked Frances. 'How much of this is Donald's work? Or are any done jointly?'

Wallace took a moment to work out his answer.

'I was into this first. As you saw from the sign outside, I'm the tenant for this shop. Once he started it took Donald a while to become proficient. So for the most part we sell individually. I make by far the most profit, but then I'm the one paying for the shop. Occasionally there are items where we've both contributed – say, one of us found the item and the other painted it. In that case we share the profit. But Donald and I never rowed over the money. It was mostly an enjoyable hobby.'

'Great,' said Frances. 'That's very helpful. One last question, then. Did any of your findings relate to Truro Cathedral?'

For a moment Walter reflected. 'Donald did produce something a while back. I couldn't make head or tail of it. Would you like to see?'

He went upstairs – the first-floor rooms stocked less sellable items. He returned a moment later with a charcoal sketch. It wasn't clear what it was: it looked like a pair of bellows.

'You can have this if you like,' he said. 'No charge. I never thought it would sell and sadly Donald won't improve it now. He didn't even give this one a name.'

Frances had no idea what it might signify. Her instinct, though, told her that it might just be important.

CHAPTER 34

Harry Jennings had wandered round Truro Cathedral on his own when he first came to Truro. He had enjoyed the grandeur of the high vaulted roofs and even higher towers alongside the simple instances of faith and hope that adorned the walls. But there was something different between reading snippets of local history in his own, rather battered guidebook and being told them by an enthusiastic and knowledgeable guide.

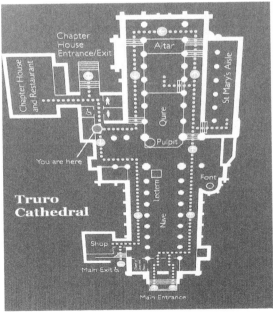

The Cathedral put on tours on most weekday mornings. They were free, conducted by informed volunteers from the congregation. The guide this Wednesday was a slim, athletic-looking man in his forties: his nametag declared he was Stephen Baird.

Harry was impressed in their preliminary conversation to learn that Stephen had run in for the task from his home, three miles away. Especially commendable given that Harry appeared to be the only member of the public who wanted a guide today.

Stephen wasn't discouraged and the two set off down the Nave.

'This pillar was taken out of the old Parish Church,' he explained, pointing to a rather darkened-stone, gnarled tower near to the West End. 'The Cathedral was built in three phases, you see. There were never going to be enough funds to build the whole thing in one go. So this stood in the open for thirty years until the Nave was completed and all the towers finished.'

Harry had decided that as the guide's sole customer it would look pretentious to be taking notes, but he made sure he made a mental note on anything linked to difficulties in building. There might well be scope here for further historical research.

They continued down the aisle, passing various military memorabilia, some linked to the First World War. The story of the Victoria Cross won on the Western Front by a leading member of the Robartes family from Lanhydrock, as he led his men into massive enemy crossfire, was noted. Then they came to a small side-chapel containing an impressively large font.

212

'This is the Henry Martyn Chapel,' said the guide. 'D'you know about him?'

Harry confessed his ignorance.

'Henry Martyn was a very clever man,' said the guide. 'He was a student down the road at Truro Grammar School, then he went to Cambridge University. He was Senior Wrangler in 1801.'

A long time ago Harry had been at Cambridge, so he had some interest in a fellow student, even from a different discipline. He recalled that wranglers were something to do with mathematics. Maybe he should ask George Gilbert if she'd heard of him? After all, she was a mathematician. Then the incongruity of what he was being told struck home. 'So why on earth does he have a chapel?'

'Ah. Henry Martyn became an enthusiastic Christian while

he was at Cambridge. He gave up mathematics, became a missionary to various parts of India and then Persia. He wasn't one for high living in a remote vicarage, he believed in being close to the locals. During his life he translated the Bible into three different languages. Then he died of some dreadful disease, I'm not sure what, it was either typhoid or cholera.'

Stephen smiled. 'Guess how old Henry Martyn was when he died?'

Harry had no idea. He recalled people didn't live too long two hundred years ago. 'Fifty?' he guessed.

'He was thirty-one.'

'Wow.' It was an amazing story. The Bible in three different languages, translated in no more than ten years. 'So that's why he's got this chapel, even though it was built long after his time?'

'That's right. And look, this font has a really well-designed cover.' Stephen slipped some catch or other then invited Harry to pull one of the chains reaching down to it from high above.

Harry did as he was asked. With hardly any effort on his part, the huge filigree font cover rose several feet, giving full access to the bowl below. Apart from everything else it was a masterpiece of counter-balanced engineering.

'Is this still used as a font today?'

'Not that often, just when anyone linked to the place needs it. We're a very pragmatic Cathedral – we like to be alongside people in a similar way, you might say, to Henry Martyn.'

The tour proceeded. Stephen sensed he'd got a keen customer and wasn't aiming to hold anything back.

They had passed the Crypt entrance and climbed the few stone steps into the Quire when there was a sudden burst of organ music from the pipes over their heads.

'That's our Father Willis organ,' said Stephen. 'Said to be the finest in the country.' They listened to some Bach Chorale music for a moment.

'Mind, that's not our main organist,' added the guide as he noted a minor hesitation. 'We have several trainee organists enrolled here.'

The historian was not as interested in the music as in any piece of local history around it. 'Was the organ here from the start?'

Stephen nodded. 'The pipes were. But the console it was played from was only moved to that position in the 1960s.' He pointed above the choir stalls, where Harry could just see signs of movement. 'The poor bloke used to be out of sight of the choir, hidden away in the North Transept. That must have been very inconvenient for all of them.'

'Quite a job to move it,' murmured Harry.

'Well, especially as they had this wonderful marble floor here in the Quire right from the start. Italian craftsmen came over to construct it. When they repositioned the console they had to get all the organ control wires to run underneath.'

Obviously there was a story here that Stephen was itching to be asked about so Harry duly obliged. He looked down at his feet. 'Solid marble, eh. It's a beautiful pattern but no doubt extremely dense. So how did they do that?'

'I wasn't here then, of course. But I'm told that they first drilled long holes through the marble, right across the Quire. Then . . .'

'Yes?'

'They got a few ferrets. They attached a long piece of string

215

to each of 'em, then stuck 'em down the various holes. Once the animals had found their way through to the other side, the workmen seized the string off them and then pulled the wires through instead. Fine twentieth century technology, I guess.'

Harry smiled. Cathedral builders here were innovative, anyway.

A little later they came to an aisle which, with its rows of traditional light oak pews, looked rather different to the rest. 'This chapel was once part of the old St Mary's Parish Church,' explained Stephen. 'D'you know about that?

'That was the church here before the Cathedral.' Harry was pleased to show off some knowledge. It was an intriguing story when he'd first heard it, especially the tussle over what to do with the old building between the bishop and the architect. No doubt his guide could add a few details.

'These days its role is to act as the town centre Parish Church. There'll be a short service here later this morning.'

'Celebrated using that massive Father Willis organ?' asked Harry.

'Oh no. They've still got the old organ. Look.' Stephen pointed into the far corner, where a more modest keyboard instrument stood.

'Mm. How old's that one?'

'1750. Actually, it's also quite famous. It was designed for the Chapel Royal in St James' Palace but it didn't quite fit, so it got moved down here.'

'Sounds like a cat with nine lives. It even survived the near-destruction of the Parish church here, when the Cathedral replaced it?'

'Well, that was a hundred years later. I guess they'd take the opportunity to install electric bellows at the same time.'

Harry was silent for a moment. There was a detail here he was missing. Then he considered the dates. Electric power hadn't even been discovered in 1750.

'So how were the bellows driven before that?' He made a guess. 'Was it all manually pumped – a rota of Sunday duties, maybe, for the scholars of the Grammar School?'

Stephen laughed. 'I hoped you'd ask. No, it wasn't manual – the schoolboys were far too busy. They had a unique hydraulic system. Somehow or other they took a flow from the mill race round the back. It would be advanced technology in its day.'

The tour continued. Harry was shown a matchstick model of the Cathedral, a metre long. 'Forty-three thousand matches,' claimed Stephen. 'The man who built it must have had masses

217

of patience – and a real love for the place.'

'He didn't include the bend though,' observed Harry as he peered along the roof from one end. 'He wanted to model the ideal structure, not just the humble reality.'

Harry had been shown the bend along the length of the building in the Quire a little earlier.

'That was forced by the geography of the area: 1880 was too recent. They couldn't modify St Mary's Street,' Stephen had explained. 'I hate to admit it but too many important people had homes already built along it.'

Harry was about to make some caustic comment on the long tendrils of power, then reflected that it was not his place to pass judgement. They continued on and Stephen made various comments on the bell tower.

It was almost lunch time by the time the tour was over. 'Thank you very much indeed, Stephen,' said Harry. 'You've made the whole place hum. It's not an old memorial at all, it's very much alive. It's been a real blessing to have it explained.'

As he wandered on towards the Chapter House refectory in search of lunch, the historian realised that he had been confronted by several aspects of engineering and hydraulics. Either might be significant and both were well outside his expertise. Whoever could he talk to that might be able to help?

CHAPTER 35

Despite studying different subjects, Harry Jennings and George Gilbert (then known as George Goode) had once been close friends in the year that they'd overlapped at Cambridge. George had been a young, bright but slightly naive mathematician, while Harry was a free-wheeling historian, already grappling with the subtler details of his PhD.

Then they'd gone their separate ways, though they'd bumped into one another occasionally. The chance meeting last Sunday in the Helzabron Inn in Gunwalloe, when Harry was staying the weekend with Joy Tregorran as her special friend, had been a slightly awkward surprise to them both.

But it had given them chance to exchange phone numbers and to learn that each currently had reason to be in Truro.

Harry had gleaned that George was normally in Truro on Thursdays and gave her a ring. Yes, she wasn't too busy, she'd be happy to meet him for lunch. Especially if he had a mathematical problem: she was intrigued.

They met at half past twelve, in the depths of the restaurant that had once been home of the Truro Grammar School and gave one another a polite hug. George felt a pang of regret, she could still recall how Harry had been such fun.

'This is my treat,' said Harry. 'What can I get you to

drink?'

A few minute later they were seated with halves of Doom Bar bitter at an isolated table towards the rear. No-one would overhear them provided they kept their voices down.

'So what's the problem?' asked George.

Harry hadn't been sure how much he was allowed to say. But he was still bursting with his idea of how an ingot of gold might have been brought to Truro in the 1790s by Eleanor. Then he recalled that George had been part of the conversation that preceded this on the previous Sunday: she was certainly as much in the loop as he was.

So as they waited for the waitress he sketched out his idea again. He was slicker than he'd been with Joy, missed out some of the finer details; but he made sure that he included Joy's novel contribution: what if Eleanor had handed the secret ingot over to her son, John?

'He was a pupil at the well-known Truro Grammar School in the 1790s. He might once have studied in this very room.'

George glanced around, sceptical. 'With his desk strategically placed next to the cocktail bar, I assume? Mixing the drinks in the various sized glasses as a chemistry lesson? And pursuing arithmetic on the dartboard?'

Harry couldn't help but smile. George had always been able to make him laugh, that was how they'd first become friends. 'No, George, I'm serious. Look at that plaque over there.'

The waitress arrived with their meals at that point and George instead checked the item with her. Yes, this had once been the schoolroom for the local Grammar School. It had been here from the 1540s and at least till the 1860s.

Once the waitress had gone George turned to Harry. 'OK,

Harry, you win. If he was a bright lad, John Kempthorne might well have been entrusted with his mother's secret ingot.' She frowned. 'But that's not the easiest thing to hide in an old schoolroom like this. He could scarcely shove it to the back of his desk; someone could easily stumble over it. So I repeat, what's the mathematical problem?'

Harry grinned. 'Well. Yesterday I had a very entertaining tour of the Cathedral with a well-informed guide. He mentioned another pupil of Truro Grammar School called Henry Martyn, said he was Senior Wrangler at Cambridge in 1801.'

George guessed the question before it was even uttered. 'You want to know about Senior Wranglers? That's easy, Harry. In the nineteenth century and thereabouts they would put the marks for students with first class degrees in mathematics in ascending order. The student with the top marks was the "Senior Wrangler", essentially the brightest student in the country. It was a tightly fought honour. Henry Martyn must have been very bright indeed.'

She thought for a few seconds. 'Wait a moment. If he graduated in 1801, then he must have been at school here in the 1790s. But that means Henry Martyn and John Kempthorne must have known one another, they'd be bright students together. So if John was his mate, they'd work on hiding the ingot together. It'd be a relaxation from their studies. So I think your real question is: where might they hide it?'

There was silence for a few moments as they made headway on their lunches, both pondering the problem.

'Actually, George, we haven't got to my question yet. One other thing the guide told me was that there was an organ in the old Parish Church which is now part of the Cathedral that was installed in 1750.'

'Oh yes?' George was slightly wary now of anticipating the historian's questions.

'Of course, it wasn't powered by electricity at the time. It is now, by the way: and still played every week in the Cathedral side-chapel. The guide told me that it was hydraulically powered, using the local mill race. So my question to you is, how might that have worked? It was there before John and Henry, you see. So is there any way that the mechanism could have used a heavy weight like an ingot to keep the thing in trim?'

This was typical of Harry Jennings, thought George. His questions were never easy. She recalled being told that this made his lectures unpopular with less able students, who wanted more standard fare. So now she had to think out how the mechanics of an organ might be driven from a nearby mill race. It sounded devilishly complicated.

'I need notice on that, Harry. It's one of your famous, non-standard questions. But we could begin with some basics. Is the mill race still running, round the back of the Cathedral? Could we go and look at it after lunch? And while we're there, could we also see the location of the old parish church and imagine where the water pipe would have had to travel.'

The mill race behind Truro Cathedral

She paused. 'But in general I'd say it's quite likely that a bellow mechanism would have needed weights to drag it down as well as flow from the mill race to pull it up. It would have been a local novelty, perhaps visited by students as part of their physics lessons. Two smart lads like John and Henry might conceive of the idea of swapping the original weights with a new one, made from their ingot.'

There was another silence, less stressful this time. Harry decided to celebrate with a pudding; there was a pause as these were ordered.

While they waited for the desserts to be delivered, George grabbed her phone and looked up the term "Senior Wrangler" on Google. Slightly to her surprise she found a list of all the winners of that accolade for two hundred years. She studied the time around 1800 carefully.

'You'll never believe this,' she remarked. 'Henry Martyn is here all right in 1801. But so is John Kempthorne, five years earlier. So these lads both were really bright.'

She studied the list further. 'In fact, both of them were in

223

the same College: that's St John's. Two lads from Truro, they'd have been really good friends.'

Harry the lecturer saw another angle. 'Wow, fancy teaching in a school with two future Senior Wranglers among its pupils. Imagine assembly with both of 'em sitting on the front row, competing to answer questions. What an amazing privilege!'

Then he remembered something else from his earlier tour. 'By the way, after Cambridge Henry Martyn didn't stick with his mathematics. He became a missionary, somewhere in the Middle East. I wonder what happened to John?'

There was some delay in desserts arriving so George continued to delve on her phone. 'What d'you know, John gave up mathematics as well. He became a vicar at a church in the Cotswolds, wrote one or two famous hymns.' She frowned. 'Hey Harry, would two such upstanding men as these two be happy to help hide a gold bar? Wouldn't they ask questions on where it had come from?'

'People change as they grow older, George. Like you and me, I suppose.' For some reason he looked slightly sad.

'These two might not have been as upstanding when they were at school – might have been the rogues of the school. And in any case, they never came back here. Maybe each of them was left with some anxieties that drove them to other places?'

CHAPTER 36

On Friday morning Frances Cober was back in Truro Cathedral, this time for an arranged catch-up with Marcus Tredwell. Though it would be pleasurable to spend more time in his company, she had decided it would be best to leave him to his own devices for a few days. She had plenty to do, back in Helston and around Truro, on the Donald McKay case. After all, she told herself, he could work through Joy Tregorran when he needed more details of current security arrangements.

Marcus was in a corner of the Nave again when she found him, still dressed unobtrusively but looking around a little more eagerly than on their first encounter. He gave her a broad smile and a firm handshake, which she sensed (or imagined?) was warmer than strictly necessary. 'Good to see you again, Frances.'

'Great to see you, Marcus. Right, shall we talk here or would you rather have another trip to Charlotte's Teashop?'

A few moments later they had once more claimed the quiet alcove looking down on Boscawen Street, as they awaited delivery of their orders.

'So how's it been going?' Frances asked.

'I love the Cathedral; and the whole town,' he replied. 'It's so much more serene than London. You know, I wouldn't mind settling somewhere round here.'

Frances smiled. 'I'm glad you like the place. Maybe we need to find you other security challenges. But no doubt your bosses will want you back sooner rather than later.'

'I fear they will,' he frowned.

Frances had expected they'd be deep into security details on the Cathedral by now, but she could afford to cut him a little slack.

'You don't sound too keen,' she remarked. 'Have you worked in the security world for long?'

'I'm not sure,' he admitted. Then realised that wasn't much of an answer. 'I've been in London for a couple of years, anyway. I'm not supposed to say any more.'

Fortunately their order arrived at that moment and gave him some breathing space. Frances was itching to quiz him further – he was being remarkably elusive – but she thought it better to contrive for him to volunteer more when he was ready.

'Let's do the official chat first then,' she suggested. 'So what have you made of security in the Cathedral so far?'

'It doesn't make a lot of sense,' he admitted. 'To be honest, I can't find anything in the Cathedral, apart from the silverware they keep in that safe in the Crypt, that would be worth the effort of pinching. Sure, there are plenty of quirky items which are much loved by visitors; but I can't see any of them would be worth much to an outsider. Their resale value would be nil.'

Frances wondered for a second whether to mention the idea from Harry Jennings, the previous Sunday, of some sort of treasure inside the building. If it existed, that would be worth chasing. She decided, though, that it would be better to keep the idea under wraps for the time being. Marcus was here to deal with known reality, not academic ideas.

Marcus took advantage of the pause to pour out their cups

of tea. Then he sat back, cup in hand, considering what else he had to report.

'As you suggested on Monday, there are many improvements that could be made to their key system. There are plenty of copies of most of them – too many, I'd say. All the ones I've had a chance to look at would be easy enough to copy – there's a local Timpson's on Lemon Quay. I expect half the keys have been here since the place was built.'

'That's what the Dean thinks, too,' commented Frances. 'So I'm sure he'd be happy enough to implement wholesale change if you told him exactly what to do. That wouldn't cost too much either, would it?'

'I don't think so. Trouble is, I think everyone is expecting a lot more from me.'

Frances pondered for a moment. How could she help him? 'What about the windows? Wouldn't it be easy for an intruder to climb into one of them round the back, say if you came along late at night with a high ladder inside your van?'

Marcus looked confident. 'I've had a careful look at that. I brought some high-powered binoculars with me, you see. I had to be let in very early, mind, before any visitors arrived, to keep my work quiet like you specified. It turns out that all the high windows have got bars across them on the inside, so that wouldn't be easy.'

'Mm. What about the lower ones?'

'Ah. The ground level ones – that's the Chapter House refectory and the Cathedral shop – are all double glazed and alarmed on the inside. It's not as bad as you might expect.'

'Great.' Then a further thought struck her. 'So exactly where do these alarms ring?'

227

'They've been put here in this century, Frances. There's a direct line through to Truro Police Station. I haven't done any homework, mind, on what happens when they ring. Maybe you could check that out for me?'

Frances puzzled for a moment. 'If I simply asked they'd probably fob me off, dismiss me as an awkward female. To be really sure we ought to conduct an experiment. Could you get an alarm to ring at an agreed time after the Cathedral's closed, while I'm watching behind the scenes in the Police Station?'

Marcus smiled. 'That'd be fun to try, anyway. But it might annoy one of the high-ups. I wouldn't want to get you into trouble.'

'My middle name is "trouble", Marcus. But it's not my responsibility, is it, if burglar alarms ring and are simply ignored?'

She sipped her cup and wondered how it could be done. 'There's a problem, though. How would you get in when the Cathedral is closed?'

'That's easy, Frances,' he replied. 'I'd say there are dozens of places in there where you could hide and not be found. This time of year it's almost dark by the time the doors close. And I've watched, I'm sure they don't go round with sniffer dogs.'

'So where would you hide?' challenged Frances.

Marcus thought for a moment. 'Behind one of the statues, say, or perhaps hiding under a tomb. In fact, you know, it'd be a good test of their security processes to see how easy that was. And if it all went wrong and I was caught, that'd be my excuse.'

They agreed a time and a date: nine pm on Friday evening. Frances knew the Station was always busy around that time.

No-one would notice if she sat writing up some of her notes in a corner of the open plan.

Frances poured them both a third cup of tea. She'd received his oral report and Marcus was looking very relaxed now. Maybe he'd be willing to share more of his murky past?

'So where did you work, Marcus, before you came to London a couple of years ago?' she asked. An innocent question, she thought. She had no idea how he would answer.

Marcus was obviously battling with conflicting pressures. But he seemed comfortable with her, so was bound to say something eventually. She just had to wait. Waiting for an answer, exploiting the pressure of silence to make someone talk, was something she'd learned to do over many years of police interviews.

'It's difficult to answer that, Frances,' he said, after a long pause. 'I'd like to tell you, I really would. You've been so friendly and kind to me: much kinder than anyone I met in London.' He was silent, looked almost like he was wanting to cry.

'The truth is that I'm not sure. I've lost my memory, you see. I can't remember anything at all of my life before the plane crash.'

CHAPTER 37

' You unfortunate man,' said Frances. 'Marcus, I'm so very sorry. No-one from London warned me about any of this. Can you at least share the bare bones of it – provided, of course, that you want to.'

Almost without conscious thought she reached under the table to hold his hand. 'Please, please, Marcus, do tell me. Take as long over it as you like.'

Now he had made the crucial admission of memory loss and received a sympathetic response, Marcus seemed almost desperate to tell her more.

'To be honest, Frances, I'm not even sure that Marcus Tredwell is really my name,' he began.

Frances frowned. 'Where did it come from?'

'The man interviewing me swore that was my name. He told me it was the name he'd retrieved from my mobile phone.'

Frances felt like she was picking up a story in mid-sentence. 'I'm sorry, Marcus, I'm afraid you've lost me. Can we start a bit further back? For instance, what's your oldest memory?'

Her companion was still for a moment: frowning, finally remembering. The experience had obviously been traumatic.

'My first memory, Frances, is waking up in a hospital. I was horribly injured: masses of broken bones and it seemed I'd been caught in some sort of intense blaze. I was strapped up, hardly able to move, with tubes inserted all over me. I was badly disfigured and could barely see. And my head hurt like hell.'

'Have you any idea where you were?'

'It was certainly nowhere in this country. Plenty of nurses but none speaking English. I couldn't understand a single word. Or remember how I'd got there. I stayed in there for ages – probably months. I guess it was the local equivalent of an Intensive Care Ward.'

Frances glanced down, found that she was still holding his hand. She gave it a squeeze. 'It sounds dreadful. But eventually you recovered enough to be let out?'

He nodded. 'That was when the interviews began. They had found a phone which they associated with me and deduced from it that its owner spoke English. Somehow or other they found a local who could converse with me. He introduced himself as "Abdul".

'At first Abdul was friendly. He told me that I'd been the only survivor from a big air crash. I'd been thrown out just as the plane exploded. The phone was found near me and assumed to be mine. Hence, he said, my name must be Marcus.

'I was in no position to argue. My headache had gone by now but my mind was still blank. For some reason I could understand him and I could voice an English reply, but I couldn't remember any more details. I had no idea why I was in a plane, where it had come from or been heading, or even my reason for travelling.'

Frances shook her head. 'That must have been very unnerving.'

Marcus smiled. 'It still is, actually. Very little has come

back and that's years later. But my real trouble was that Abdul didn't believe me.'

Frances blinked in surprise. 'Why ever not?'

'The trouble was that he knew something else about the real Marcus Tredwell. For some reason he thought he was some sort of British intelligence agent – a spy. So he assumed, with some justification, that my memory loss was simply a spy trick which I'd been taught, to use if I was ever captured and interrogated.'

'Oh, no.'

'Yes. In consequence he put me through a long interrogation to try and restore my memory, so I could give away all my state secrets. It was a nightmare.'

Nightmare was hardly the word, thought Frances. No doubt Abdul and his cronies had been extremely brutal with Marcus for months on end. She didn't think she could bear to be told all the details. Not yet, anyway.

'How ever did all this end?'

'Well, a couple of years ago there was a clandestine prisoner swap agreed between the country I was in and Britain. I think they happen behind the scenes from time to time. Abdul and his mates claimed that they were holding the notorious Marcus Tredwell. That person – allegedly me – was offered up in exchange for a genuine spy of some sort being held by the British.

'I found myself on a plane being sent to some neutral airport, probably Nicosia, in the middle of the night. Where I was taken out and swapped with a Middle Eastern gentleman with an equally large beard who came off another plane. I got onto the second plane and was escorted back to the military airfield at Northolt, in West London. From there I was driven off to the back of beyond for further cross examination.'

'How peculiar,' said Frances. 'Of course, British Intelligence wouldn't take long to realise that you weren't their Marcus Tredwell at all.'

'The real trouble was, they daren't admit that,' said Marcus. 'They had swapped a real terrorist for me, couldn't admit even to their bosses that they'd been tricked. In fact, I'm not even sure they were tricked. Everybody where I was being held thought I really was Marcus Tredwell.'

'So what happened next?'

'Well, they produced fresh copies of all the documents that went with the name Marcus Tredwell – passport, driving license, bank statements, last year's P60, the lot. Told me some of his back story – but that was mainly so I wouldn't go anywhere near any places where he was known. Then they offered to employ me, at a modest salary, as a security contractor based in the United Kingdom, on condition that I kept my tale secret. They taught me a few skills then put me onto low-level tasks like assessing security at Truro Cathedral.'

'You poor, poor man,' said Frances. 'What a dreadfully sad story. And you have no idea who you really are?'

'Occasionally I hear words or places that sound faintly familiar. The name "Cornwall" was one. That's why I volunteered for this work. But what my old connection was I have no idea.'

CHAPTER 38

Before they parted Marcus had sworn Frances to total secrecy on the tale he'd just told her. 'That was the key condition of my being employed by the Security Services,' he said. 'I might have some other qualifications, but I don't know what they are. In the meantime I have to hang on to this job. If the story ever got into the public domain, you see, my life would be destroyed from all sides.'

Frances couldn't completely see why – what if he got his memory back, for instance? – but of course she had agreed. For some reason the man had trusted her enough to share the remembered part of his life with her and she had to honour that. She also felt a deep sympathy towards him – almost affection. She resolved to research into memory loss and its restoration further, once she had more time.

In the meantime, Frances reflected, as she headed back for her car, her own employers were expecting her to resolve the case of Donald McKay. To her horror she realised that it was now over a fortnight since his inert body had been found in Shortlanesend. That must be her priority for today.

Not long ago, she recalled, she had imagined that they'd had a breakthrough. Walter Wallace, McKay's close friend (and/or partner?), had seemed almost too good to be true, with his tiny shop over in St Agnes. Assuming that McKay, too, would spend days serving behind the counter, the police could now plausibly account for most of the dead man's time.

With his interest in old machinery – Frances could make no sense of the bellows sketch at this point – it still seemed possible that McKay could have learned something profitable – or at least pursuable – about some sort of treasure around the Cathedral.

The notion made the police officer think about dates. Could they tie together? Exactly when, she wondered, had McKay applied for the Assisted Dying conference? Was that before or after the completion date she'd seen, scribbled on the back of his sketch?

If the bellows had been seen and sketched only after he had applied, that made any link unlikely. Whereas if that came first, maybe close behind, that might point to a purpose for coming to the Cathedral that was really nothing at all to do with "Assisted Dying".

Frances wondered where Joy Tregorran was today. Was she still tidying up from her conference, or maybe doing other jobs to help the Dean? It would be good to chat, anyway, about Marcus's work on security. She pulled out her phone: there was one way to find out.

Twenty minutes later Frances was seated in Joy's small, temporary office, adjacent to the Dean's grander workspace, as the vicar made them both mugs of filter coffee.

The police Officer felt a tinge of guilt: what was she doing, talking to Joy rather than exchanging comments with her own policeman, over in Helston?

Then she reminded herself that Joy had met McKay, had

worked closely with him in drafting the conference drama, whereas Tim had never met the man at all. He could only guess what McKay was like: Joy actually knew. And seeing her would be more use than talking to Inspector Marsh, anyway.

'So how's it all going?' asked Joy as she handed over the mug to her visitor.

'We have one or two lines of inquiry open,' replied Frances. Then she grinned, 'I'm sorry, I'm sounding like a press release.

'To be honest, Joy, we've a few ideas but nothing definite. Can I bounce a few thoughts off you?'

Joy smiled. 'Well, the Dean asked me to take the lead for him on Cathedral security. I suppose that anything that helps with McKay might help on security as well. So be my guest, bounce all you like.'

'Right,' said Frances. 'My constable and I have been trying hard to make sense of Donald McKay,' she began. 'Yesterday we went over to St Agnes to meet the first friend of his that we've come across, apart from the conference delegates. An old work mate, from before they both retired, called Walter Wallace. Apparently they would paint Cornish machinery together. Did he ever mention that?'

Joy sipped her coffee, considered for a moment. 'I don't think so. Certainly he never talked to me about St Agnes. But that's not suspicious: some people like to keep different strands of their lives distinct. He and I only really discussed issues relating to our drama.'

'Can I ask a bit more about that, Joy? Was the drama your idea or Donald's?'

'Oh, he sparked the idea when he mentioned drama as an interest on his application form. Then I saw it and fanned the flame. He was very enthusiastic, you see. But then, to be honest, so was I.'

The prime mover wasn't clear, thought Frances. 'D'you still have the forms?' she asked. 'Could you tell me when his got here?'

'Certainly.' Joy reached into a pile of material on her desk and retrieved a red folder from near the bottom. 'I kept them in arrival order: Donald's was the first: September 18th. We'd only advertised the conference the previous week. To be honest, I was glad there was any response at all.'

'So when did you start on the drama?'

'Only after it was clear there was plenty of demand for the Assisted Dying course – and a couple more delegates who might help to enact it. Mid October.'

Joy stood and peered at the calendar on the wall behind her. She flipped back a month. 'Yes, that's right. We first went into the Crypt on Wednesday October 15th. We stuck to Wednesdays for rehearsals as the conference was to begin on a Wednesday. It helped the drama group to keep the same weekday free.'

'Did they like the idea of performing in the Crypt? Didn't they find it creepy?'

'Well, I had no alternative. I think it was Donald that first suggested it. I got a key and he and I went down there to check it out a week later.'

'Did you ever lend him the key?' Frances held her breath: this was a crucial question.

'Donald suggested it would be good for the drama group to

237

have their own copy. There'd be rehearsals when I didn't need to be there. I mean, the place was hardly a bullion room. I gave him one straight away.'

Frances noticed that Joy was looking puzzled. Perhaps she'd better explain.

'I'm asking about dates, Joy, as I found a sketch by Donald in a back room of their shop in St Agnes. It was of a pair of old bellows, which Wallace told me had something to do with the Cathedral. On the back I spotted a date: September 3rd. The thing is, everything you've just told me would fit with Donald coming here in pursuit of the bellows, and also contriving a way to gain unsupervised access to the Crypt.'

Joy looked shocked. She was silent for a few moments, cogitating. She was also reflecting on her conversation earlier in the week with Harry Jennings. That had discussed hidden treasure as well.

'Alright,' she said. 'I agree. The dates do fit – although that might just be coincidence. Let's assume for a moment that you're right. How does that help explain his death?'

Frances paused, drawing various ideas together. 'It only helps, I'd say, if Donald broke his silence and told someone or other what he was planning. Maybe the excitement of the chase got to him? What if he boasted that he'd almost found the hidden item: would bring it home, say, after the drama.'

Joy continued the projection. 'So that person was watching – and waiting for him to bring home his find. That same evening, before he'd had a chance to take it somewhere else, they went round to his bungalow, poisoned him and walked out with it. What if that person was his good friend, Wallace?'

Frances had already explored the same thought. 'What

makes that a bit unlikely, Joy, is that the police knew nothing about Wallace until he came to McKay's bungalow on Tuesday afternoon and was amazed to hear the news. It wasn't that we found him, you see. He found us.'

Joy wasn't going to give up her theory that easily. 'But Frances, you've managed to keep the death out of the media. There was no reason for Wallace to think the police were involved at all. Perhaps he'd come to make sure he'd left nothing that would give him away? He'd pretend to ring the door bell but use a key if he had to. You say he appeared to be amazed. But if he was the killer, he'd have planned out a suitable response anyway.'

Frances nodded. 'There was one thing I did notice, actually. He managed to give my policeman the shop address in St Agnes but not his home address. So he led us to St Agnes but we'll need to do more work to find his home. If he did need the time then he's had another day to hide anything too revealing.'

She continued, 'But there is a real weakness with the theory.'

'What's that?'

'Well. Remember how George and I were nearly poisoned. How could Wallace put more of that poison into the wine sold in Diocese House? As far as you and I know, he has nothing to do with the Cathedral at all.'

CHAPTER 39

On most Friday mornings Harry Jennings would listen to the team's presentations to one another: today he was looking forward to hearing from Ben Williams. What progress had his student managed to make on the legacy of the virtuoso violinist, Joseph Emidy?

'Last time I reported to you all on the mid-life crisis of Emidy himself,' said Ben. 'I accept, though, that there's plenty more to be done on his early life in Conakry – it's just possible he was there the same time as the visit by Eleanor Kempthorne that Ellie told us about, for example.'

Ellie interrupted him. 'Hey. Maybe that was the real reason Eleanor volunteered to go looking for him in Falmouth, many years later?'

Ben frowned. 'Just possibly. The trouble is we've no primary sources from that part of the world. Unless ECHO would fund Ellie and I on a research visit there?'

Harry shook his head. 'Sorry you two, we can't afford that right now. The Royal Cornwall Museum is about the furthest we can get to at the moment.'

It had been worth a try, anyway. Ben smiled at Ellie and then continued. 'As I told you all last time, Joseph Emidy died in 1835. There's a massive headstone in his honour at the Anglican Church up in Kenwyn. So I went there with Ellie. We took some time to visit the place and then unravel the church records of his family.'

'Emidy is a pretty unusual surname,' observed Harry. 'The

UK Census, which happens every ten years, starting in the nineteenth century, might help track the family as well.'

'That's what I thought,' said Ben. 'Trouble was, I soon found I needed to consult the census data for the United States. For some reason or other all eight of his children emigrated there straight after his death.'

'That in itself is worth further investigating, Ben,' said Harry. 'What made them all leave? They wouldn't have been children. Could it be racial prejudice? Say, a bias hidden from view while Emidy was in his heyday, but very clear once he'd gone?'

'His wife was Cornish, I believe,' said Ellie. 'Maybe being of mixed race in those days was more difficult to manage than being just black or white?'

There was silence as ideas were considered.

'Did any of them inherit Emidy's musical genes?' asked Bill.

'I expect so,' said Ben. 'Emidy was a musical genius. Mind, they might have been keen to find a different career, not simply follow in their father's footsteps. I can't find any mention of them in the annals of the Truro Philharmonic Orchestra, for instance.'

That prompted a wider discussion in the ECHO team about legacy talent. It was definitely a factor but was by no means guaranteed. Ben let the ideas run for a while. Then he took back control.

'I managed to construct several generations of family tree for the Emidy family in America. But I wasn't sure how far to take it. It was much harder to follow up sources over there, so I'd almost given up. Then, last week, I had a breakthrough.'

There was an anticipatory silence. Ben had the floor.

'Like Harry suggested earlier, I had kept tracking successive editions of the census for the name Emidy, in and around Truro. Did any of 'em ever come back? Finally, I found the name: it was in the 1911 Census. I realised that might be linked to the completion of Truro Cathedral.'

Simon Quentin, who was researching Cathedral development, took over. 'Ben asked me what I'd found about the celebrations to mark the completion of the building project. I told him the work was finished in 1910 but it took them nearly a year to find a suitable way to mark the achievement. Lots of VIPs needed inviting, of course – including the next Duke of Cornwall. His dad had been here at the start of the building work in 1880.

'But this was a Cathedral intended for ordinary people, so they wanted everyday Truronians as well. Eventually, in a file in the Royal Cornwall Museum, I found a list of all those invited. It was very long. But one of these was a representative of the Emidy family, who were still spoken about in awe, over half a century after Joseph had died.'

Ben took back the narrative. 'I would imagine it took a lot of effort to track an Emidy down in America. No computer in those days, no Facebook either. But eventually they found a great grandson of Joseph. Another noted musician, in his case a pianist. He was invited over to Truro and was happy to accept the invitation. Given the local name recognition, he had an active role in the celebratory service: he was one of those allowed to play the new(ish) Father Willis organ. Of course that hadn't been thought of, let alone built, in Joseph's day.'

'So it all ended well?' asked Harry.

Ben shook his head. 'I'm afraid that, even after this welcome and recognition, the younger Emidy didn't settle here. A short while later he had sailed back across the Atlantic. It was May 1912. He was lucky, I suppose, that he hadn't set out a month earlier on the SS Titanic. But I'm afraid I haven't managed to track down any more visits from the family in recent years.'

There was the usual substantial discussion after Ben had concluded his presentation. He and Simon had found out some interesting facts and raised some challenging questions, but they were by no means at the end of the trail. There was probably plenty more left to discover.

Harry did his best to suggest fresh lines of inquiry and other possible sources. Then he noticed it was after one o'clock and shepherded his team out for a pub lunch. He bought all their drinks, in some cases twice over. In his mind these gatherings were all part of the ECHO team building.

When they came back Harry shut himself in his office. He wasn't drunk, not even befuddled, but he needed time to think. Might he have just glimpsed another stage in the story of the ingot (or whatever it was) that had come from the Caribbean?

The key thing, of course, was his team's finding that Eleanor Kempthorne had been a close associate of Joseph Emidy. They had both been alive for some years after James Kempthorne – by then a Rear Admiral in recognition for his behind-the-scenes work in Hispaniola – had passed on. Harry glanced at his notes. Yes, that was right: the Rear Admiral had died in 1808.

After leaving Cambridge, Eleanor's son, John Kempthorne, had moved away from Truro, becoming a vicar in the Cotswolds. His ally Henry Martyn had gone even further, to the next Continent but one. Neither could be relied on to give earthly treasure much attention. Their eyes were fixed on higher things.

But Eleanor was a feisty woman. So what could she do?

Ben's presentation had given him this wonderful new idea. What if Eleanor, towards the end of her life, had shared the secret of where the treasure had been stored (which she'd been told by her son) with her close friend, the virtuoso violinist?

That was plausible. But if so, was it not equally likely that, when Eleanor had died, Joseph Emidy would pass the information on, in his later years, to his own children?

The trouble was, all eight children had left Cornwall suddenly for America. Harry had a sudden thought, a moment of enlightenment. What if there had not been enough time for them to find, recover and deal with the treasure? It would sit, more or less abandoned, where John Kempthorne and his friends had hidden it, somewhere inside the Old Parish Church.

No-one else in Truro had any reason even to suspect its existence. Not for years and years. Not even when the Cathedral was first being built.

That was until another musical Emidy came to Truro, early in the next century. If the secret had been passed down the Emidy generations, might this Emidy not have seen a chance to look for the treasure; and to hide it somewhere else, somewhere he thought safer, inside the new Cathedral?

Harry imagined how Joy might respond to his latest idea. Why on earth, she would ask, would Emidy Junior bother? He could almost see the scorn on her face.

His answer: it was the effect of the Cathedral on the Old Parish Church. Harry was reasonably sure that had been the first hiding place, in the pumping machinery for the 1750 organ. But the organ was now in the Cathedral, powered by electricity. So what would happen to the waterpower links and the ingot weights? They could well have been dumped in some corner of the Crypt. In that case, Junior would have to choose between taking them back to America or hiding them somewhere else.

But these were ingots. They'd be hard to take home. It might be a lot easier to hide them somewhere else in the Cathedral.

Harry Jennings went round his idea again and again. It was nothing like certain but it had merit. He needed someone to bounce it off, face-to-face: probably one of his friends who was also concerned with the recent crimes associated with Truro Cathedral.

He seized his phone. A few moments later he had got through to Joy Tregorran and lodged his recurrent plea for a weekend together. But once again he was disappointed.

'I'm sorry, Harry,' she replied. 'I can't afford the time to have you stay with me in Gunwalloe this weekend. At the moment I'm trying to do two jobs at once. The Dean has me managing the security audit for him in Truro, while my church continues to expect an active presence from me in Gunwalloe. I'm sorry, but right now, I'm afraid, there's no time left for you.'

There was an awkward pause. Harry didn't quite know

what to say. He was surplus to requirements. But Joy continued to dig herself in.

'In any case, Harry, I'm back now in Gunwalloe so I can't offer you a lift over. I won't be coming into Truro again till next week. I'll try and give you a ring on Monday, Harry – if I have time. Things might look a bit better by then. Bye.'

Harry sat for a few minutes staring at his phone. There was no doubt that everything Joy was telling him was true. And all the stretching of body and mind, with demanding loads across two locations, was no doubt stressing her out. But he wasn't used to rejection, even when justified, and it hurt.

He paused and cogitated. Then he reached for his phone again. This time he dialled the number he had rung for the first time only two days before. Would a very old friend at least give him a hearing?

But this time the disappointment was even more abrupt. The phone he'd called was switched off. It would not even accept a voice message.

CHAPTER 40

As it happened, George Gilbert had been thinking quite a lot about Harry Jennings and their lunch together the previous day.

The historian had asked her (eventually) some mathematical questions. How might the old Parish Church organ have been powered, in the 1750s, by the nearby mill race? What sort of design was involved? And might it include a heavy weight?

George had walked round the back of the Cathedral after their lunch and seen the same mill race in its present form. The water was certainly running fast and gurgling noisily through the narrow, five-foot channel.

She had judged the flow was fastest under a footbridge heading towards the Chapter House. Then she'd paced out the distance from there along the road, back to the old church. It was about thirty metres.

She had mused on the problem when she was back with British Telecom and that evening in her Premier Inn room, but with only limited success.

One of the incidental pleasures of her lunch with Harry, she realised, had been the re-discovery of the joy of leaving her workplace and its distractions for an hour and wandering around outside. She had come back to the office a lot fresher and had resolved to do the same thing more often – even if she didn't receive any more invitations to lunch with the handsome

247

historian.

As she strolled around Truro City Centre on the Friday – it was cold but at least not raining – a thought came to her. If Harry was right, or to be more precise his tour guide had been correct, the bellows would once have worked for decades in the old Parish Church. Would that not be an item of interest, even today, to the Royal Cornwall Museum?

Though she had often intended to do so, George had never actually visited this Museum. She had always been working too intensively on the days she was in Truro. And by the time she had left the office in the evening the Museum itself was closed.

George braced herself. Today, she decided, would be different.

It wasn't far. The Museum was set back slightly from the

main road, with a teashop next door. That would be her treat if she was successful.

George went into the main entrance and paid the modest charge to go in. She was told that the street level galleries dealt with many aspects of life in Cornwall and were intended for viewing by the general public. More specialist topics were handled in the Courtney Library upstairs.

George glanced at her watch: she could afford to stay here for an hour. She resolved to have a quick look round downstairs – what sort of things did they cover? If that didn't look promising she would visit the library.

One room was associated with Cornish geology and George wandered in. It was a subject that she regretted not having studied in earnest. There were all sorts of diagrams with linked photographs of Cornish cliffs and other idiosyncrasies.

Suddenly she found herself looking at a picture of Port Isaac and her heart missed a beat. This was where she and her long-gone husband Mark had come for their honeymoon, twenty five years ago. She'd not thought of it for years but now she was drawn towards it. Looking more carefully, she could see the guest house where they'd stayed, even the window to their room. A burst of sadness enveloped her and she started to cry.

A few moments elapsed before she had regained some sort of control and could make her way out.

The main gallery was huge and presented interesting items from the history of Cornwall, all in chronological order. That was better: she could go at once to the displays covering the eighteenth and nineteenth centuries.

There was a mass of fascinating stuff here. George noticed

a small display which mentioned Joseph Emidy, a former black slave with a genius for playing the violin, who became leader of the Truro Philharmonic Orchestra. Perhaps she could ask Harry about that, if they ever had lunch together again?

She must be disciplined, she told herself. Concentrate on aspects of the tale that Harry had told her. Suddenly, as she walked along, her attention was taken by a large, well-dressed cardboard figure hanging down from the ceiling. The caption below told her that this was Sir Humphrey Davy.

She knew Davy had invented the mining lamp but she saw that he had done a great deal more. He had been one of the early Presidents of the Royal Society – he was one of the top scientists of the early nineteenth century. And she observed, with amusement, that he had been brought up in this part of Cornwall and had also attended Truro Grammar School.

Then suddenly, more intriguingly, she saw Davy's dates. He was born in 1779, the year before Henry Martyn. All at once it hit her: Sir Humphrey was an exact contemporary of the man Harry had been exulting over. There weren't just two very clever lads at the famous school, there had been three. She assumed that Harry hadn't known this or it would certainly have been part of his story.

George was about to ring him to tell him – it would be some answer to his concerns, if not the one he'd intended – then she remembered her schedule. She must first go to the library upstairs to enquire what they knew about pre-electrical bellows and organs.

The Courtney Library certainly had a grand staircase, thought the analyst. She could imagine it being used in the century before last by ladies descending gracefully in their long flowing dresses. George wandered round the gallery upstairs until she came to the library entrance. It had various notices of academic interest which didn't apply, so she knocked and went in.

The librarian, a trim, white-haired lady with a badge saying "Angela", was having her own lunch – a small cheese baguette. George walked over to her desk and introduced herself.

'Have I come at the wrong time?' she continued.

'No, no, we're open all the time. But we have to eat occasionally. They still let us do that. How can I help you?'

'Well, someone asked me about how the old organ in the Parish Church of St Mary's was powered, in the days before electricity.'

George had little hope of an answer but she had underestimated the librarian, who smiled.

'You're not the first person to ask me that recently,' she began. 'As it happens we already had a folder on the subject. Would you like to see it?'

Abandoning her baguette (which made George feel slightly guilty), Angela slid off her stool and headed to the far side of the room. There were masses of filing cabinets there, all carefully labelled. The librarian studied a list carefully. Then she chose one, opened the top drawer and pulled out a beige cardboard folder.

'This might help you,' she remarked. George followed her to the large table in the middle of the room.

Angela opened the folder. It contained a number of sheets. One was a sketch of two bellows, side by side. Another was a series of equations, handwritten in an older style of English. The third was a typed document which George judged must be modern. That would probably explain how it all worked in an everyman form of English.

George gave a sigh of satisfaction. 'That looks to be exactly what I was after, Angela. Wonderful. Is it possible to photocopy them all so I can take them away to study at my leisure? I'll happily wait till you've finished the baguette if you like.'

The woman acknowledged the courtesy. 'Not many visitors are that considerate. The last man to take a copy of that folder was polite enough, mind.'

She seized her baguette and continued munching. George took the chance for a first look at her treasure. This was exactly what Harry was after – well, provided she added an interpretation. She didn't think the historian would make much of the mathematics.

Suddenly a thought struck her. Angela had finished her lunch by now and was doing the photocopying she had requested.

'This man, my predecessor,' she began. 'You don't by any chance have a name for him, do you? I wouldn't mind swapping notes. I'd have thought this was a specialist subject.'

Angela sighed. 'I expect so. We usually take people's names. That's exactly so they can share their enthusiasm. It'll be in the book here.'

She pulled out a black visitors' book and flipped back the pages. 'It was about three months ago. August, probably.' She continued to scan the pages. 'Ah, yes. Here it is. On August 25th: a Mr Donald McKay. He took copies of everything too.

He was some sort of Engineer, I believe. It takes all sorts, I suppose.'

'I suppose it does,' said George. She picked up the bundle of photocopied papers about the bellows and made a generous donation to the collecting tin on Angela's desk. 'Thank you very much indeed.'

As soon as she was outside George tried to phone Frances. An early trace of McKay was surely of significant interest. However, Frances phone was off. She would have to try again later.

CHAPTER 41

It was as she was walking back from her frustrating, late morning conversation with Joy Tregorran that Frances had asked herself an obvious question.

Assuming that McKay was killed by the same tranche of poison that had later afflicted her and George – and hence by the same person – why wasn't she putting more effort into getting hold of Barry? After all, he knew where McKay lived, had been in the man's bungalow (in company) on the Thursday morning and was also a conference resident in Diocese House. Didn't that make him a prime suspect?

Frances had tried to interview Barry herself, along with all the other delegates. She had his mobile number and had tried phoning him regularly, without any success. Over the last two weeks, chipping away, she had made good progress on seeing – or at least phone-interviewing – the rest. And the drama group. But she hadn't managed to get hold of him.

His application form had told her that in real life Barry was a doctor, living in Truro. Perhaps that was why he had chosen, or been chosen, to take the role of the grumpy doctor in the Crypt drama. But to the police officer it was rather a surprise.

She had contacted his surgery. But the receptionist there was quite clear: Dr Parsons (as it turned out Barry was known) had gone away for a long-planned autumn holiday. He

254

wouldn't be back till "the following weekend".

Now Frances scrutinised that phrase again. Receptionists at doctors' surgeries were used to massaging messages at their employers' direction. When did a weekend actually start? Was it not at least possible that Dr Barry Parsons was already home from his no-expense-spared holiday? It was certainly worth another try.

Half an hour later Frances had eaten a packed lunch, collected her car from the Police Station and driven out south towards Devoran, a pretty, boat-obsessed village just outside the main city.

She had decided, on balance, not to contact the surgery. If Dr Parsons was actually home but still officially off duty, there was no point in forcing the loyal receptionist into a complicated lie. It would also give the doctor advance warning of her approach.

It would be interesting, anyway, to see where the man lived.

Frances suddenly realised, as she parked outside his house and gathered her thoughts, that she didn't even know if Barry was married. She had assumed from his closeness to Roberta the social worker during the conference that he was unattached, but maybe that was a short-term liaison? She hadn't had chance to quiz him on the point directly in casual conversation at the conference.

Then Frances saw a curtain twitch. Someone was in, anyway. She eased out of her car and headed for the front door.

'Welcome home, Dr Parsons,' said the police officer, as the door swung open and Barry stood before her. He blinked, looking half asleep and very surprised to see her. Behind him two large suitcases, each held by a bright red strap strewn with luggage labels, took up half the hall.

Frances saw a massive pile of unopened post on the hall table beyond. Given that she had come without any warning, she was certain that the doctor was indeed just back from a holiday. The poor man was probably suffering from jet lag. She decided he needed one of her smiles.

'Have you been home long?' she chirruped.

Parsons blinked again and glanced at his watch. 'Thirty one minutes,' he replied. 'Before that I was in the air for fourteen hours – non-stop from Singapore – but I never sleep properly in a plane. I'm always fearful the intercom will crackle and they'll start asking for a doctor, you see. That's my worst nightmare.'

He made an effort to pull himself together. 'You'd better come in. It is Frances, isn't it? I didn't realise you were a police officer.'

Ten minutes later he had made them both a pot of tea and they were seated in the lounge. The menial task seemed to have restored his brain a little.

'Are you here about Donald?' he began.

'I am, sir. I've been interviewing all the delegates from the Assisted Dying conference in turn. But I couldn't get hold of you: you were away.'

'Yes. I always leave the summer holiday weeks to my colleagues who've got children, you see. But then, if you go away in November, you've got to go to the southern hemisphere to get the sun. When England are playing I like to watch some Test cricket. But there's none on at the moment. So this time I went to Bali, on a trail into the depths of the jungle. My phone didn't bother me at all – that was delightful. I even saw a couple of wild elephants.' He gave a rueful smile. 'And now you can see: I'm home with a bang.'

The man didn't seem that worried, thought Frances. But then, she reminded herself, he was a member of a drama group, used to acting a part. She needed to rattle him.

'If you're a doctor, sir, why on earth didn't you say, as soon as you saw Donald McKay's body?'

Barry considered for a moment. 'Well, most of all, I was upset. I'd known Donald for years. We'd clash over details of how parts should be played but at heart we were both drama stalwarts – and friends.'

He glanced across. 'You and I, Frances, are both professionals. We probably don't have many close friends. Doctors are no more immune to emotion when an old friend dies than anyone else. It hits you most of all when, like this, it comes out of the blue.

'Then there was my work-life balance. I work jolly hard at the surgery but when I'm off duty I like to stay that way. I value my time off: as, for example, when I'm on an aeroplane.'

'In any case,' he went on, 'I didn't need to examine Donald. I could see at once that he was dead, had been dead for hours. Roberta was ahead of me, had already got hold of his doctor. By the time she handed me the phone I realised that it would be neater all round if his own GP saw him. She'd know his chequered medical history, wouldn't hesitate to sign a death certificate. As in fact she did.'

But he could see the police officer was not yet satisfied.

'Finally,' he said, 'I had a plane halfway round the world booked, going as soon as the conference was over: my main holiday of the year. I wanted to avoid fresh complications.'

Was this convincing? Did Parsons have other reasons for getting someone else to sign the death certificate?

'So you don't like complication?' she hazarded.

Dr Parsons could see the police officer wasn't satisfied; more was needed. 'The thing was, Frances, I'd just played an unsympathetic doctor in the drama the night before. If the delegates found out I really was a doctor, they'd assume I had just been playing myself and that I believed all those heartless things the drama-doctor had uttered. Whereas in fact I'm all in favour of mercy killing, I wish the law allowed it. Just between ourselves, Frances, I wanted freedom to go on expressing that view.'

Frances wasn't totally convinced but she would need to check. If Dr Parsons had simply kept quiet until the local doctor arrived, that surely wasn't a crime? After all, there was a post-mortem a few days later and it had confirmed that Donald had indeed been dead for hours. In the end his silence hadn't mattered at all.

Frances decided that she would accept his story for the time being. 'Right sir. Thank you for making that clear. Just a few more things then, I've been asking everyone. Firstly, what's your make of car and its registration number, and where did you park during the conference? Secondly, at what time did you go to bed on that first Wednesday evening? And thirdly, I know it's a long time ago, but can you remember who else was around when you did so?'

As with her other interviews, the results of these standard questions were unrevealing. She couldn't really expect sharp answers, two weeks after the event.

Frances came away far from satisfied. As soon as she'd seen that Barry was a doctor, she'd realised that he could easily get hold of methadone but she hadn't wanted to reveal that at this stage.

She decided it would be best to ask Tim Barwell to check for his car on the traffic cameras before taking any further action.

CHAPTER 42

In the end George Gilbert had been the one to ring Harry. Her phone had remained off for the afternoon as she wrestled with complex calculations linked to her project. It had been late on Friday afternoon by the time she had finished and could make a call.

By now she was preparing for a trip back to her cottage near Tintagel. She'd bought cereals, bread and milk on the way back from the Museum. With the weekend sleepovers with Frances Cober she hadn't been home for three weeks.

Harry had sounded sorry for himself when she got hold of him. She sensed he was feeling on his own and forgotten.

'I got some stuff from the Royal Cornwall Museum that you might find interesting,' she began. 'But you'd need to see it. I can't do it justice over the phone.'

'You can come to ECHO to show me if you like,' he offered. It's very quiet now. Everyone but me has gone home.'

'And you're hanging about, waiting for the slow boat to China. Or at least something heading for Exeter? You poor old thing.'

Suddenly, out of the blue, without forethought, an idea struck her. 'Hey Harry, would you like to come for a weekend in Treknow? I have to go home this weekend.'

The thought had been planted without deep thought but was readily welcomed. Ten minutes later George's Mini Cooper was pulling into the car park outside the ECHO Portakabin and she was welcoming her old friend on board.

Harry didn't dare speak as George picked her way through the Friday-night rush-hour. The task needed her full concentration. But twenty minutes later they had reached the edge of Truro and the line of traffic was moving rather faster.

'Will this seat go back a bit?' he asked. 'I'm probably a bit taller than most of your passengers. Or at least, I was when I climbed in.'

George giggled. 'Oh sorry. I should have done it before you got in. There's a rod somewhere below you. Squeeze hard, raise it up and then give a great big shove.'

It occurred to her that the words sounded like something out of an old sex manual and the thought made her giggle again. She and Harry had once been very close when both were at Cambridge but that was a long time ago. For some odd reason the thought made her feel almost light-headed.

Harry huffed and pushed, swore under his breath and eventually got the seat into a more comfortable position. 'Thank you so much for inviting me, George. I'd lost enthusiasm for a weekend on my own. So we're heading for a cottage in Treknow? Hey, I didn't know you were a woman of property.'

George took a moment to reply. 'Yes. It's almost ten years ago now to the day. My uncle left me some money when he died and I wanted to have something more permanent down here. North Cornwall was where Mark and I used to come for our holidays.'

Harry realised that by pure accident he had traversed onto delicate ground. He had never heard her talk about Mark

261

before, didn't even know if the two were divorced or the man had simply died. Maybe breaking into the subject like this without warning had caught his friend out too? He sensed that she was crying. No-one could do that and retain full control of their car.

'Hey George, why don't you pull over for a few minutes?'

He glanced up. It was almost dark but in the gloom he could just see a break in the hedge, not far ahead. 'There's a lay-by coming up. Why don't you stop and have a good cry?'

George had no problem in following his advice. Signalling her intentions, she jammed on her brakes; a moment later they had come to a halt in a small lay-by as the evening traffic thundered past. She put her head in her hands and started crying, with deep, deep sobs.

For a minute Harry didn't know what to do. Then instinct took over. He leaned over to the driver's seat and put his arm gently around her. With his other hand he reached into his pocket and pulled out a clean handkerchief. George was crying tears by the bucket, this would certainly be needed. Then, for fifteen minutes, he just let her cry.

'D'you want to tell me about it?' he asked, once the tears seemed to have subsided to a trickle.

George sniffed, loudly. For a moment she said nothing. Then she began.

'Mark and I had had our ups and downs but we'd grown really close. He was a very caring husband and we had one daughter, Polly. She was a teenager and we both doted over her. But his business often took him abroad. We were both of us so busy, practically all of the time. My consultancy role had taken off and my firm were sending me up and down the country like a yo-yo. I guess I should have given him more time, but apart from Cornwall, family time together was the one thing we never seemed to have. And of course we never will.'

She started crying again, less frantically this time, and for a while said nothing. Harry was wise enough to stay silent.

'Then one day, just after I got home from work, a policeman came round to our home in Kilburn – North London. Checked who I was, then said he had some bad news. Mark had been killed in an air crash. Somewhere in Iran, he said. It was so far off the beaten track that it hardly made the national news. Of course the Iranians were never ones to encourage journalists to come and see for themselves. The whole crash site was blocked off. There were rumours that the plane had been shot down by one of their own military rockets – it was alleged they mistook the aircraft for an American bomber.'

Harry recalled that something similar had happened again recently. He thought it was safe to ask a question now. 'So Mark came home in a wooden box?'

George nodded. 'Most of Mark did, anyway. He was dreadfully burnt, unrecognisable. The Iranians had worked back from the flight manifest and the seat positions in the wreckage. They weren't all that helpful. I was told they were secretly embarrassed by the whole thing. They knew deep down that it was their fault. Most of those killed were Iranians, of course.'

'But wasn't there a post-mortem – here in the UK?'

'There was a post-mortem, Harry. It was conducted quickly and was far from revealing. It was a female Coroner and she didn't ask too many questions. I think the British authorities had told her they wanted it all to die down as soon as possible and not to make too much fuss.'

'Didn't you challenge that?'

'Harry, I was in far too bad a way to argue – even with a female Coroner. I hadn't started on my career as Miss Marple of the West in those days. I had no idea what questions to ask.'

'But later?'

'I did my best. I wanted to understand what Mark was doing in Iran. Whatever it was for, it didn't make business sense. Mark's uncle helped me some of the way and then I decided to leave it and move on. Talking of which . . .'

George seemed to think that the break had lasted long enough. She braced herself and then pulled the Cooper out into a tiny break that she had spotted in the traffic.

Harry gave a gasp as the car behind almost rammed into them. This weekend away was going to be more unexpected than he had ever imagined.

CHAPTER 43

Sergeant Frances Cober had spent the rest of Friday afternoon, after talking to Dr Barry Parsons, in Truro Police Station.

First she had contacted Tim Barwell. She had told him about her interview with Barry and asked him to check for any traces of Barry's car, travelling between central Truro and Shortlanesend, on the fateful Wednesday evening.

Tim was currently in Helston. But he was happy to accept the challenge. The constable had worked out a way to do that directly from his own office desk. With the various passwords and code words that he'd acquired in Truro, he could transfer the relevant traffic camera shots onto his own computer and then peruse them at leisure.

He promised to ring her back once he had anything to report. But he warned, 'It might take some time.'

After that Frances checked her notes from the Thursday afternoon, after McKay's dead body had been found. She had plenty from her interview with Joy. She was glad she had not skimped on the recording.

Joy had been explicit about her lunchtime conversation with Barry and Roberta. The sequence of events in McKay's bungalow had been clear. No doubt the shock of his death had anchored the whole thing in Joy's mind and she'd been happy to offload it.

It was all as Barry had told her. Frances checked with a colleague on the next desk, who was more au fait than her with the law on post-mortems. Yes, Barry had been right: a victim's own doctor, familiar with his condition and its treatment, could sidestep a post-mortem if they were satisfied that all was in order.

So Barry would have been quietly satisfied that Thursday lunch time. He had met the regular doctor and she was untroubled. McKay's poisoning would never be suspected at all.

And it wouldn't have been, Frances told herself, if she hadn't been on the Assisted Dying conference as an off-duty police officer; and her crime antennae, even when supposedly off duty, hadn't started to twitch.

So why on earth, wondered Frances, had not Barry left well alone? Was one death not enough? Why had more of the same poison been used at Diocese House, where it had come close to killing her and George?

It was late afternoon now. Most of the police officers at Truro were heading home for their weekends. There was no-one left that she knew well enough to bounce ideas off. There was still a light on in Kevin Marsh's office, but she doubted that talking to him would do her much good.

On an impulse she tried to ring George Gilbert. Perhaps she'd like to come to stay for the weekend: that would give her someone she could talk to and relax with? Maybe they could go for a long walk round Frenchman's Creek? But she tried and found that George's phone was off. The analyst was obviously hard at work or else engaged in deep discussion.

Six o'clock. It was quieter now. Frances found an empty interview room down below, took her laptop and notebook and shut herself in. Why, why, why would anyone choose to use the same poison twice?

Frances took a deep breath, eased her position and relaxed her muscles. To think creatively, she'd been told, her body had to be at peace. Then, slightly less tense, she tried to recall the scene in Diocese House.

What if Barry had returned to Diocese House late on Wednesday evening with unused poison hidden inside his coat? He wouldn't want to chat to anyone with that on him, he'd have gone quickly up to his room.

But he would have something to dispose of. This was before he'd met McKay's own doctor: he wouldn't be sure that he would get away with the crime. He had to get rid of the evidence. It wouldn't be enough to flush the contents down the sink. He was a doctor, would know that forensic scientists could analyse a recently emptied bottle – or access the U-tube under the sink.

What if . . . what if a bottle of Cathedral Red had always been part of the plan? Was that what Barry had taken to offer Donald? Maybe there only ever was one poisoned bottle, which had already been to Shortlanesend, helped Barry perform the killing and then returned with the poisoner? He wouldn't want to leave it in the bungalow, anyway. Even the dimmest plod might gather it as potential evidence.

So now it was vital for Barry, back in Diocese House, to get rid of the remainder. How would he do that?

No doubt he would worry. If, next morning, McKay's poisoning was suspected, the police might descend on Diocese

House and search the premises – every guestroom. They mustn't find anything in his room.

He didn't have long. He had already volunteered to Joy that he would go to Shortlanesend and check McKay's bungalow. Then Frances remembered, he wouldn't be doing that on his own: Roberta had volunteered to come with him. He could hardly stop on the way to put a half-full wine bottle into an empty dustbin.

Wouldn't the most elegant way to do this be to add more wine so the bottle was once more full and screw the top tightly back on? Then slip the full, apparently untouched bottle into the line of half a dozen bottles on the shelf behind the Diocese bar?

What if the bar was locked? It was supposed to be. That would have stymied him. But the conference was in full swing. Frances recalled the hesitancy of Patricia Townsend: had she left the bar unlocked by mistake, late on Wednesday evening?

If so, Barry might have noticed that, on his way back to his room. Had that even been what gave him the idea?

If the bottle had been left in the bar, by that mechanism or some variant of it, then it was pure bad luck for Barry – and equally (for different reasons) for Frances – that the evidence had found its way to a police officer.

On this scenario she hadn't been assigned the bottle because she was a policewoman. Any random delegate, buying a bottle of Cathedral Red to take home for their family, would have been an acceptable way of disposing of the evidence. And if they'd drunk it in modest quantities, they might not even notice its sleep-inducing properties.

There was no proof of any of this, of course. The poisoner

would have wiped the bottle before returning it to the bar. But even if he hadn't, Frances, George – and then Joy – had all handled the bottle repeatedly, without even considering the possibility of fingerprints. At that point it was simply a bottle with suspicious contents.

The best hope for evidence was if Tim could spot Barry's car making that extra journey to and from Shortlanesend. That wouldn't be proof but it would be reason for a much more searching interview with Barry Parsons.

Frances made sure her phone was on and eyed it hopefully as she settled down to wait. Tim would be very thorough. He had warned her that the search could take some time.

In any case there was only another couple of hours to wait before the alarm set by Marcus should go off in the Cathedral.

CHAPTER 44

Neither George nor Harry were buzzing with conversation for the rest of the journey, up to the A30, along the Atlantic Highway to Wadebridge and finally through Delabole and down to the hamlet of Treknow.

Now the old memories had been triggered, George was recalling all sorts of incidents in this part of Cornwall with her former husband. Thinking about that was an indulgence, she told herself impatiently: life was very different now.

But the mental struggle made her drive a little erratically. It was completely dark by now and Harry dare not speak, did not want to disrupt her concentration. In any case, he could see that his friend needed time to reflect.

No streetlights: Ivy Cottage was in pitch darkness when they arrived. 'There's nothing valuable in here,' George told him. 'It's not worth bothering with security lights, so far off the beaten path.'

She opened the front door and ushered Harry in. In her introspection she forgot that there was a step down. Her friend stepped forward, stumbled and sprawled across the hallway. For a second he thought he might have broken his ankle. He managed to control himself, not to swear out loud.

The incident broke the ice, anyway. And restored the mood between them, closer to what Harry had been expecting.

George gave him a short tour – the cottage wasn't large. 'You can have the smaller bedroom,' she told him. 'Min overlooks the sea.'

Harry was an old friend but she didn't want any misunderstandings over the basis of his visit.

'I bought milk and cereals in Truro, but I haven't got any meals in,' she told him cheerfully, once they'd reached the kitchen. 'But there's a pub down in Trebarwith Strand. I usually treat myself there when I arrive on a Friday. It's called the Port William.'

'That's fine – as long as you've got a good torch to get us there,' Harry replied. His ankle was still hurting. He could only hope that the exercise would do it good.

It was half a mile down to the Port William. The pub was fairly noisy when they got there but there was still plenty of space. George seized a vacant table for two, close to the log fire.

'You hang on to this and I'll get the food,' she told him. 'I assume you've not gone vegan or anything?'

'Beef and ale pie and chips would do me fine,' Harry replied, noticing the same items being eaten on the next table. 'And a pint of Doom Bar, please.'

George returned with their drinks a few minutes later. 'They'll bring our meals in a few minutes.' She held up her glass of cider. 'Right, Harry. Cheers. Welcome to North Cornwall.'

Harry glanced around. 'What a great place, within walking distance of your cottage. I'm very jealous.'

'It's a pity it is dark,' she told him. 'There are crashing waves outside, and a view along the coast. I'm very happy to

271

relax here on weekends off. I'll show you more of it tomorrow.'

In the end they did not get to discuss anything about the Royal Cornwall Museum and what George had found there until they were enjoying a leisurely breakfast next morning.

'What a great Museum,' said George. 'It had some very good displays of Cornish life. I discovered another top-notch student at the Truro Grammar School, by the way: Sir Humphrey Davy. He's an exact contemporary of Henry Martyn. Imagine teaching a physics lesson with those two on the front row. You'd need to be on good form.'

'I'd heard of him, of course,' replied Harry. 'But I hadn't realised that he coincided with Henry Martyn, with John Kempthorne just a year or two older. A gang like that makes it more likely, doesn't it, that Eleanor would make use of their brains to hide her treasure?'

'And coming at it from the other end, I found details in the Museum which they claimed showed the bellows for the 1750 organ in St Mary's. Look.'

George opened her brief case and produced a series of diagrams.

The first was of a pair of bellows. The second showed pipes leading into a mechanism that drove the bellows, linked to a distant mill race.

Finally, with Harry agog, George showed him the third. In this one the bellows were pumping into a large rectangular box, with half a dozen pipes coming out, heading for the organ. On its top was a lid, held down by two heavy weights.

'There's also a page of mathematics but I haven't made

much headway on that yet. The diagrams give the main idea, though.'

Harry was intrigued. 'Go on, then.'

'The fast-flowing water from the mill race is used to drive the bellows. One pumps while the other recovers. The bellows in turn pump air into this box, to a substantially higher pressure than the atmosphere around it. Air from the box then goes into the organ pipes and makes them produce a sound, as the organist plays.'

'So what does the box do?'

'The heavy weights on top limit the maximum pressure. If the mill race is running too fast and the bellows are driven too hard, the box lid will rise and some of the air will escape. It avoids over-pressuring the organ pipes.'

George turned to her friend. 'This is only a schematic. Making it work in practice is a lot more complicated.'

Harry was entranced. 'You can imagine that clever students like the ones at Truro Grammar School would have found this a lot of fun. But from our point of view the most important thing is . . .'

'– the weights on the air box.' George gave him a big grin. It was good to be on the same wavelength.

'This mechanism wasn't inside the organ, it was somewhere out at the back. So if you understood how it worked, you'd come along and replace the lead weights which had been there at the start with gold ingots of a similar size and weight. Maybe paint them grey so it wasn't obvious that anything had changed.'

'Brilliant. Well done. All we need now is some hard evidence that this was part of the secret trail, not just a clever academic idea.'

'I'm not sure I can prove that. But I did find out one thing more that might help.'

'What's that?'

'The RCM librarian keeps track of her visitors and exactly what they take an interest in. Guess who was the last person looking at these organ bellows?'

Harry shook his head. He needed more clues. 'I've no idea,' he said. 'Tell me.'

'It was Donald McKay. That was in late August. Ten weeks ago. But someone else must have been on the trail after him. No wonder the poor chap got himself killed.'

Between them, from either Frances or Joy, Harry and George knew most of the details of McKay's death. The fact that he was known to have been interested in these bellows, alongside Harry's inspired guesses about the actions of Eleanor Kempthorne and her son, made it almost certain, they felt, that this was why he had been killed.

'So the question for the future, Harry, is: when McKay was killed, did his killer manage to find and remove the secret object at the same time? We're guessing that this was one (or maybe two) ingots of gold.'

Harry smiled. 'D'you recall, I made some comments about that last Sunday? If the killer was successful and the secret has been removed, then there's no reason to expect any more deaths. Whereas, if they weren't successful, I'd expect them to go on searching.'

'But now they'd be even more desperate. If they've killed once they would be far less inhibited about killing again.'

George considered for a moment. 'I'm very glad, Harry, that you've come with me this weekend. I'd say two of us are a lot safer than one.'

CHAPTER 45

A t quarter to ten on Friday evening, sitting mostly alone in the main office at Truro Police Station, Frances Cober was still waiting for a call or an alarm.

The call, if it came, would be from Tim Barwell. It might be that he had found a sighting of Barry Parson's car, travelling at a crucial time, to or from Shortlanesend. But if Barry hadn't travelled that journey, or had done it avoiding all Truro's traffic cameras, there would be nothing to find. She'd told the officer to stop looking if he'd not found anything by nine pm. Even the most zealous constable couldn't be expected to work all night.

More disturbingly, she hadn't heard from Marcus, or the Cathedral alarm that he had intended to set off. Frances had made discreet inquiries and had established that all the Truro alarms linked to the station were bundled together in a box in the corner of the office. That was why she was stuck here but finding her position increasingly uncomfortable.

The most obvious cause of delay for Marcus would be that he had been held up – either getting into the Cathedral or the shop, or perhaps as he sought to disrupt the alarm system on a window once he was in there. The thought crossed her mind, had the alarm itself been made burglar-proof?

On balance that seemed unlikely. Marcus had the chance to

inspect the wiring in daylight and would know what was needed to trigger the alarm. He was unlikely to be thwarted by a standard gadget. And nothing else in the Cathedral seemed to be more advanced. It would be amazing if the alarm itself had beaten him.

So Frances considered a wider view. What if the Cathedral alarm link had itself been broken – maybe years ago? There was no record that it had been triggered in recent times, in any case.

In some ways it would be good if a fault was found. That would vindicate Marcus' security auditing work, anyway. Mildly embarrassing for the police but in the long run it would be good for the problem to be recognised and then, presumably, sorted.

Frances pondered for a few moments. Were there other causes why she might not have heard from her co-conspirator?

What if Marcus had been spotted by a tour guide as he had tried to hide in the darkening building? Maybe there was more security in the place than he'd been led to believe?

In that case there would be a fierce argument, a clash between differing authorities, after which, no doubt, he would be evicted. But then, surely, he would ring her and explain what had happened?

What if the indigenous guard had not only thrown him out but also taken his phone? That would have been inconvenient. No doubt there were items on that phone that Marcus wouldn't want to lose. But there was no reason why he couldn't walk round to the Police Station and find her. They could go for a consoling drink together.

Frances went round the various options for some time

without finding any of them remotely convincing.

Then she had a more promising idea. Marcus would have had his daily chat with Joy Tregorran that afternoon. What if he had told her what he was planning to do that evening? And she had explicitly instructed him, for some reason or other, maybe some nuance of Cathedral politics, to do no such thing?

That didn't explain, of course, why he hadn't then contacted Frances to tell her that the whole plan was off.

Frances wrestled with the idea for a few minutes. Then decided that there was one way to check it out: she could ring Joy Tregorran and run the idea past her. And even if Joy said it was nonsense, there was just a chance that she would have some different idea that could explain the whole thing.

Frances had seized her phone and rung the Gunwalloe vicarage before she had even asked herself if it wasn't rather late to be ringing at all.

Joy Tregorran had had years of experience dealing with worried callers at all hours of the day or night. She had been schooled in the importance of being polite on all occasions. But she didn't sound best pleased when she realised it was Frances making the call.

'Frances! What's the matter? Are you alright? Is this an emergency? You do realise the time, don't you?'

'Joy, I hadn't realised it was so late. I'm sorry to be bothering you. It's just that I had an idea . . .'

'If you sleep on it, Frances, you might have another one. Then the two could talk to one another, perhaps become friends.'

This was probably the nearest Joy got to being cross.

Frances gave a sigh. 'I'm really sorry, Joy. It's just that I'm worried about Marcus. He was supposed to be ringing me this evening and I haven't heard anything. I don't suppose . . .'

'Well, he's not here, if that's what you mean. I had to turn Harry away earlier. I'm not running a men's refuge, you know. I need a weekend without external pressures. I've got an infant baptism in the Cathedral on Sunday afternoon – for a delegate from Assisted Dying, actually. They asked me during the conference and I was feeling soft-hearted – didn't like to refuse.'

Frances would have liked to ask who the delegate was, but it sounded like Joy was already stretched to the limit.

'You have no idea where Marcus might be?'

'Sorry, I've no idea. He might have been taken ill, I suppose. He's staying in the Premier Inn, so they might know. Or else you could try Truro General Hospital. As a police officer you might get a faster response than most of us.'

'Thank you Joy. I'll try them both. I'm very sorry indeed to have disturbed you. See you next week, I expect. Bye.'

Frances slammed down the phone harder than usual and ran her hands through her hair. She felt highly irritated. Then she glanced at her watch. By now it was well after ten pm. She resolved to try phoning the Premier Inn and then Truro Hospital. If Marcus was not in either of those she would simply go home.

Maybe a good night's sleep was as important for her as it sounded like it would be for Joy Tregorran.

CHAPTER 46

Frances Cober was still sleeping the "rest of the righteous" in her former fisherman's cottage in Gweek at half past eight next morning – Saturday – when her phone rang.

'Hello,' she said sleepily.

'Frances Cober?' It was a female voice with an Irish lilt.

'That's my name. Who wants me?'

'This is Truro General Hospital. I'm speaking from the Intensive Care Ward that's attached to Accident and Emergency. We have a patient here carrying an ID card which also mentions your name.'

Frances heart sank. 'Who is he?'

'The card says he's called Marcus Tredwell. But we can't ask him yet, he's still unconscious.'

'Right. I know him, he's a colleague. I'll come straight away. Be with you in forty-five minutes. Thank you so much for letting me know.'

Thirty-five minutes later – traffic was light at that time on a November Saturday – Frances had raced to the hospital on the hill overlooking Truro, parked her car and made her way to Newlyn Ward, as the nurse had specified.

There was just one senior nurse at the entrance desk, with the name tag "Morag". Frances recognised the voice that had called her as soon as the conversation began.

'Hello, Morag. I'm Frances Cober. You called me half an hour ago about Marcus Tredwell.'

'My, you haven't hung about getting here. The patient's this way.' She led Frances round the corner, to a bed currently hidden behind hospital curtains. Frances braced herself for what she was about to see.

The two stepped inside the curtain. Frances saw Marcus the security expert, his head swathed in bandages and with various drips attached to him and also to devices beside the bed.

'We don't believe there are any injuries to him, apart from the head. External ones, anyway.'

Frances instinct was to give the comatose man a gigantic hug but obviously that wasn't appropriate at this stage.

Instead she turned to the nurse. 'How long's he been here, Morag?'

'He was found inside the Cathedral, in the Nave I believe. Just after the refectory opened its outside door for those wanting an early breakfast. Someone who was looking for a toilet spotted him lying on the ground; the staff there called an ambulance straight away. He's only been in here for half an hour, we called you as soon as we'd found his card. The consultant hasn't seen him yet. He should be here in a few minutes.'

'So you don't know the problem?'

'I'd say the problem, Frances, was that a massive stone fell from a great height, straight onto his head. But you'd need to have studied medicine for a decade to be sure.'

Marcus was lying very still. Frances swallowed hard. 'Is there much chance that he'll survive?'

Morag wasn't one to mince words. 'Without the headgear, Frances, he'd have been a goner. But he was wearing something slightly odd which might have saved him.'

Frances followed the line of her gaze and saw a lightweight climbing helmet placed on the bedside table, an unlit torch mounted at the front. She could imagine Marcus would have been wearing that when he was wandering round last night, primarily for the convenience of the torch. Maybe, in some bizarre way, he was a lucky man.

'Should I wait in here?' asked Frances. There was one visitor's seat.

'Best to leave the patient to the consultant, Frances. He doesn't much like dealing with visitors – you're all too healthy. I'll let you know what the great man is planning to do as soon as he's gone.'

'In fact,' she went on, 'you might as well go to the hospital canteen and buy yourself breakfast. You'll probably be in here for some time.'

Frances reckoned that it would probably be an hour before the consultant had completed his round in the Intensive Care Ward. She might as well have a decent breakfast, she might not have the chance to eat again for some time.

While she was munching her sausage, bacon and eggs, Frances decided she'd call Tim Barwell, find out what progress he'd made on the traffic camera evidence. The number of rings before he answered made it likely that he, too, had been asleep, but once he had emerged he quickly pulled himself together.

'Hi, boss.'

'Tim, I'm in Truro General. Marcus Tredwell, our security

expert – I don't think you've met him – was hit by a falling stone as he patrolled the Cathedral last night. He's unconscious but they reckon he'll pull through. He's waiting to be checked by the consultant, so I may be here for some time.'

'Right. Is this yet another accident or was it deliberate?'

'At this stage I've no idea. How did you get on with the traffic photos?'

'I couldn't find any evidence of Barry's car, in either direction. So either he didn't do the journey at all, or he dodged the cameras. But he lives in Truro, you said? He'd know how to avoid them, anyway.'

There went the most likely method of trapping Barry Parsons, she thought. 'Thanks for looking, anyway, Tim. I'm not quite sure where we go next.'

'If you're saying I'm due a day off, boss, I'll go for a cycle ride today and maybe another tomorrow. But I'll take my phone in case you need me.'

Frances found it hard to concentrate on anything as she took time to finish her breakfast and then walked slowly back up the stairs to Newlyn Ward. The accident to (or perhaps attack on?) her colleague made it hard to think in a cold and logical manner.

She wished her friend George was around, thought of ringing her, then decided it was unfair to involve her, once the analyst was away from Truro. George needed some rest too. Lack of relaxation was a potential enemy for them all.

Once she had reached the ward Frances noticed an increased buzz of energy from the staff and deduced that the consultant had been and gone. Then she glanced over to

Marcus's bed and saw it was no longer surrounded by curtains; it was empty. A horrible thought struck her: did that mean her colleague had died in her absence?

A moment later she spotted Morag walking back to the central desk and managed to catch her attention.

'What's happened to Marcus?'

'Oh, don't you worry, Frances. The consultant said that the patient needed a head X-ray to check if the skull was fractured, so he's been taken down there. There'll no doubt be a queue, you'd best take a seat in the annexe. Have you something to read?'

Frances didn't have anything fictional to help her pass the time, but she still had her investigation notebook. It always travelled in her handbag. The annexe was quiet; she decided it was a good chance to review the entire McKay case afresh.

The problem with the whole thing, she told herself, was that it was not recognised as murder from the start. Even though McKay had gone straight home from playing a man who'd been poisoned and then died, no-one else had thought it suspicious at all. If she hadn't stuck her nose in, the doctor would have signed the death certificate and no-one would have known any better.

True, she had managed to get her constable over to Shortlanesend, but not in time to see the body. There was no hard evidence to point to poisoning until well into the following week and even then her boss had been more interested in the threat to the Cathedral than the death of McKay. She'd battled on with minimal resources, distracted by a parallel investigation by Harry and his team into lost treasure

284

from the Napoleonic era.

But if the search for Cathedral treasure was behind Marcus's attack then that made it a more significant crime. For it implied, surely, that the search for the treasure, whatever it was and wherever it was hidden, was not yet over.

Frances glanced over to Marcus's bed. He'd just been brought back but was still inert. Before she investigated any further there were some core facts that she needed that only he could tell her. For example, exactly where had he been standing when the stone had descended? Had he any evidence that someone else might have caused it to fall?

Her mind flipped back to her own inquiry. The other oddity in the whole thing was the half-hearted attempt, two days later, to poison her and her friend. That had to link back, surely, to one or other delegate on the Assisted Dying conference.

In desperation, Frances turned back her notebook and started looking through her interviews, starting a week too late, with every delegate who had been there. Was there anything that she had missed?

It was fortunate, she told herself, that earlier in her career she had developed the habit of recording everything. Otherwise twenty-five similar interviews, half via the phone, would have merged into a soggy recollection that meant nothing at all.

She worked diligently through the names, one by one. There was nothing there. Or there. Or even there.

Then Frances came to a name which was slightly less detached. There was a strong reason why she had ignored it before. But now she forced herself to find a way round the difficulty. And found a possible loophole.

She could be in the hospital for some time. Marcus was as still as ever. If the X-ray, when it finally came through, showed that his skull had been fractured, then he could be in here for weeks. It might even provoke another memory lapse.

But once she was finished here, Frances resolved, she needed to take her latest idea further.

CHAPTER 47

Harry's stay in Ivy Cottage was no long-planned event. But now he was here, George wanted to make the most of it, to show the historian something of North Cornwall and its rugged cliffs. After all, this was why she had bought a cottage here. It had also given her plenty of experience of paths along local cliffs which started at her front door.

'Looks like it's going to be a fine sunny day,' she predicted, as their breakfast drew to a leisurely close. 'Can I take you along the local Coast Path?'

'I'm in your hands,' he replied.

Twenty minutes later they set out: down the path to Trebarwith Strand, past the Port William and then up the other side. Both were puffing hard by the time they reached the top.

As they paused for a break, George annotated the landscape. 'That's Port Isaac over there. Beyond are the Rumps, followed by Pentire Head. We could do those another time.'

Harry did not demur. He would be very happy to come here again if he was invited.

They pressed on, down a to-and-fro path into another valley, this one occupied only by sheep. 'There used to be slate works here on the coast,' she told him. 'We'll take another footpath now, up the other side.'

287

This was another path which zigzagged steeply up, regaining all the height they had just lost. Both were glad of a rest by the time they'd reached the top.

'That's the worst of the climbing over,' claimed George. As with most hopeful statements in walking it wasn't entirely true. But Harry had to admit that the next couple of miles were relatively level.

'There's no-one else around,' he observed. 'Great. The only sound is the steady roar of the waves far below.'

'You'd see plenty more walkers here in the summer months,' George replied. 'But visitors to Cornwall are fairly seasonal. That's the joy of being down here at this time of year.'

Then their path crossed over one which led from a farmhouse on the hillside above them, over to the cliffs down below.

'Right,' said George. 'We've got a choice. D'you want to carry on over the cliff tops, or to go down to the beach? We could have our lunch there. But remember, Harry, if we go down, we've got to come back up.'

'Which beach is this?' he prevaricated.

'Tregardock, Harry. One of Cornwall's hidden treasures. The folk of Delabole think it's their own. Mind, I doubt anyone will be here today.'

Harry glanced up. The sky had darkened. It was threatening to pour. The folk of Delabole had some wisdom, anyway.

'Go on then. We might find something unusual.' He followed his friend as she weaved her way down the grassy slope, was surprised when they had to hang on to an old rope to negotiate the last rocky descent. Then they were on the beach – just as it started to rain.

George had spotted a small cave around the side. 'Cornish weather is very fickle, Harry. This might not last. We can eat in here, anyway.'

George had brought Cornish pasties for lunch, which went down well, followed by an apple each. But as they ate the rain got steadily worse.

'Could we swim in the sea here?' he asked.

'Sure. Are you game for skinny-dipping then? The only thing is, it'd be rather cold at this time of year.'

'Maybe not today, George. The spring, perhaps?' The chat wasn't serious, but the idea was fun.

The climb back to Ivy Cottage was less fun. George had a heavy cagoule which kept her fairly dry but Harry only had a shower proof jacket, which was virtually useless.

As George had warned, the pull back to the cliff top seemed hard. Then she led them up another slope, over to the hamlet of Treligga. Harry, soaked to the skin and frozen, just kept plodding along behind. The rest of the journey seemed to last forever. It was late afternoon before they reached Ivy Cottage.

By this time Harry had determined that he would never, ever, visit this part of Cornwall again.

George, though, seemed to thrive in adversity. 'Right, Harry. You need a long, hot bath. Good job I left the water on.' She led him upstairs to the bathroom and made sure he had a towel. Then she left him for her own room. In reality she was soaked and cold as well. But at least she had something to change into.

Five minutes later the sonic boom was heard. There was a raucous noise from the loft and the whole cottage seemed to shudder. A howl of panic came from the landing. George grabbed her bath robe as she headed out.

Harry was standing there, stark naked, hands over his ears. He looked terrified as the noise persisted around him.

'What the hell is that?' he screamed.

'Didn't I tell you to be patient as you filled the bath? One tap at a time, Harry. Alright,' she conceded, 'perhaps I forgot. There's something wrong with the plumbing, I'm told, but I've never managed to sort it. Here.'

She threw him the bath robe. 'I told you skinny-dipping was for later.'

A few minutes later George had suppressed the noise by flushing the toilet and turning down the taps. She left Harry and retreated to her room to continue changing. Only a pair of Cambridge graduates, she thought, could make such a pig's ear of an unplanned striptease.

That evening Harry insisted on taking George out for a meal. 'Anywhere you like, George, as long as it's warm.' George suggested the Riverside Inn in Boscastle, 'They do great grilled steaks. We can try booking ahead. It shouldn't be full at this time of year.'

It turned out that Harry had no dry clothes at all, he was still wearing George's bathrobe. He wasn't that apologetic: 'I didn't know I was coming here on Friday morning.' George was a much smaller build so she had nothing in her wardrobe she could lend him.

It was time to improvise. 'I do have some other clothes here, Harry. In my actor's costume chest which we use for the Gilbert and Sullivan sketches we do at Christmas.' She giggled, 'I'm a Gilbert so you'll have to be Sullivan.'

A few minutes later, from a limited choice, Harry found himself dressed as the Captain of HMS Pinafore. The uniform was for a broader figure but fortunately it came with a belt.

'I guess it's better than Little Buttercup,' he muttered.

'They're very friendly in the Riverside,' she reassured him. 'As long as you can pay they probably won't even notice.'

By now their friendship was warming nicely. Harry shoehorned himself into George's car and they presented themselves at the Riverside. Harry ordered rib eye steak with brandy and peppercorn sauce and George pork medallions.

Inevitably the conversation moved on from the obscurity of Tregardock Beach to the continuing suspicion of hidden treasure inside Truro Cathedral.

'The weights over the organ bellows might be the first place used for hiding. But there's no reason to think it was the last one, Harry. I mean, someone must have moved things on at some point. Do we have any ideas on other hiding places?'

Harry pondered for a moment. 'Well, there was one other bit of interesting mechanics that I saw on my tour last week.'

'What was that?'

'Henry Martyn's font. It's a carved wooden piece, in a small chapel at the side of the Nave. Somehow or other it's got a counterbalancing system. A minister can pull the cover up without effort if he's conducting a baptism. How d'you reckon that works?'

George took a mouthful of pork. She smiled to herself, the meal was even better than usual.

'Let's assume the whole thing is mechanical. In that case, as the font lid rises up an equivalent weight somewhere else

291

must come down. And, of course, vice versa: the weight is pulled back up again as the lid is lowered. There might be several weights involved. But did you see anything move as the guide adjusted the lid?'

Harry considered. 'I didn't, George. It all happened like magic.'

'Right. So the question then is, where in that chapel might these counterweights be hidden?'

There was a thoughtful silence as they continued to eat. 'This is really good, George. Thank you for suggesting we came here.'

'Within the chapel itself I can only think of one solution,' said the mathematician. 'Let's imagine stone pillars in the space around the font. In that case the chains might go up from the font lid, across the ceiling and then down inside the pillars. Say one at each corner. It'd be complicated, though.'

It took Harry a while to grasp the idea. 'It sounds really tricky. In that case, the balancing weights would all be inside the pillars?'

Suddenly George had an epiphany. 'Hey. Remember the kerfuffle in my bathroom?'

Harry had several memories from the bathroom. He wondered which one she was referring to.

'That racket was caused by a pressure-surge in the loft,' she went on.

'Well, that was what you told me, anyway.'

'In the Henry Martyn Chapel, all the work might be done in the space above the chapel ceiling. As long as there's enough height, the chains could go up to the higher roof, over a set of pulleys and down again to the balancing weights.'

Harry frowned. 'Take me through that again, George. This time a bit more slowly.'

There was a pause while both ate more. Harry hoped for mental sustenance. As she ate, George tried to think out how to make the idea more accessible.

In the end she resorted to a sketch, drawn on her serviette.

As they talked it through, some refinements emerged. 'It's unlikely they'll bother with gearwheels, Harry. So the amount the font lid goes up will be same as the balancing weights come down. How high did it go?'

Harry mused. 'It could probably have been pushed up by four feet or so.'

'In that case the weights could come four feet down. That might make them reachable. But is there that much space above the chapel and below the roof in the aisle of the Nave? I wonder, Harry, if we could get up there?'

A short while later they'd finished their main courses and had ordered desserts: a brown sugar meringue for Harry and salted caramel ice cream for George. But the topic of hidden treasure remained on their minds.

'When was the Henry Martyn Baptistry completed, Harry?'

'Well, the Nave wasn't finished till 1910 so it wouldn't be much before then. Maybe it was the same time? You know, it could be the great grandson of Joseph Emidy who put the weights up there – or who swapped the ones that were first used.' He explained his thinking to George.

'We'll need to check it out when we get back to Truro,' she observed. 'But I think we should drop the subject now for the rest of this evening.'

Harry was not minded to disagree.

CHAPTER 48

Frances had spent nearly all Saturday in one section or another of Truro General Hospital as Marcus had lain still and out of reach.

The X-rays had come back late morning. The Consultant and Senior Nurse Morag had studied them together carefully and later Morag had passed on their findings. By what she had said could "only be termed a miracle", Marcus had managed not to fracture his skull. 'There's nothing fundamentally wrong with him,' she said, 'that rest and time won't cure.'

Late in the afternoon, bored out of her mind, Frances had gone back to Gweek via Sainsbury's in Helston and bought herself a luxury Chinese banquet. She wished she had someone to share it with, but none of her local friends would respond to an invitation without advanced warning.

The police officer made as much as she could of the task of cooking it (though that was mostly heating it up). Then, eating it slowly with several glasses of Sauvignon, she managed to give herself a pleasant evening. After that she slept like the proverbial log.

By nine o'clock on Sunday morning there was still no call from the hospital. Morag assured her, when she rang in, that 'Marcus was likely to come round sometime today.' Frances promised that she would pay a visit later on.

Then it occurred to her that Joy Tregorran might enjoy lunch out. It would be good to smooth the relationship, anyway. Two phone calls later a table had been booked for them both at the Ship Inn in nearby Mawgan.

Joy looked more rested than she had last week, possibly a quiet weekend on her own was what she'd needed. They got through most of the meal talking about anything except the events at the Cathedral.

But it could not last. Frances decided that she must tell Joy what had happened to Marcus – after all, the vicar was the designated local link.

'And what's behind this, d'you think?' asked Joy, once the police officer's account was complete.

'I've no evidence until Marcus can tell us what happened,' Frances began. 'It might not be relevant, but I don't know exactly where he was standing. But the chance of a random stone falling exactly on Marcus is utterly remote, especially in the context of all these other events.'

'In that case, Frances, it must have been someone else on a night time search in the Cathedral, who feared that Marcus would catch them.'

Frances had thought the same thing for twenty-four hours but had had no-one to share with. She gave a reluctant nod. 'Which in turn means that the secret – the ingot or whatever – is still waiting to be found. It couldn't have been discovered by McKay.'

There was a pause then Joy asked, 'I don't want to pry into police matters, Frances, but are you making much progress?'

'Not as fast as I would like. I'll tell you what I'm thinking,

Joy, if in turn you could tell me the person who called for this afternoon's baptism. It'd be interesting, wouldn't it, if we both had the same name.'

Frances and Joy both had reasons to be in Truro that afternoon. They agreed it would be sensible to travel over in the same car. After all, if there was a call from the hospital, they each knew Marcus better than anyone else in the city. It might cheer him up, once he stirred, to have not just one but two female visitors.

Joy had a staff permit allowing her to park behind the Cathedral and hastened off to the Crypt to robe up for the service. Frances wandered around inside, keeping an eye on those starting to gather round the Henry Martyn Chapel. She recognised one of them but decided not to converse until the baptism was over.

A few minutes later Joy appeared, wearing a white surplice over a dark blue robe. She walked over to the Henry Martyn Chapel and greeted the family whose small child was to be baptised.

It was time to begin. Joy reached underneath to release the hood of the font and raised it as high as she could; the service was under way.

Harry and George had woken up late on Sunday morning. But they could see the rain had cleared and the sun was shining.

'I'd like to show you a bit of the Coast Path, going in the other direction,' said George as they tucked in to their cereals.

Harry was still dressed as Captain of the Pinafore: his own clothes had been completely drenched yesterday. Even after overnight drying they were still damp, warming on the heated towel rail.

'I'd love to, but I really don't want to get soaked again,' he responded. 'The only other costume in your chest that might fit me was the Pinafore's Lookout, and the lower half of that was a pair of sparkling tights.'

George could think of several bawdy responses but daren't say them out loud. He might be a historian but she didn't want to offend him.

In the end they agreed to walk to Trebarwith Strand, then up the coast as far as Tintagel. 'You'll see the oldest church building in Cornwall – St Materiana's,' said George. 'It won't take long, we'll be back around twelve.'

Before they set out, George booked them into Trevathan Farm Shop at St Endellion for a traditional Sunday Roast. 'Lots of locals go there,' she explained. They would continue on to Truro after lunch.

At this point they had no idea a baptism service was planned for that afternoon. Their aim was to check out their ideas on how the font mechanism might be linked to an ingot hiding place.

As they drove along the A39 after a splendid lunch – there'd been no need to hurry so they'd also managed a dessert – Harry recalled his tour guide saying something about a high-level passage inside the Cathedral.

'He said, "It would need a lot of tidying before it could be opened to visitors".'

'Mm. Had he been up there himself?'

Harry thought for a moment. 'Yes. He'd admitted he'd been on a special tour for the Cathedral guides, earlier in the year. It must be possible for a determined person to get right round.'

'Did he happen to mention how he got onto it?'

'No.' Harry pondered for a moment. 'But he did point out the bells in the North West Tower, said they were rung from a higher platform. So you must be able to get that far. You'd probably get onto the Passage from there.'

George quite often stayed in Truro on Sunday night, it gave her a useful early start on Mondays. The Premier Inn had plenty of vacancies in November, she would clock in later. She parked at the rear of the inn, then they walked across to the Cathedral and into the Nave. It was quarter past three.

The place wasn't crowded. Harry led them to the chapel under the North West Tower and they glanced around. Then Harry spotted a doorway, let into the outer wall. The door was closed but it turned out it wasn't locked.

'You game?' murmured Harry. George nodded; at this moment there was no one else around.

Swiftly they opened the door and stepped inside, closing the door behind them. A steep staircase rose ahead. George was glad that she was wearing her trainers, could climb up almost silently. Harry, still dressed as Captain of the Pinafore, was a little noisier.

A minute later, forty foot up, they had reached the mezzanine floor used by the bell ringers. Glancing quickly round, George was pleased to see no-one was there at the moment. Then she spotted doorways in two of the tower pillars. These must be entrances to the Upper Passage.

'Which one should we use?' she asked.

Harry stood for a moment, peering across the Nave. The

Henry Martyn Chapel was tucked into the opposite corner. A small crowd, more smartly dressed than they were, was gathering around it. Was the Chapel about to be used for a service?

'You know, George, I reckon they'll be using the font shortly. It'd be good to see the hood actually moving. Why don't you go that way – it should lead round to the space over the font – and I'll try the other. I might see things looking across that you miss. But for goodness sake don't make any noise.'

George followed his gaze to the Henry Martyn Chapel. She could see the Upper Passage did get to the point above it on its route up the aisle. The late afternoon was gloomy and the Cathedral lights were underwhelming. Nothing shone onto the Passage, anyway.

George kicked herself for not having brought her torch. She doubted Harry would have one, either. She shrugged, nothing could be done about it now; she turned and clambered through the Passage doorway.

As she picked her way carefully along, George could see why the tour guide had said it was unsuitable for visitors. The passage was extremely dusty for a start, with a distinctive smell that she associated with older church buildings. There was a load of clutter and she had to watch carefully where to put her feet. At times, especially where it threaded a Tower pillar, the Passage became very narrow indeed. A plump visitor might not make it.

Slowly, steadily, George moved forward. She glanced across the Nave and could just see the shape of Harry in the passage opposite. It was too dark to see his face but she recognised his sober outfit: a good job, she thought, that Gilbert and Sullivan didn't require extravagantly gaudy costumes.

All at once she could hear voices below. She was almost over the Henry Martyn Chapel now, mustn't make any noise during the service. Just one more pillar to squeeze through.

Suddenly George was aware that she was not alone. There was someone else ahead of her, in the section over the chapel. She froze in mid-pillar, hoping she'd not been heard; and thanked heavens for well-designed trainers.

It was gloomy ahead. Her night vision, which had been getting better, was reduced again by a light shining up through the floor. There was also a chain, which she assumed would take the weight of the font hood. It disappeared into the darkness above.

Suddenly she heard a familiar voice. It was Joy: she must be conducting the service below. A moment later came a faint clinking sound and the chain started moving: presumably the hood was being lifted. Above her head, she assumed (but couldn't see), matching weights would be dropping down.

Down below the service continued. Up in the next section of passage, George sensed her fellow intruder was reaching for the weights that must have dropped down as the hood rose.

But George the mathematician deduced they wouldn't be easy to remove. For it couldn't be done without taking out the counterbalance, which in turn would cause the font hood to crash back down. In the worst case that might even crush the infant being baptised in the bowl below.

Instinctively, George stepped forwards. 'You have to leave those weights alone,' she whispered.

Her disembodied voice came without warning out of the pillar. It clearly gave her fellow intruder a nasty shock. For, a few seconds later, she sensed the person had stood up and squeezed out of the far Upper Passage doorway.

Now the bigger picture dawned. This was probably the criminal behind the whole thing – almost within her grasp. A few seconds later George had crossed the intervening section and was hot on the trail.

CHAPTER 49

Harry Jennings had not made out much of the confrontation above the Henry Martyn Chapel from the other side of the Nave. It was too dark. But he had seen a darkly-clad figure slip out of the other passage doorway and, a few seconds later, a second figure – smaller, he presumed it must be George – head after them.

If the tour guide had been correct, the passage ran all the way, at one height or another, round the inside of the Cathedral. So if he carried on he would be able to meet and hopefully help catch the intruder, as he came from the opposite direction. They wouldn't expect two Cathedral safe guarders to be chasing them from different angles.

Moreover, he needed to play his part in the capture. He couldn't expect George Gilbert to do it all on her own. If his suspicions were correct, the dark figure had already killed Donald McKay and almost poisoned a Police Officer. George was small; the villain would almost certainly beat her in a one-on-one fight. As far as he knew his old friend didn't go in for the likes of karate or kick boxing.

But it might not even be a level fight. There was no reason why the villain would not be carrying a weapon of some sort – possibly a knife?

Of course, Harry could simply have called the police on

999. Later in the day he would ask himself why he hadn't. But it was unclear how quickly the authorities would respond, late on a Sunday afternoon – and at this moment he could see that speed was of the essence.

Harry threaded his way along the Upper Passage, ignoring the stale smell and doing his best to avoid the debris that had accumulated over the years. Some of it must have been here since the Cathedral was built. There were plenty of loose slates and stones; it would be easy to trip, maybe sprain an ankle. No wonder that the tour guide had not been enthusiastic about allowing visitors to tramp around.

Harry found he could not progress quietly and at the same time keep an eye on events in the other passage. He decided that silence was the more important. As he watchfully placed his feet in the open spaces, he could only assume that over the opposite aisle the chase was continuing.

By now Harry had passed the Central Tower and was picking his way along the passage high above the Quire. There was no service under way here so very few lights were on: it was almost dark. Next time you go on a murder hunt, he told himself severely, make sure you bring a torch.

A few minutes later he reached the North East corner, where the Passage widened out into a small chamber. Harry started thinking harder now about exactly how he was going to catch the intruder. It would be best, surely, to accost them here, rather than in a narrow passage?

The historian stopped moving and forced himself to think. You're the surprise element in this chase, he told himself. What's the best way to exploit that?

Suddenly he had a flash of enlightenment. A moment later he had undone his belt and was pulling it out from the loops on his Pinafore trousers. Then he fastened the buckle end onto a hook that he'd felt, next to the doorway, about a foot off the ground.

He couldn't hold it for long, but if he was at the right angle he could keep the belt pulled tight. He positioned himself on the other side of the doorway and crouched down, hanging tightly onto the belt end. To his horror he realised that his Pinafore trousers were starting to slip down. But with luck they'd hold up for long enough, the belt was just the right height to make the intruder trip. After which, loose trousers or not, he would leap on top of them. That would surely give him a few seconds precious advantage.

Slowly, Harry's breath returned to normal. He was stationary and virtually inaudible.

Then he heard the sound of someone coming quietly towards him from the other direction. This was it. Was this how soldiers felt in the trenches, seconds before their attack began?

He crouched on tiptoe, preparing to leap. Then it all happened. The intruder came through the door, stumbled over his belt and crashed face down to the ground.

With a primeval howl Harry leapt on top of them. He seized one of the figure's arms and then the other, pulled both behind them as hard as he could. It'd hurt but that was too bad. He had to minimise the risk of a knife emerging.

But the figure wasn't struggling as hard as he'd expected. Had they given up? Or been winded in the fall? While he had chance, he needed something to fasten their hands together – his belt?

He glanced round: where was it? In the darkness he couldn't see. He let go of his captive with one hand and felt on the floor behind him.

It was a dreadful mistake. Somehow or other, as he let go, the intruder wriggled, swung a leg and then kicked him hard in the groin. He wished that his trousers hadn't slipped down to his knees and removed his main layer of protection. For a second his interest in proceedings faltered. As he lost focus the figure twisted round and kicked him again, this time even harder.

Now, for Harry, it was dark no longer: the historian could see a whole galaxy of stars. Then, as the pain engulfed him, he fell unconscious to the Passage floor.

305

CHAPTER 50

George Gilbert thought she'd had a lucky escape from being beaten up on the pursuit. She'd done some damage in return and wasn't hanging about for a match replay. Harry presumably was still somewhere ahead of her, she would feel safer once they were together.

She struggled round the Upper Passage, wondering, as she got further and further, where her friend had got to. Surely he wouldn't have retreated to ground level and left her to face the intruder alone?

She was past the Central Tower and back in the Nave by now. Five minutes later she had completed the Upper Passage circuit of the whole Cathedral and was back in the Bell Tower where she had begun.

How could she have missed him? And how had they lost the intruder who was behind all the assaults and difficulties?

The answer to both questions might lie in a better knowledge of the Upper Passage. She and Harry had understood that the Bell Tower was the only way on and off. Was that right? Perhaps there was some other exit point that, blindly ignorant, she had simply struggled past?

There was one person who would know. Someone who she knew was here this afternoon, conducting the baptism service: Joy Tregorran. She glanced down across the Nave. The service was over now but if she was lucky she might still catch her.

George hastened down the stone staircase and back to ground level.

Somewhere along the line the analyst had gleaned that robing and its inverse (disrobing? Was that the right word?) took place in the Crypt. She hurried along to try to catch Joy there and was surprised to come across Frances on the way.

'What on earth are you doing here?' she asked.

'I might ask the same of you,' Frances replied, 'Right now I'm on my way to find Joy.'

They hastened together towards the Crypt and encountered Joy as she came out, locking the entrance carefully behind her.

'Look who I've found,' said Frances.

'Were you at the baptism service too?' asked Joy, surprised. 'I'm sorry, I didn't see you.'

'It's a long story,' said George. 'I was almost with you. Within twenty feet, anyway. But the most immediate thing is that I've lost Harry.'

She turned to the vicar. 'D'you know about the Upper Passage here, Joy? Crucially, how many ways are there off it? Besides the two routes out at the Bell Tower, I mean.'

It was hardly an obvious starting point and it would have been natural for Joy to respond with a few clarifying questions of her own. But she could see that George looked distraught and needed answers.

'I personally have never been along it,' she began. 'It's said to be in a bad state of repair. But I do recall being told something about an emergency way down, via that smaller tower in St Mary's Aisle – you know, the one holding the old bell. Shall I show you?'

Without waiting for an answer she led them up the steps,

across the Quire and down the other side towards the chapel that was once part of St Mary's.

'The tower doorway's over here,' she said. 'But I expect it's locked.' Joy was surprised a second later to discover that it wasn't.

George, though, was not surprised. She had been computing the logistics of two people traversing the Upper Passage from opposite ends, while the person they were chasing had slipped away in the middle.

'I'm afraid I know now where Harry is,' she began. 'He and I attacked one another by mistake when we met in pitch darkness, half way round. I can only hope I haven't killed him.'

Harry's special friend over the past year and the policewoman who knew them both could only stare at her in horrified amazement.

It was an hour later, just after six. Frances, Joy and Harry were seated in the residents' lounge of the Premier Inn. George was returning from reception; she had just booked herself in for the night and thus authenticated her friends' access. As she passed the bar, she stopped to order them all coffees. The ensuing conversation might take some time.

In the end, the rescue of Harry had been straightforward. Frances had taken charge. She had despatched George to the North West Tower in case Harry made his way there, stationed Joy to guard the old church tower for the same reason, and then climbed the narrow tower herself.

As a diligent police officer, even when off-duty, Frances was carrying a torch. That made her task much simpler. She had found Harry more or less where George had left him. He was sitting, awake but bemused, on the Upper Passage floor. He had also worked out what must have happened. Frances had led him back the way she had come.

Frances sensed Harry was embarrassed to see Joy at the bottom though she didn't understand why. But there wasn't time to talk. The three of them had headed through the Nave, picked up George and found their way out: they were the last ones to leave the Cathedral.

It was George that had suggested they could continue their conversation more comfortably in the Premier Inn. So now that dialogue could begin.

'I think we'd best leave the skirmish between Harry and George to the historians,' said Frances with an impish grin.

'Just one question, George,' said Harry. 'Where on earth did you learn to kick like that?'

'Last summer my firm arranged for me to go on a Defensive Tactics for Women Course, put on by the Metropolitan Police. I hadn't had the chance to put it into practice before but it seemed to work. Mind, being attacked by a man with his trousers round his knees did give me some advantage.'

The women giggled. Harry could see this was a line he wasn't going to win in present company and signalled capitulation. Frances decided it would be best to move the conversation on.

'We've all got different insights into this whole business,' she declared. 'Let's start by each of us sharing new findings. Then, maybe, we can make some dependable deductions.'

Joy opted to go first. 'The person who asked me to arrange

today's baptism service at the Henry Martyn Chapel was Roberta Thomas. She chatted to me during the Assisted Dying course, on behalf of her nephew and his family. It was me that picked late on Sunday as the time to have it. I had to avoid the regular Cathedral services, you see. And it was an afternoon when I had no service at Church Cove. So was that a mistake?'

Frances responded. 'You had no choice, Joy. I had my own suspicions of Roberta. That's why I wanted to be here, to keep an eye on her. But as far as I could tell she did nothing wrong at all.'

'All the mischief was happening above you,' said George. 'That's what Harry and I were after. We'd worked out, you see, that the counterweights on the font hood meant there had to be extra weights somewhere above: they'd come down, be within reach, as the hood was pushed up. And there were. We ended up chasing someone from two different directions. Trouble was, we didn't know about the escape route down the old church tower.'

'So Roberta was innocent?' asked Joy, confused.

'Not at all,' said Harry. 'She was the facilitator for whoever was above. There needed to be a baptism service at a known time for that person to have any chance of recovering those weights. What we don't know is if they were successful.'

'But now I know where to look, I can check that tomorrow morning,' responded Joy.

'There'll need to be two of you, I think. One below, to raise the font hood and hence lower the counterweights, the other in the Upper Passage to check if they're still there.'

'But they'll have to be,' protested George. 'Once they're removed, the hood will come crashing down, won't it? That was what made me intervene. I didn't want the baptised infant to be crushed to death.'

There was a short pause as the others grappled with the mechanics.

'But we can't arrest Roberta just for arranging a baptism service,' observed Joy. 'The person we really need is her co-worker. Did either of you two get any idea who the Upper Passage person was?'

George shook her head. 'It was so gloomy, you see, and I didn't have a torch. I couldn't even tell if it was a man or a woman.'

'For some peculiar reason I had a sense I'd seen the outline somewhere before,' added Harry. 'But don't ask me where. As George says, it was too dark to see much at all.'

The conversation would have continued for some time but at that moment Frances' phone started to ring. It was Truro Hospital.

'Marcus Tredwell has just regained consciousness,' the nurse reported. 'I think he'd love to have a visitor. You could come and chat with him for a few minutes if you liked.'

'Right. I'll be there in twenty minutes.'

Frances started to collect her belongings. As she did so Joy interpreted her actions and began to do the same.

'Frances and I came in the same car,' Joy explained to the others. 'We might as well both go and see him. We're the only people Marcus knows here, anyway. Perhaps this conversation could continue tomorrow evening?'

CHAPTER 51

There was a moment's silence after Frances and Joy had left. But George could see that the discussion was by no means over.

'Harry, why don't you go and book yourself a room here for the night. It won't cost you any more than a round rail trip to Exeter. They've got a drying room – you could stop pretending to be Captain of the Pinafore. Then perhaps you and I could give the whole thing one more run through?'

The ten minutes while he was gone also gave George time for a profitable think.

When Harry returned, he was carrying another tray of coffee, 'To give us a mental boost.' George smiled as he poured them both a cup. It seemed they were friends again.

'Let's start with Donald McKay,' she said. 'We know from Frances' trip to St Agnes that he had made his own sketch of the organ bellows. But it might only have been one sketch made from another. The Royal Cornwall Museum said he'd found the details in there – the librarian showed me his name on their visitor list.

'We also believe the bellows were around in John Kempthorne and Henry Martyn's school days and could well have been used to hide a couple of gold ingots. All that must mean, surely, that the dead man was one of the search party.'

'Could it be that he was killed because he'd found the ingots, George? Had he found them hidden in the Crypt?'

'Or else he was judged a danger to his fellow-searcher and had to be silenced. But it gives us possible motives, anyway.'

There was silence as other ideas were evaluated. The challenge was going to be meshing them all together

'But McKay can't have found the ingots, Harry. If he had, there'd be no need for someone else to go hunting for them in the Henry Martyn Chapel. Which we saw happen this afternoon.'

'Right. Maybe it was his failure to find anything in the Crypt, despite all his searches, that meant other lines had to be considered?'

'Mm. Someone else had to be involved in the hiding, then. The ingots must have been moved. When did Joseph Emidy first come into your thinking?'

'Last Monday,' said Harry promptly. 'We had a seminar on him in ECHO. It occurred to me afterwards that he was in a position to take Eleanor's secret forward. But it would still need a jump, the Cathedral wasn't built yet. That came when Simon, he's one of my students, revealed that Joseph's great grandson had been invited back to the Cathedral for the final opening. So the ingots could have been moved in 1911.'

George mused, then shook her head. 'That can't be right Harry. Sure, Emidy Junior could have put them there in 1911; but "last Monday" is too late to realise it. Joy was asked about a baptism service at the Assisted Dying conference, you see. So the idea was around more than two weeks earlier.'

Time was against them. There was a longer pause for thought.

'That's when I first knew about Emidy's great grandson, anyway. That means the prime searcher must have known before I did.' Harry frowned: something was wrong here.

Suddenly George saw a way through. 'Harry, you've encouraged your students to work together, haven't you? That was one of your chief aims. You've not been present in the Chamber all the time. So some of the ideas presented at the ECHO seminars would have been known by the ECHO students for a while, informally, before they were disseminated.'

There was another silence as Harry thought the idea through.

'The thing is, George, it wouldn't be enough for someone just to have clues on where to search – the bellows and all the rest. Even the intervention of the great grandson. The crucial thing needed to start it all off was a solid reason on why there was something to search for.'

'That only came,' he continued, 'when we heard from Ellie about Eleanor's escape from Hispaniola. I was the one to link all that to the Louisiana Purchase and letters between Thomas Jefferson and Napoleon Bonaparte. And I only did that a week last Monday . . .' His voice faltered in confusion.

'Which is still the week after Joy was approached about the baptism. This is a real conundrum, Harry. We seem to have landed ourselves in a time slip.'

A short while later more coffee had been ordered and consumed, this time with biscuits. But the puzzle remained.

'The thing is, Harry, did you tell the ECHO students any of your ideas – about the Louisiana Purchase and so on?'

314

'No. I only came to it myself after the conversation with Frances and Joy that we'd had on Sunday. And I was sworn to secrecy.'

'So the idea of the ingots didn't get to anyone else from you. But don't you see, that means your personal timeline on it is irrelevant. Could the students have thought of it for themselves?'

Harry frowned in concentration. 'There was some mention, I recall, of the diplomat having a heavy courier bag. I suppose that might have given an idea to someone. But you'd have to be looking first.'

George took a deep breath.

'To go back a step, Harry, we believe that Donald McKay was part of this search. Someone else was interested in it as well. Isn't it possible, even plausible, that the connection between them was made through a meeting at the Royal Cornwall Museum?'

Harry considered and then nodded.

George continued, 'So why don't we go in there first thing tomorrow morning and find McKay's date of entry. Then we could keep on looking, see if we find another name, anyone else we recognise, who was researching local history there at the same time?'

In truth it wasn't much of a plan. But for the time being it was all they had.

CHAPTER 52

Frances and Joy had been pleasantly surprised by the sight and demeanour of Marcus Tredwell in Truro Hospital on Sunday evening.

The security man was still heavily bandaged, of course, but he was awake. And, clearly, he recognised both of them – and remembered their names. Frances had feared that his waking up, heavily bandaged, in an unknown hospital might spark terrible memories with all sorts of dire consequences.

'Frances! Joy!' he whispered. 'Ladies, thank you so much for coming. I can't say how glad I am to see you.'

'The nurse says we can't stay for long, Marcus. But it's good to see you conscious again.'

'Can you recall anything of what happened?' added Frances. She knew she had to make the most of their limited access.

'Frances will tell you later, Joy, what we were trying to do,' he began. 'I'd managed to hide in a toilet cubicle when they cleared the Cathedral at six o'clock. The staff team are not all that thorough, you know.'

'And there was no-one around after that?' asked Frances.

'I didn't think so – not that I was aware of, anyway. It was very dark. I made myself comfortable, sitting at the back of the Nave and keeping pretty still. Suddenly, I heard a noise, it sounded like someone tiptoeing up a narrow staircase. It seemed to come from the North West Tower – the one where the bells are. I wondered if they were going to do something to the bells, maybe ring them loudly as a token of protest.'

'But they didn't?'

'No. Then I heard them moving quietly along the Upper Passage, over towards the Henry Martyn Chapel. I followed them from down below but kept close to the outer wall so they wouldn't see me if they looked down. I didn't know if they had a torch, but I feared they might.

'When they got over the Chapel they stopped. I had no idea what they were going to do but I was sure it hadn't been authorised. Then I made a stupid mistake. I moved out into the aisle to hear them better. Trouble was, that meant they could look down on me, directly below.'

Marcus paused, recalling the sequence. 'I stood still to make myself harder to spot. The trouble was, once they had spotted me it gave them a stationary target to aim at. A second later a heavy weight landed on my head. That was it. I remembered nothing more till I came round here this evening.'

'You poor man,' said Frances. She reached across and held his hand, gave it a squeeze. 'But that's a very clear account. Joy and I will go and have a closer look tomorrow morning.'

'It could have been even worse,' added Joy. 'At least your skull isn't fractured.'

At that point Nurse Morag came over and joined them. 'Marcus is doing well, better than we dared hope. If he had somewhere to go to we could even let him out tomorrow evening.'

Frances realised an answer was required. 'You could come

and stay in my house for a few days if you liked, Marcus. It's over in Gweek, near Helston. I wouldn't be there all the time, of course, but you'd be comfortable and warm.'

Marcus looked overwhelmed, close to tears. 'That's very kind of you, Frances. I could write version one of my report while I was there.'

'I'm not far away either, Marcus,' added Joy. 'I'm not usually in Truro. I've only been here this week to help you. I'm mostly based on the Lizard, around Gunwalloe. So I could keep an eye on you too.'

'Sounds grand, ladies,' said Nurse Morag. 'You're going to be well looked after, my friend. It's all going to work out just fine.'

As they returned to the Lizard a short while later, Frances and Joy agreed they had better travel separately into Truro on Monday morning. Once there they would start by gathering evidence in the Cathedral.

Frances and Joy met in the Cathedral at half past nine – later than planned, but the Monday morning traffic into Truro had been unusually slow-moving.

Before setting off from Gweek, Frances had taken the chance to call for a Forensics team. She knew she needed help to look for traces along the Upper Passage. It sounded from Marcus's account that he had suffered a serious assault – if not attempted murder.

She felt sure that when she had the chance to tell him about it, Inspector Marsh would take this case seriously. After all, Marcus was being sponsored by his bosses in Exeter. Truro needed to show they could look after someone loaned to them if required.

At long last, Frances felt, she had a crime scene to work on. She'd had misgivings over McKay's bungalow: perhaps that was a missed opportunity? On the other hand a week had gone by after the death before she'd any hard evidence that a crime had been committed. In that time there'd been several visitors and no proof that the bungalow was precisely where the crime had occurred.

Here the combination of Marcus's testimony and the events of yesterday focussed attention on the space above the Henry Martyn Chapel. Joy was part of the search, though. A minister was needed as it would be important to experiment with raising and lowering the font hood, and observing the effect on the counterweights above.

An hour later Frances was satisfied. The Forensics team had found several fingerprints on the chain linked to the font which led up out of the Chapel. That had inspired her to show them the emergency stairs leading from the Passage down to the St Mary's Aisle. There they'd found further copies of the same prints on the handrail. Frances was relieved that she'd thought to wear gloves when she'd gone to fetch Harry on her climb up and down the stairs yesterday.

The question now was whether the fingerprints could be matched to anyone on the National Crime Database.

CHAPTER 53

Harry couldn't really see why he needed George with him at the Royal Cornwall Museum on Monday morning. He was the only one who stood any chance of recognising aspiring historians on the visitors list.

But George wanted to come. She felt she'd started a good relationship with the Museum librarian, Angela, on the Friday afternoon. And she'd been the one to take an interest in the bellow diagrams, which had led on to crucial discovery of the name Donald McKay.

George also felt that this was a joint inquiry. She and Harry had made progress over the weekend and she wanted that partnership to continue.

'But don't you need to be in the office?' asked Harry.

'I work late often enough, Harry. One morning coming in late won't ruin my reputation. I can spare an hour with you in the Museum. If it takes longer I'll leave you to it.'

From earlier conversations with Frances, George could also see that the opening dialogue would need to be carefully managed. 'Remember, Harry, the death of Donald McKay isn't public knowledge yet. We need another reason to be interested in him.'

'OK. I can sort that. ECHO.'

The Museum had just opened when they got there at half

past nine and they went straight up to the Courtney Library.

'Hi Angela,' said George. 'This is a friend of mine, Dr Harry Jennings. We'd like to do a bit more work around those bellows.'

'I was here a few months ago,' Harry reminded the librarian. 'Exeter University asked me to start a historical research unit here. We are currently in a building up near the Cornwall Records Office which we've called ECHO. But I'm interested in anyone living in Truro with a passion for history.'

Harry paused for breath and then continued. 'George told me about someone else she'd found with an interest in the old Parish Church organ bellows, called Donald McKay. But there might be others. Could we have a glance through the visitors' list, see if there was anyone with him whose name we already know?'

It was a broadside for first thing on Monday morning. If both had been complete strangers to Angela they'd have got nowhere. But the fact that the librarian had met them both before, and that Harry was a senior history lecturer, smoothed the way.

A few minutes later she had handed over the visitors' book and parked them at the far end of the large work table.

George consulted her notebook. 'I found Donald's name as a visitor on August 25th. As far as I could see, that was his first visit. But he might have come on later days as well.'

She seized the visitors' book and flipped back the pages. 'Here we are. Donald McKay, here on August 25th. Right, is there anyone else who came on that day that you also happen to know?'

She handed the book over and Harry started browsing. He

turned over one page, then another. Then he gave a start. 'Wow. What a coincidence.'

'You've found someone interesting?'

'This one.' He pointed to a visitor who'd come on the same day as McKay but arrived half an hour later.

George looked over his shoulder and read, "Ellie Masters". The name meant nothing to her. 'How d'you know her?'

'That's the student who's been leading us through the diary of Eleanor Kempthorne.' He frowned. 'This needs a great deal of thought.'

Half an hour later the two were seated in the coffee shop beside the Museum. Harry had looked at all the dates when Donald McKay had visited. On no less than four of them Ellie Masters had also been present, always at almost the same time. There was no other name on any of these days that he recognised.

'So I'd say that this is the crucial partnership: Donald McKay and Ellie Masters. It probably started in this coffee shop.'

'You don't look very happy, Harry. What's the matter?'

'It's the dates. They are far too early. Ellie hadn't even been selected for ECHO on August 25th. I suggested a visit here would be helpful to all of the students, but that was when we first gathered in late September.'

'But she's a history graduate, Harry. What better way to spend her summer holidays than in the local Museum? She probably found the diary of Eleanor Kempthorne in here long before the name emerged in ECHO. Maybe she'd skimmed it, got the edited highlights, weeks before she gave you the polished transcription?'

'She wouldn't have got my subtle add-ons, though. About Jefferson and his letters to Bonaparte – and the advance on the Louisiana Purchase, sent via Hispaniola.'

'Those weren't in the diary?'

'No. Well, not the part she read out. Hold on a minute.' There was a pause.

'Ellie told us all that the diary had finished. It was when Eleanor was about to come home. That would have been a natural point for it to stop so we accepted it. But . . .'

George completed the thought for him. 'The real diary might not have ended there; it might have detailed the journey home. Explained how Eleanor got the ingots from the French diplomat's courier bag. You wouldn't need to know about the Louisiana Purchase if you'd seen that in the diary. You'd have had Eleanor's own witness to gold ingots. The diary might even have said what she did with them when she got home.'

Harry snorted. 'It might even have mentioned telling Joseph Emidy to take care of them after she'd died. In that case she's been way ahead of us all along.'

There was a pause as thoughts were collected.

'The thing is, Harry, the damage to your ego isn't the problem,' George giggled. 'Not the big one, anyway. What all this means is that we know the killer of Donald McKay. It's as clear as day. All we need now is the hard evidence to prove it.'

At that moment George's phone rang.

CHAPTER 54

The call was from Frances Cober in Truro Police Station.

'George, we've got clear fingerprints from the area above the Henry Martyn Chapel. Trouble is, they're not from any known criminal.'

'Harry and I know who they'll match, Frances. It's Ellie Masters, she's one of Harry's students at ECHO. The one who was presenting the diary of Eleanor Kempthorne – or at least, shall we say, the edited highlights. You'll probably find her up in the ECHO Chamber. They're all there on a Monday.'

'Right. Thank you, George. I'll go and bring her in. If the prints match I'll hold her for interview. Is there any chance you and I could have lunch together, say in the Truro Grammar School restaurant, before the interview starts?'

George saw that Harry was still beside her as the call ended; he'd picked up the gist of the conversation.

She turned to him. 'I'm sorry Harry, but I had no choice. D'you think it would be best if you were in the ECHO Chamber when Frances comes?'

'Probably. I can reassure the other students, anyway. I did have one more idea though, while you and Frances were talking.' He outlined his thought.

'But you could check that before you leave. Ask Angela for sight of the Eleanor Kempthorne diary for a few minutes and check how far it goes. That'd be useful material for Frances' interview. I'll be in touch later.'

She gave him a conspiratorial grin and set out for her office. She might get a couple of hours paid work done before lunch if she was lucky.

Frances was seated at the isolated table at the rear of the restaurant, where they could talk freely, as George arrived. She was wearing a huge grin.

'I've got her, George, and the prints match. I've got enough to deal with the Marcus Tredwell assault. What I'd ideally like is a good understanding of what really happened in the McKay case, before I start the interview.

In truth, George's two hours in the office had been spent as much on pulling her ideas together as on assessing telecom security.

The regular waitress came and took their orders. Then they could begin.

'I don't know anything about Ellie's home situation,' said George, 'but for some reason or other she was desperate for a way to make some money. I think it all began when she met Donald McKay, by chance, in the Royal Cornwall Museum back in August. At any rate, the record shows they were both there at the same time on August 25th. McKay was after mechanical subjects to sketch and came across the organ bellows; Ellie was looking for early Cornish feminists and had come across Eleanor Kempthorne's diary. They probably fell into conversation about nineteenth century Cornwall in the coffee shop next door.'

There was a pause as lunch was brought to their table, then George resumed.

A Cornish Conundrum

'The two met several times at the Museum in the coming weeks. Ellie wouldn't be allowed to take the diary away but she managed to skim-read it there. It went a lot further than she ever read out at ECHO. It was clear that Eleanor had returned to Truro with one or two gold ingots in her possession. McKay found out the history of the organ bellows. They both realised the bellows were there at the right time to make a good hiding place in the Parish Church. Of course, this was a hundred years before the Cathedral came into being, but they learned – maybe from a guided tour – that the south aisle of the old church was now part of the new Cathedral. They could even see the old organ, powered by electricity, working in the St Mary's Aisle.'

'You'd better stop talking and eat something,' said Frances. It'd be a shame if your toasted sandwich went cold.'

A few minutes later George resumed. 'At that point – mid September – one or other of them spotted the advert for the Assisted Dying conference, in and around the Cathedral. And they thought, was this a way to access the Crypt and search for the ingots?

'Ellie was just about to start PhD studies with ECHO. But McKay was retired, no reason why he couldn't enrol. On the off-chance he mentioned his drama skills when applying and to his delight they were picked up. In truth, security in the Cathedral was pretty slack. It didn't take long for McKay to acquire a Crypt key of his own. At that point he and Ellie could start a systematic search.'

'I remember talking to one of his drama colleagues,' said Frances. 'She mentioned him claiming a room for himself in the Crypt. "It took him so long," she said, "to remove his makeup.""'

Frances gave a sigh. 'Whereas in reality his slowness was to give him time after rehearsals to search the place on his own.'

'In the meantime,' said George, 'Ellie brought edited highlights of Eleanor's diary to the ECHO chamber. It had to be broadly accurate, but she hid any suggestion that Eleanor had returned with gold bars. But Harry was interested. In the end, desperate, she had to pretend the diary finished earlier than it really did.'

'She didn't want to give anyone even a hint there was treasure to be found here, George. Trouble was that their boss Harry was too bright. Once he'd got an idea, he discovered all sorts of other historical details that would support it. They're probably not in the diary at all.'

A short pause and then George resumed. 'One other thing to note that Harry told me is that Ellie lives in Kenwyn. That's on the way to McKay's home in Shortlanesend. Crucially, she's a keen cyclist. So when they stopped meeting in the Museum she'd cycle over to visit him in his bungalow. Probably only after dark. A traffic camera might spot her but it wouldn't collect a number anyway.

'So now, Frances, we come to the evening that McKay died. Our evidence isn't too strong but I can think of several plausible scenarios.

'We know that McKay came back in his car after the drama, on his own. It's possible that Ellie was already waiting for him with her fatal additive. If so, they might have had a terrific row which ended with her poisoning him.

Frances frowned. 'It couldn't be that noisy, George. No reports of shouting from neighbours, anyway. My constable,

Tim Barwell, went round all of 'em. I've read through their statements.'

'OK. Here's another idea, then. What if McKay swore there were no ingots in the Crypt and Ellie accused him of not looking hard enough? He'd take umbrage, threaten to tell the authorities what was going on. At that point a desperate Ellie might decide she had no choice but to silence him.'

Frances frowned. 'But the poisoning had to be planned, George. The stuff had to be brought from somewhere. It wasn't just an act of desperation.'

George considered this objection and then nodded reluctantly. 'OK. Well, what if McKay had been successful? He'd show Ellie the ingots but she wasn't planning to share them, wanted the lot. So she'd have taken them off him and left him poisoned.'

Once again Frances voiced a problem. 'But he wasn't successful, George, was he? That was why she had to go on looking in the space over the Henry Martyn Chapel. It's not that easy, is it?'

George was silent, putting her remaining idea in its best order.

'It's most likely, I'd say, that Ellie joined him after he was home. So how about this as a scenario? McKay's depressed that no ingots have been found: suicidal. Ellie has no reason to thwart him: he's no use to her now. She helps him take the poison, then, once he's dead, she removes his suicide note, tidies the place a little and disappears.'

Frances pondered for a moment. 'That'd certainly be a line for Ellie to take, George, given a good lawyer. Assisting a suicide is less serious that administering poison. You know, that might be hard for us to disprove.'

'What you haven't done yet, with any of these ideas,' she added, 'is to explain how a bottle of tampered wine found its way to the Diocese House bar and almost killed the two of us.'

George had exhausted her ideas. She smiled. 'I don't have all the answers, Frances. I'll leave that one to you.'

The waitress came again to take away their plates and desserts were ordered. In truth there was more talking to be done.

Frances began. 'It sounds fairly plausible, George. Trouble is, despite the fingerprints, there's not much hard evidence to back it up. We can probably prove that Ellie knew McKay and the two were in some sort of partnership. Maybe the Courtney librarian will remember them working together? But we've no proof that Ellie even went to McKay's house at all, let alone on the vital Wednesday evening. Unless she interviews badly, I don't think we'd even get the case to court.'

George could see what she meant.

'Have you personally interviewed the occupants of the Close where McKay lived? Are you sure there's no-one living there that could help us?'

'To be honest, I had no choice but to leave that to my constable. I had to concentrate on interviewing the conference delegates.' Frances sighed. 'That's taken me long enough.'

'As a last resort, is it worth a trip there yourself? After all, you've got a much clearer idea now on what you're after.'

'I could go right away, I suppose. Ellie's interview will wait a couple of hours if it has to.'

Fifteen minutes later Frances was on her way.

CHAPTER 55

On the basis of cold logic, Frances told herself, this trip was clutching at straws. Constable Barwell was a diligent police officer, there was almost certainly nothing for her to find.

Somehow, though, her instinct told her to expect more. It only took twenty minutes to pick up her car and drive out to Shortlanesend. Her Satnav quickly found Donald McKay's bungalow. She wondered about going inside, then decided what she was after today was witnesses. She would start with Jim Temple in the house opposite. And his wife. Tim hadn't given any description of her, she noted, and wondered why.

'Good afternoon. Mr Temple?' she began, as a casually dressed, middle-aged man came to the door.

'That's me.'

'I'm Sergeant Frances Cober. Could I possibly come in and ask you a few more questions about Donald McKay? And also, maybe, talk to your wife?'

'Come in, Sergeant. I knew the police were hard pressed but Donald's death hasn't had as much coverage as I'd have expected.'

'We've been covering other angles, sir. Could I talk to your wife at the same time, perhaps?'

'I'm afraid Annie doesn't come downstairs anymore. She's

in her bed, next to the window. The doctor thinks she may not have long left to live.' He gave a sad smile. 'But we've had a good life and I suppose that nothing lasts forever. Do come on up.'

No wonder Tim hadn't met her, thought Frances as she followed Jim up the stairs.

Annie turned out to be a woman in her mid-fifties with alert eyes operating out of a frail body.

'My name is Frances. I'm very pleased to meet you.'

'Good to meet you too. Is this about poor Donald?'

'I'm afraid so. We're still making enquiries – and making some progress, I hope.'

'So how can I help you? I keep a fairly good watch on the Close, and of course Donald's bungalow is right opposite.'

'Were you watching on the Wednesday night, just under three weeks ago? It was the day before Donald's body was found.'

'I was. There's nothing I much like on television on Wednesdays, you see.'

'Besides McKay's own car, did you see any other cars come to his home that evening?'

Annie frowned in concentration. 'Not cars, no.'

'Some other vehicle, perhaps?'

'Ah. I don't know if you'd call it a vehicle.'

Frances knew she mustn't push her. This could be the vital evidence that would settle the case.

'What would you call it then, Annie?'

'I'd call it a racing bike. Driven like the wind by a girl. She raced in, jumped off and parked it round the side. Then she rang the door bell. Donald obviously knew her; he let her in straight away.'

Frances was tempted to give the woman a hug but knew she mustn't.

'What time was this?'

'It was mid-evening, I'd say. Jim hadn't come to bed yet, he was still downstairs with his crossword. It'd be around ten o'clock.'

'And did she stay long?'

'No more than an hour, I'd say, Sergeant. She let herself out.'

'This is very helpful, Annie. Can you remember anything about the girl? Or her bike?'

'D'you remember, Jim, I commented on it to you when you came to bed? Not much goes on in the Close, I have to make the most of what there is. Her bike was a pink fluorescent colour. She was wearing a cerise cagoule and a pink cycling helmet.'

Frances was writing this down as fast as she could. One last question occurred to her. 'Had this girl visited Donald before?'

'She started coming in mid September, I'd say. Came fortnightly or so. But only ever after dark. If we hadn't known Donald fairly well we might have been suspicious, even teased him about her.'

'I did ask him about her once,' contributed Jim. 'Donald said she was a history student he'd met that wanted to learn some engineering.'

'I don't suppose he told you her name?'

' 'Fraid not. He just referred to her as Ellie. But she was his only visitor – apart from Walter Wallace of course. That was his friend. The two of them were into painting machinery. I'd hoped to go to their shop one day but St Agnes is such a distance, if you don't have a car.'

'I don't suppose, Annie, that you would recognise Ellie if you saw her again?'

Annie looked like she'd been insulted. 'Sergeant, my body is failing fast but there's nothing wrong with my mind. Course I'd recognise her. Why, d'you know where we can find her? She might not even know that Donald is dead.'

'I think she probably does,' replied Frances. But wiser, she thought, not to elaborate.

CHAPTER 56

The agreed meal between Harry, George, Frances and Joy took place in the Old Truro Grammar School restaurant that evening. Plenty to share, with many developments since the previous evening.

Frances took the lead. She had spent much of the afternoon interviewing Ellie Masters. Of course her account was highly confidential, but that was hard to maintain in this context since all the others had made massive contributions to her arrest.

'Ellie started off full of self-confidence but I gradually chipped it away. Her fingerprints in the Upper Passage of the Cathedral were hard for her to account for, but of course I couldn't prove they'd been left there on the night Marcus was assaulted by the carefully dropped stone.

'Harry's discovery – that Eleanor Kempthorne's diary went on a lot further than she had claimed – was harder to explain. Even so, the fact in itself was hardly illegal.

'The crucial sighting came from Donald McKay's neighbours – thank you, George, for prompting me to go there. His wife is bedridden but she watches everything that goes on like a hawk. She'd seen Ellie arriving on her bike the evening that McKay died and leaving an hour later. Even gave me her name. That more or less finished Ellie off. I'm hoping for a successful conclusion to the interview tomorrow morning.'

'So what was the link between Ellie and the tampered wine bottle in Diocese House?' asked George.

'That was quite subtle,' replied Frances with a grin. 'It turned out, you see, that Ellie's aunt is Roberta Thomas.'

They had all heard the name. But the puzzled faces of her companions told her that much more was needed.

'What happened was this. Ellie arrived at McKay's bungalow with a small flask of poison tucked into her cagoule. McKay already had a bottle of Cathedral Red. He'd either bought it in the Diocese House or else pinched it from the store in the Crypt during one of his searches.

'Somehow or other – it's a detail I'm hoping to extract tomorrow – Ellie poured her poison into McKay's already-opened wine, persuaded him to have another glass and the combination finished him off. But you can't easily carry a full wine bottle on a bicycle – especially if you don't have a carrier basket to hold it. So she left it beside the wine glass, on the table.

'But when she got home, she realised it was a giveaway. Without it, the death might be taken as natural. She knew McKay had major health issues. She also knew her aunt was at the Assisted Dying conference. In desperation she rang her, asked her to pick it up. Which, somehow or other, she managed to do.

'I knew that Roberta didn't have a car. That was why I hadn't given her much attention. But she managed to persuade Barry to take her with him. She got into the kitchen while he was still crying over McKay's body and then responding to the GP. She had a large handbag and it just fitted in.'

'OK. So that got the poisoned wine bottle out of the

bungalow and over to the conference,' said Joy. 'What happened next?'

'You'll recall, Roberta got back to the conference at lunch time and you whisked her away with Barry for an off-site lunch. At this point the doctored wine was still in her handbag.

'There was a minute between the return to Diocese House and the start of the afternoon session. Roberta went to her room, wondering where to hide the bottle. She was afraid that if McKay's death was declared suspicious, hordes of policemen might descend on Diocese House, looking to search every room – and every handbag.'

'That's an over optimistic view of the police force, I reckon,' said Harry.

Frances nodded. 'Then, desperate, she had an idea. A variant on "the best place to hide a car is in a carpark". Everyone else was in the meeting room and the lunch-time bar wasn't locked. She first topped up the bottle with tap water. Then she crept in, bottle still in her handbag, and added it to the others on the shelf behind the bar. After which she joined the rest of the delegates to hear about Donald McKay's death.'

'So the notion of trying to finish off an alert police officer wasn't true at all?'

'No. In her panic, the risk that the bottle might be resold, and go on to poison someone else, simply didn't occur to her.'

'Have you had time, yet, to find out what was driving Ellie?' asked Joy.

'I think so. Ellie told me that her mother has incurable cancer. She needed the funds to send her to Switzerland, either for specialist treatment or else, if that didn't work, for a managed form of "assisted dying". Either of which, you know, is very expensive.

'Aunt Roberta is Ellie's mother's sister and was equally concerned. So to both of them the notion of finding hidden treasure in the Cathedral became very attractive.'

There was silence round the table as the account was absorbed. There were still some gaps but it seemed fairly comprehensive.

'I've been talking for far too long,' observed Frances. 'Who's going to go next?'

'This afternoon was our regular ECHO sharing session,' said Harry. 'Simon was talking about the history of funding for the Cathedral. Given all this talk of treasure he had some interesting findings.'

'I'd love to hear,' said Joy, trying to sound loyal. Frances sensed there might be trouble ahead for her and Harry.

'Simon had been studying the building fund as the Nave was completed. Most donations were small amounts, from all over Cornwall. It was very humbling, he said. Tiny churches in the middle of nowhere, all wanting to play their part. But even so, in 1910 the fund didn't match the final building costs. It looked like the Cathedral would head into the future with a significant debt.'

'Not the best of starts,' observed Joy.

Harry nodded in agreement. 'But then Simon went on to look at the performance of the fund after the Nave had been completed. To his amazement, in 1912, there was a massive donation from the United States. It covered the debt and left the Cathedral in substantial profit. It's been self-sufficient ever since.'

'Could he tell where it had come from?' asked George.

'It was marked as anonymous, apparently. And no-one liked to inquire too closely. But Simon did some what you might call financial archaeology. It's not certain but he reckons it was probably a gift from Joseph Emidy's great grandson, sent once he was back home. That was the end of the tale as far as he was concerned. But . . .'

'We can guess where Emidy got the funds from,' guessed Joy. 'I'd say it's cash derived from ingots – the ingots that were bought from Hispaniola by Eleanor Kempthorne. So in fact, today, there's no hidden treasure left at all.'

'Aren't you disappointed by that?' asked Harry.

'Not really, Harry. You know the Bible verse, "The love of money is the root of all evil." It certainly seems to have been true in this case.

CHAPTER 57

A fter all the excitements of Monday, life in Truro returned to a more normal pace.

George Gilbert continued to investigate the risks to internet links across Cornwall between Newquay Airport and Goonhilly Earth Station. Most of her time was spent at the Newquay end. When she had time to dream it wasn't of her long-gone husband but of Harry Jennings. Might they get together again one day? She didn't have cause to stay with Frances Cober in Gweek for some time.

Harry Jennings went back to the ECHO Chamber to encourage his remaining three students on their research projects. The disappearance of a fellow student on a murder charge was a blow to morale but also a salutary lesson.

Harry decided he would complete the analysis of the life of Eleanor Kempthorne himself. He'd learned to decipher old script years ago. The early stages were much as Ellie had transcribed. The sequel, after Eleanor bade her husband farewell and left with diplomat Pierre, was far darker.

In her own words, once they were on a homeward-bound vessel, Eleanor had thrown herself at Pierre in an attempt to seduce him. But the diplomat had known the risks and had resisted. Then she had discovered that the Captain of the ship, like his crew, was a Dutchman. The Dutch had been invaded by the French and hated them even more than they hated the English. The Captain would be delighted to have an excuse to turn on Pierre.

So, close to Europe, she had accused Pierre of a brutal rape. He had been summarily tried by the Captain and found guilty. He was severely flogged and then keel-hauled. The combination of the two had been fatal and the man had not survived. As a result there was no problem in Eleanor landing at Truro with all of Pierre's possessions. She'd been able to make use of his coins but cashing ingots in any bank of the time was much trickier. She had handed them over to her son for safe keeping.

He might have told her some details but she didn't record them. For years Eleanor lived in fear of being abducted by French agents, taken to France and interrogated. There were times when it was best not to set down the whole truth and this was one of them.

Frances Cober continued with her interview of Ellie Masters.

'An eye-witness tells me McKay let you into his bungalow late that Wednesday evening, but you came out alone. You were the last person to see him alive, Ellie. So what really happened?'

Ellie held out for some time but in the end she confessed. She and McKay had different motives for the search. His interest was intellectual and waned as the search dragged on, hers was deeply personal. But by now he knew too much, she couldn't afford for him to tell the tale. She seized the methadone prescribed for her mother and brought it with her to

McKay's. The poor man had no chance.

Her confession led to her being charged for McKay's murder as well as Marcus's attempted murder. Inspector Kevin Marsh commended her for both. Frances managed to obscure the fact that it was her that had encouraged Marcus to wander the Cathedral at night in the first place.

Frances took Marcus to Gweek for recuperation once he was discharged and the two became good friends. Occasionally she sensed slivers of his memory starting to return, but it would be a long haul: in any case, she very much liked the present version.

Before he returned to London, Marcus completed a report on security at the Cathedral. It was a workable critique full of practical details, which the Dean was pleased to accept and later implement.

As the Cathedral's coordinator Joy Tregorran benefitted from the report's tone. It wasn't a damning indictment; nor was it an unaffordable dream. She was recognised by the Dean as a competent ally for the future. She wouldn't be Associate Vicar in Gunwalloe for ever.

It was on a visit to the Cathedral to discuss the report, as she made her way through the Nave, that an idea occurred to Joy. One item which had been in the Crypt from the beginning and was now standing in a quiet corner of the Nave was the Black Madonna. Could this also hold treasures from the past?

She recalled the tale: it had been moved stealthily into position by two tour guides. It couldn't be that heavy. One strong-looking guide, Stephen, was still on duty so she approached him. There was no-one else around and he was happy enough to help.

Slowly, carefully, they leaned the statue over until it was lying on the Nave floor. The base was now accessible. There was a circular hole in the middle, two inches wide, blocked by a well-seasoned cork.

'Interesting,' murmured Stephen.

'Could we get it out?'

'I expect so.' Stephen drew a penknife from his pocket with

a corkscrew on one end. He applied it to the cork and twisted.

A moment later they could see inside. The hollow ran a long way up the statue. But it was far from empty.

'Looks like rolls of manuscript,' said Joy, 'tied up with a ribbon.'

'Help me lift the statue onto a tilt,' said Stephen. 'We might be able to joggle it out the end.'

It took five minutes gentle persuasion but in the end the roll slid down far enough to be reached by Joy's slim fingers. A few seconds later it was out and in her hands.

'Why don't we put the statue back up, where it came from?' said Stephen. 'Then we could go away and look at what we've found in better light, say in the refectory.'

Ten minutes later they were at a side table in the Chapter House refectory, a tea tray on the table beside them.

'It looks very old,' said Joy. 'Shall we open it?'

They cleared an empty space on the table, making sure it wasn't moist. Then Joy grappled with the knot on the ribbon. Eventually it came undone. Slowly, with infinite patience and delicate hands, she started to unroll the documents.

Stephen seized each one as it was released, laid them out across the table. The outer one was a letter, written in a slanted style by a polished hand. Inside that, slightly less old, were pages and pages of a musical score. Neither Stephen nor Joy knew quite what they'd found.

'See what you can make of the score, Stephen. I'll try the letter. But we mustn't pick them up.' There was ten minutes of serious silence.

'Wow,' said Joy. 'This is a hand-written letter from Thomas Jefferson, you know, the author of the United States

Declaration of Independence. It's addressed to Monsieur Napoleon Bonaparte. I think it's anticipating the Louisiana Purchase.'

'That'd be worth something at auction,' responded Stephen. 'But I reckon this'd be worth more. Here, look at the title. It's a concerto for violin and orchestra, written by Joseph Emidy. We knew that he was a composer as well as a virtuoso performer. It's always been regretted, you know, that none of his works survived. I wonder how this got here?'

Joy had a good idea of how it might have happened. But she judged this was one insight that she had better keep to herself.

Reflecting over the past fortnight that evening, Joy could see several life-beyond-the-grave incidents which had come to light. James Kempthorne and, two hundred years later, Marcus Tredwell had both re-emerged from deadly predicaments in the back of beyond. Now a once-lost musical score had done much the same.

In all three cases the return would be a cause for surprise and celebration. There was sermon material here. Even when things seemed to be at their worst, she mused, there was still hope for the future.

EPILOGUE

It was several months before the frequently resettled Emidy Violin Concerto was first performed. Early comments from those given the chance to preview the score were exceptional. It was a cultural event that would arouse a great deal of interest across the nation.

It was to be broadcast by BBC Two, live on Saturday evening. Nigel Kennedy was the solo violinist, plus the London Symphony Orchestra conducted by Sir Simon Rattle. It would become one of the landmark concerts of the year.

The finders of the unsettled score, Joy and Stephen, became locally famous. As did Joseph Emidy himself. He progressed from mention on a small label within the Royal Cornwall Museum to becoming a Cornish legend. There was already talk of turning his remarkable story into a film.

'Why ever did you think to look inside the Black Madonna?' Joy and Simon were asked. The question came repeatedly. Stephen attributed the find to Joy, but her lips were sealed: she dared not spell out the full background. The trial of Ellie Masters was still in the future and many things could not yet be revealed.

The Dean insisted that Cathedral security was checked for the performance and invited Marcus Tredwell back down to take charge. Of course, Frances saw the opportunity and invited him to stay with her in Gweek. For the first time she had found someone who took her police work seriously but was also great fun to be with. His friendship had enriched her life as well.

George's project at Newquay was completed so she no longer had reason to visit Truro. But the relationship with Harry Jennings had re-ignited. Harry's ECHO work was based in Truro. By now he had acquired a flat in the city, which made it easy to invite George down for the concert.

The whole city was awash with excitement. When the orchestra was in its place under the Central Tower and the concert was about to begin, Frances and Marcus found themselves seated on one side of the Nave, close to the Henry Martyn Chapel where Marcus had almost been killed. George and Harry were on the other side.

George glanced across and saw her friend. She was more smartly dressed than usual. 'Look, Harry. That's Frances over there – in a dress! Hey, she seems to have found a friend.'

Harry followed her arm. 'The bearded man is Marcus. The security expert who conducted the great audit. Did you never meet him?'

George shook her head.

In turn Frances spotted George and gave her a wave.

'Who's that?' asked Marcus.

'That's George. She's a friend of mine, down for the weekend from near Tintagel. You wouldn't know her.'

'Oddly, I think I ought to. But only from a long time back, in an earlier life. Don't worry, Frances, I'm glad to be here with you.'

AUTHOR'S NOTES

As with my earlier Cornish Conundrums, this novel is a work of fiction in a visitable location. Where possible I have drawn on actual events and you will find some fact and fiction intertwined.

Eleanor and James Kempthorne lived in the late seventeen hundreds. He was a naval captain until shipwrecked in Samana Bay in 1782. Their oldest son, John, attended Truro Grammar School, was Senior Wrangler (top mathematician) at Cambridge in 1796 and later became a vicar in the Cotswolds. He wrote the hymn "Praise the Lord, ye heavens adore Him."

Henry Martyn was also at Truro Grammar School and was Senior Wrangler at Cambridge in 1801. He became a missionary to Persia and translated the Bible into three languages before his early death in 1812. There is a chapel and an elegant font in his name in Truro Cathedral.

Sir Humphrey Davy, a President of the Royal Society, was a contemporary of Henry Martyn and another student at the Grammar School – all at the same time. What a trio!

St Mary's Parish Church, next to the old Grammar School, dates from the thirteenth century. Its organ was transferred from the Chapel Royal in St James' Palace in 1750. It is still in regular use today.

Work on Truro Cathedral started in 1880 and was finally completed in 1910. It incorporates St Mary's Aisle, part of the old Parish Church; its Crypt and near-inaccessible Upper Passage are roughly as described.

I am grateful to Stephen Baird for a guided tour of the Cathedral, the source of many features included in the novel. He suggested a few corrections but it is, in the last resort, a work of fiction.

"The Story of Truro Cathedral" by Miles Brown has been a useful source of data, as have many sources on the Internet.

Thomas Jefferson, author of the US Declaration of Independence, was Ambassador to France in the 1780s. Later, when President, he bought the central third of the United States from Napoleon Bonaparte in 1803 – the "Louisiana Purchase". Its cost was a mere $16 million.

The idea that an advance on this fund might be sent from America to France in the 1790s is pure fiction, as is Eleanor's trip to the West Indies.

Joseph Emidy, a slave from Portuguese Guinea, was put ashore at Falmouth in 1799. He lived in Truro as violinist, leader of the Truro Philharmonic Orchestra and composer till his death in 1835. Sadly, none of his compositions survive. His eight children all left for the United States on his death.

The notion that his great grandson returned to play at the opening of the Cathedral in 1910 is my invention, as is the idea that he had any role in re-hiding treasure – or even re-settling his great grandfather's score.

Truro Cathedral itself is in many ways the hero of this book and I have done my best to do the place justice. It is a magnificent and welcoming structure which is well worth a visit. I am unaware of any financial or security shortcomings.

I am grateful to friends and relatives for wise comments on early drafts of this novel, especially Simon and Karen Porter, Les Williams, Chris Scruby; also my wife Marion and daughter Lucy Smith. Dr Mike Pittam gave valuable advice on poisoning and on post-mortem variation. Angela Bamping was a highly efficient copy editor. All errors, including those remaining, are mine.

If you have enjoyed this book, please consider putting a one-line review on Amazon to encourage others to read it. If you have any detailed comments - or ideas for future conundrums - please contact me on the website below.

David Burnell   *website: www.davidburnell.info*
May 2020

EARLIER CORNISH CONUNDRUMS

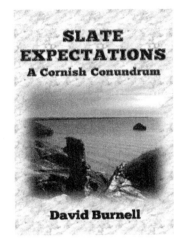

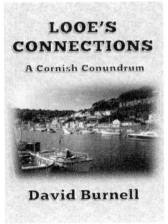

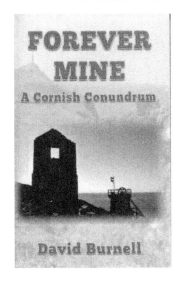

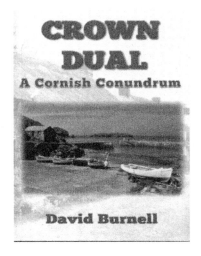